The Pearl in the Darkness

Santana Saunders

The Pearl in the Darkness

Formatting by Let's Get Booked

www.letsgetbooked.com

Published by Hummingbird & Tree Publishing LLC

www.hummingbirdandtree.com

Paperback: 978-1-7356305-0-2

E-Book: 978-1-7356305-1-9

For my grandmothers, Floraine and Jean.
Thank you for being the heroines of your own stories
so I can write mine. The chocolate covered cherries and
fried chicken were an added bonus.

1

WHERE ONE BEGINS AND ONE ENDS

What once was a soft, white sandy beach, a sea of smiling faces lounging under umbrellas now sits a ravaged waste land. The ground is an odd gray, black crystallized grit that will slice the bottoms of our feet if we don't wear shoes. The color of the sky blends in with the ground, so we can't tell where one begins, and one ends.

I had spent summer vacations here. There were rows of high-rise condos along the beach. We picked a new one every other year. It was the only time I recall feeling truly unburdened. My father didn't answer his phone. My mother went without styling her hair or putting on makeup the entire time. The days were never planned. Meals were sporadic and often consisted of just ice cream or deep-fried grouper from one of the local huts. I would lay back onto my towel, listening to the waves crashing on the beach and the chatter of children building sandcastles. My eyes closed and tiny, round flashes of light danced behind my eyelids. When I was younger, I thought they were the magic inside my mind sparking to life. I spent hours creating an elaborate sand village and imagining what characters lived there. Firefighters who raced into their trucks to save families trapped in burning buildings. A round, jolly baker filling his shelves with cupcakes and fresh bread. A young, brave girl who secretly protected the people and battled supervillains. This was the place where I had all my best ideas.

Today, the silence is swallowing me whole. If I breathe, the sound of my saliva moving up and down my throat will be too loud. The typical buzzing of people on their phones, the internet, vehicles in the background racing here and there is all gone. In its place, a deafening, dim void.

My father was always known as a gentle giant. He stood six feet five inches tall, but he wouldn't harm a fly. He was always so patient with me and my childhood friends who frequented our house. Every so often, we would reach that edge of his ability. We stormed through the house, romping and roaring around, nearly destroying any breakable knick-knack of my mother's in our path. One of us would inevitably break something or someone would get hurt. All the roaring fun would halt into silence. When he snapped, we all knew we had gone too far, and felt more guilt than our little child psyches knew how to apologize for. He was the one parent we all truly felt bad about disappointing. I remember hoping if I froze in that moment it would erase what happened, or maybe it would lessen the transgression.

Today, the ocean is eerily still, like a lake at the crack of dawn. The still air is so thick and stale, as if all the elements know. We went too far. Father is mad. No one make a sound.

2

WHISKEY AND DONUTS

Hollis was by far my number one choice for a roommate, but days like today make me question that decision. He tends to turn what should be a 20-minute task into a day-long quest.

"Why can't we just settle on the coffee table in the front of the store?" I asked.

"It's padded. Then we have to buy some nonsense tray to set our drinks on. It has to be solid and the right height," he replied.

Finally, a salesperson approaches. She shamelessly tosses her hair and bats her eyes at Hollis as she shows us every single solid coffee table in the showroom. He naively follows her around as if she really doesn't understand the description of the table we are looking for. Idiot.

I intervene before she convinces him to buy a hideous bachelor pad room set. They line up a delivery date, and we hit the road. It took two hours, but at least he hasn't mentioned it being my birthday. I don't mind turning thirty. Actually, I look forward to feeling more respected. It's not easy earning respect as a twenty-something female. Now, I'm a thirty-something proud owner of a new coffee table. Take that, world.

Usually I am the one behind the wheel, but Hollis insists on driving. We pass the old strip mall shops lined with palm tree landscaping. Every building has a pastel shade and the same stucco textured siding. The streets are so tight I hold my breath every time someone cuts over into our lane. Florida is a state that doesn't really have one set of driving rules. Sure, everyone who grows up here takes the same driving exam, but our state is packed with people from all over. That's the funny part about growing up in a vacation town. Everyone moves here for a life of paradise, but really there isn't just one culture here. It's a melting pot. That must be why I'm such a well-rounded individual.

By the time we pull into the parking garage, it's near dark. Our neighborhood used to be lined with vacation rentals that snowbirds would flock to every winter. Now, it's mostly rows of run-down rental condos that could use a fresh coat of paint or two. Maybe one day a developer will swoop in and clean this mess up. It doesn't hurt that there are some local businesses in walking distance, so I don't always have to brave the scary melting pot streets. Hollis looks down at his phone and lets out a horrendous breath.

"She's canceling our plans again," he says.

"Your mother?" I ask.

"The one and only. I know it's been a long grueling day of coffee table shopping, but would you join me for a drink on the roof? I could use some fresh air."

He knows I'll amuse him. We are like family, Hollis and I, and his mother is a constant disappointment. She doesn't deserve him. The only praise she will get from me is for giving birth to him. We grab a couple premixed margaritas and trudge up to the roof. As we bust open the door, "SURPRISE!!!!!"

Of course, he remembered.

There are colorful lanterns hanging between airy curtains in the theme of a bohemian oasis. It takes my breath away.

Upon the right side of the table sits my favorite bottle of scotch. The Macallan 18-year-old sherry oak single malt scotch whisky. It's a blend of spice, orange and cloves straight from Scotland. The left side of the table is adorned with pitchers filled with sangria, vodka lemonade cocktails, strawberry prosecco punch; basically, all the fufu drinks most people enjoy. In place of the typical birthday cake, sits a three-tiered tower of my favorite Krispy Kreme glazed donuts. They've set up a projector aimed at a large white sheet upon the stucco wall. Chris Pratt dances around the galaxy to that old song, "Come and get Your Love." Great, now they will all know about my infatuation with Marvel movies. I don't remember how old I was when my obsession with them began. There is something comforting in the idea of people with extraordinary abilities defending those who can't defend themselves. I look down at the hideous—but typical—leggings and tank top I'm wearing. It's moments like this that having a female best friend would come in handy. She would have suggested I change into something more appealing. My parents tackle me with hugs and affection.

"We couldn't let you sit out your thirtieth, you old lady!" they laugh.

"If this makes me old, what does that make you two?" I retort.

My mother lives for these major life events. Her blonde hair is perfectly wrapped up in a sleek French twist, and her dress is a vibrant fuchsia that compliments her fair skin. She is always the life of the party, and I'm certain she was in charge of designing this rooftop oasis. She has a way of taking any ordinary, plain space and making it beautiful. My father, on the other hand, takes his rightful place in the back of the crowd where he is content. His shirt matches my mother's dress of course, and he is perfectly satisfied being the back seat to her shining presence. They are a living Barbie and Ken doll set. I have a theory that every second he is not cutting someone open, he is letting his brain cells recharge until the next surgery. My college dorm mate, Nina, pushes past them.

"Let me at her! All the humidity in the world couldn't keep me from my Leo!" she exclaims.

"I can't believe you are here. How are things in San Francisco?"

She grabs both of my arms. "It's insane. People are terrible, but that's pretty much everywhere these days. The job is my life. On the bright side, things are still looking very early

2000s in this old, Kourtney and Khloe Take Miami style vacation tower! I can't believe you two left the flamingo wallpaper up. You know, living in Florida does not give you a license to live this way." She huffed.

Still the same old Nina. We didn't exactly hit it off right away. On my first day in the dorms, she told me that she couldn't imagine if her parents had given her up. I wish I could say that she was the first to make that mistake.

Our neighbor from down the hall, Lorenzo, casually strolls up.

"You know it wouldn't have been a party without me, birthday girl," he says with a wink.

His date of the evening chimes in with all the perkiness I can imagine someone to muster. "Happy dirty thirty, Leo!"

I hate to make assumptions—okay, actually I love to make them—but she has got to be the girl who peaked in high school. She hangs on every half compliment Lorenzo shoots her. She keeps tugging down on her dress because it stops just short of her butt cheeks. I look up and see she notices me observing her. *Well, she knows what I think about her now.* My face is a tell-all for any emotions, and I'm pretty sure she just got a glimpse at my disgust face. Lorenzo doesn't pick up on it.

He's not the most observant, but he certainly has a way with the ladies. He just doesn't really care if they stick around long. I'm sure there's a story there that a therapist could uncover, but I don't really care.

And here comes my landlord.

"Hey Dale! We're not late on rent are we?"

"Oh no! Hollis asked me to help decorate the roof, and I just had to wish you a happy birthday."

Dale doesn't get out much, but I clearly don't either since Hollis had to stretch him an invite to fill space. *Note to self, make more friends in your thirties.* The night goes on without a hitch. Nina fills me in on her brave, solo adventure on the West Coast. Which, ironically, mostly involves her searching for Mr. Right. Lorenzo's date drinks far too many glasses of champagne, and he regretfully has to take off early so she can get into a clean change of clothes. My parents take that as their cue and head back to the suburbs. I take a seat next to Hollis in front of the projector.

"Nice work, buddy."

"Before you get mad, consider the fact that I can't control the sheer passion all the people in your life have for celebrating the day of your birth," he says.

14

"Right. All six of them. You know what really made my night?" I ask.

"Watching vomit spray out of Lorenzo's date's nose? Because that was most definitely the highlight of my night," he laughs.

"That was right up there with Dale taking me through all of his favorite comics once he knew about my love for Marvel films."

"Had I known, I may have joined in, to keep it going of course. I always knew you two were soulmates."

He spends the next hour wrapping up the last Marvel movie and finishing the scotch with me in a pile of colorful, beanbags scattered for seating. Hollis doesn't even like scotch. I place the milky pearl hanging from my neck between my fingers and roll it back and forth. It's the only thing I have left from her. It was passed down from three generations of women in my family. I picture my ancestors scouring the dark sea floor in search of that one special oyster. I read that it takes two to four years for the pearl to form. A lifetime when your survival depends on it.

***

We grew up in the same cul-de-sac. I was adopted when I was four years old. Hollis has always looked more like my very Scandinavian parents than I do. His hair is a dirty blonde shade, his skin is fair, and his eyes are bright, cobalt blue. My brunette locks, olive skin and hazel eyes are a far contrast. A black bird in a flock of swans, so to speak. Our parents share many of the same skills, but oddly enough, hold very different family values. His parents are more like the "bad guy" version of mine. His father, Alec, is a surgeon, but the kind who drives a beamer and spends every free minute showering himself in his riches on vacation without Hollis or his wife. My father, Raph, is the surgeon who gives his extra money to multiple charities, and his idea of a vacation is committing a substantial amount of time to Doctors Without Borders. Hollis's mother, Blake, shared my mother's love for transforming something ugly into something beautiful; however, her transformations typically consisted of multiple plastic surgeries. First, she didn't like how wide her nose was, so she told everyone that she had a deviated septum and somehow that operation left her with a much smaller, upturned nose. Then she opted for larger breasts, sucked the fat out of her thighs and abdomen, and last but not least, she had her upper arms lifted. It must have been so strenuous for her to lift her arms with all that dead weight hanging around. Occasionally, she threw out her entire closet and bought a brand-new wardrobe for spring cleaning. My mother, Jo, would take a dismal, outdated room and fill it with gorgeous handmade furniture, potted plants, throw blankets and wall décor, and still find time to make us a delicious meal at the end of her day. She would have made a phenomenal interior decorator, but she insisted that taking care of my father and I was her passion.

I was seven when we moved into the new neighborhood. I thought our new house was a mansion. In reality, it was a 2,700-square foot, two-story home with a two-car garage and a modest back yard. It was the most money my parents had ever spent on anything, and I was in heaven. My bedroom was twice the size of the one in our last house, and I had a playroom with ample space to roam and let my imagination run wild. Hollis' house made ours look like a guest house for staff. Looking back, it's odd that our homes were in the same cul-de-sac. They had a four-car garage, a rounded terrace off the master bedroom overlooking a professionally landscaped yard with a huge, kidney-shaped pool and pool house. It must have been a couple of weeks after moving in that Hollis invited me to ride bike with him. He was showing off, popping a wheelie, and managed to bang up his knee pretty bad. His father was not home, per usual, and his mother was not good with blood. I brought him to my house and my mother patched him up.

"Good as new, buddy. I've been meaning to come over and introduce myself to your mother. Can I walk you home?" she asked.

"Oh, no. I'm fine, Mrs. Smith. She's probably taking a nap or something right now. We don't need to bother her," Hollis replied.

"You know, it's almost dinner time. Would you like to join us, Hollis?"

"Sure. If you don't mind."

From that night on, we had family dinners with Hollis at least five nights out of the week. Some nights his parents would have something catered in for a party and he would miss out. He craved the structure my parents gave him. They couldn't really punish him, since they weren't his parents, but he rarely gave them a reason to. I was adopted so young. I can't feel sorry for myself for being abandoned by my biological parents when their replacement was so superior to anyone's parents that I knew.

My father was there for Hollis when he needed advice. I would be willing to bet that he gave him the birds and the bees talk. I can't imagine the man he would have become if his real father had any part in raising him. The world doesn't need any more men like him. Hollis didn't have any issues getting attention from girls, and his father would have simply thrown a box of condoms his way with a pat on the shoulder. He would have been lucky to get through high school without contracting at least one sexually transmitted disease.

The only time I recall his parents vocalizing their right as his parents was when he asked to attend church with us one Sunday. They were adamant that he not go because they did not believe in God, and they didn't want him to be influenced by a church. I always wondered if they were mostly concerned that Hollis would learn all the ways they were morally wrong. As if he didn't already have eyes and ears of his own to figure that out.

It wasn't long after his tenth birthday that his parents got divorced. Lucky for us, his mother got the house in the settlement and we could remain neighbors. His father had an affair with a long-time mutual friend of theirs, and his mother made the mistake of returning home early from her yoga class. It wasn't the first time his father had a strange woman over. Over the years, roughly half of our class ended up becoming a product of divorce. Those classmates always seemed to struggle. Some had regular visits with the school counselor or their family therapist. Not Hollis. He was thrilled. His mother was definitely negligent, but his father was always the negative energy in the house. Now that he was gone, he could breathe again. His mother went through numerous boyfriends, and even one fiancé, but she called that off. Now that she had her divorce settlement, she didn't really need a man for anything but fun. She didn't need a nanny for Hollis, either. She had my parents for that. I'm relieved that she didn't make an effort to get to know us. It may have made it difficult after everything changed.

3

A-DAY

I was a freshman in high school when we were sent to our school auditorium, in lines by class. The echo of a couple thousand teenagers romping through the halls at maximum volume was irritating my third period social studies teacher more than usual. He was sweating through his button-up shirt and snapping at students who were not getting to their seats on the bleachers. Our principle, Mrs. Max, approached the podium and demanded everyone's attention for an important announcement.

"Before I begin, you need to understand that these new rules are now federal law. The school has not made these decisions, but we must enforce them. As of today, no students will be allowed to practice prayer, speak of their religious beliefs or have possession of any religious property on school grounds. If any of these rules are broken, you will be sent home and any religious items will be confiscated and disposed of. We have placed large bins at the end of every hallway, so you can eliminate any items that are currently in your possession or stored in your lockers."

There were some random bursts of laughter from a couple students who clearly thought this was a joke. They were shut down immediately. As she stepped down from the podium, the chatter picked up louder than before. I had nothing to say. All the commotion around me was drown out into a faint buzzing in both of my ears. I could see mouths moving, but all I could hear was buzzing. As the news began to sink in, most of my classmates could care less. They carried on with their normal gossip and making plans for their weekend. The few who would care appeared to be in the same daze I found myself in.

Typically, Hollis and I walked home together, but that day my mother was waiting for me when the bell rang. I loaded my bag into the car. Keeping her eyes straight ahead, she casually says, "Keep a smile on your face, like everything is normal. Your father is waiting for us and we will all discuss this once we get home." I pasted on a fake smile and stared ahead in silence the rest of the ride home.

My father takes my bag as we walked through the door and asked that we take a seat in his den, so he can lay out our new ground rules. I cautiously take a seat on the sofa next to my mother and place my hands on my lap. He closes the blinds behind us and takes a seat.

"I have scoured the house and I can confirm that we have not been bugged. Other residents in our area were targeted as potential terrorists, and their homes were infested with them. We will not give up our faith, but we will be smart about the way we practice it. Moving forward, there will be some ground rules that we all need to abide by. If asked how we feel about the new laws, your response will always be that it was an adjustment, but we understand why our government felt the need to make these changes. You are not to pray aloud. Not outside of this house or in this house. Ever. We will continue to take time to pray, but it will be internally. When referring to prayer use the code word "meditate." We cannot risk being recorded and taken into custody. Every Sunday, we will have brunch as a family, followed by a brief Bible study in the den.

This will only be conducted by myself, and I will have our Bible encased with the same wood as our floor paneling. It will be placed under the floorboards in the den. I will perform a search of the house for any bugs prior to each weekend, since that is when we spend the most time at home."

None of us cried. I thought he might be taking this all a little too seriously. Did we really need to worry about someone planting a bug in our house? I mean, how dangerous could a small suburban family like ours be? I didn't have a clue how bad it would get. I was an ignorant, fifteen-year-old girl, and I couldn't imagine it would result in such hateful violence. Later that week, we relay the rules to Hollis since he usually took part in our family gatherings. He understands that he can never repeat anything to his mother. Not that she would make meaningful conversation with him, but better safe than sorry.

At school, kids were being sent home for quietly saying a prayer. Any personal items with religious connection were confiscated and destroyed. There were riots throughout the city. People were running through the streets burning Bibles. Police force and Army troops were beating those standing in protest at church doors as they attempted to replace the stained glass with standard windows. Children were ripped from their parents' arms and placed into foster care. Their parents were hauled to prisons designated specifically for "religious criminals." There are rumors of the religious prisons exceeding the abuse endured in federal prisons, but no proof has surfaced. The borders were slammed with swarms of people fleeing the country, and others lining up to get in. Eventually, Immigration Customs put a freeze on the borders. Christmas Day became "Winter's Day." The lights, snowmen, gingerbread cookies, and presents all stayed the same; as if to say, "Don't worry everyone, we don't have to miss out on all the fun, even though the meaning of the season is no longer a thing."

It was three months in, and the riots finally started to die down. The Shepherd family lives two houses down from us in our cul-de-sac. Their daughter, Maggie, is four years younger than me. She is your typical, awkward preteen. We didn't know each other well since I am older, and decidedly too cool for her. Our parents were always friendly, and we had gone to the same church. I have just finished shoveling a pile of pancakes in my mouth and was racing out the door to meet up with Hollis when she comes bolting up our porch stairs. I nearly trample over her. Her whole body is trembling. Tears are streaming down her face. Her eyes look permanently pried open with terror. Two government officials restrain her before I can ask her what had happened. Her arms are stretching toward me, reaching for a lifeline. I just stare at her as they cart her off to their vehicle, surely to become a foster child with an agnostic family. Her mother is screaming so hard the veins in her neck were bulging. I'll never forget their faces, and that I just stood there. I didn't do anything. The next day, a for sale sign appeared in their front yard. A few months later, another family moved in. I keep Maggie in my prayers every day. I pray that her foster parents are kind to her.

Some countries wait to see the results before jumping on our bandwagon. They are interested in the concept. Crime rates and terrorist acts dropped, or so they say. There are rumors that the government is fudging the statistics and covering up attacks in an effort to polish their image, and it has worked. This encouraged other countries to follow suit. The ones that don't believe their initial feelings about our country are justified. They are obviously the countries plotting the terrorist attacks, so I guess only they really know if our government is being forthright.

As years pass, more and more civilians no longer identify with any form of religion, making the transition for the government much easier. The people who stand their ground are all gradually beat down. Down to a silent follower, or just gone. Now, the majority believe that religion was an illusion that individuals developed for personal benefit. I overhear whispers comparing believers to uncivilized barbarians of the prehistoric era. It feels wrong, practicing our faith in whispers, behind closed doors and covered windows. Generally speaking, if you find that someone is hiding something, they are usually ashamed of the thing they are hiding. That couldn't be further from the truth in this case. My faith teaches the importance of sharing your beliefs with those around you, but here I am, walking on eggshells. Keep your prayers to yourself, and your Bible hidden deep in the floorboards.

My daily walk to my local coffee hut takes me by what once was a small Methodist Church. I imagine that it had the most vivid stained-glass windows, strong, golden walnut pews and piercing natural light. Now it is an HQ Workit. Basically, a communal workspace for people who don't have their own office or don't prefer to work at home. Where the pews would have been are cubicles. Where Communion was taken now sits a coffee station. I wonder if it haunts any of them to know they are working in what should be a sacred holy space. I doubt they even know that it used to be a church.

There is the man with salt and pepper hair seated in his usual corner near the window. A chill run from the nape of my neck clear down the tips of my toes, as if someone funneled a gallon of ice-cold water into my veins. My fingertips clear down to my feet fire up with the tingling that comes with going numb. It keeps getting worse. Even worse than the episodes that came from my sessions with Mrs. Stonedale. When I was eight, the adoption agency advised my parents to send me to regular meetings with the school counselor to ensure I was properly dealing with my issues. I had to bring an extra jacket or sweater with me on the days I needed to meet with her. She seemed nice enough. Like most school counselors, her demeanor was always poised and understanding. There was just something about her that set me off every time. I would focus on the string of beads she always wore, doing my best to answer her questions amidst my teeth chattering. (They couldn't have known she would one day murder her husband and hang herself from her foyer balcony.) The first time it happened, they thought I just had caught a virus or bacteria of some kind.

They took me to numerous specialists, and they ruled out anemia, hypothyroidism, blood vessel conditions and diabetes. What good is having a prodigy doctor for a father if all he can come up with is a diagnosis of an acute psychological nervous reaction, stemming from my tragic early years?

Luckily, my parents felt it would work its way out of my system, deciding I no longer needed therapy sessions after Mrs. Stonedale. It never did work its way out, though. Hollis's diagnosis is that I am a superhero, and I clearly have the power to shoot icicles out of my fingertips. When we were younger, I would try with all my might, imagining some powerful force to come flying through my body, to no avail. He was convinced I just didn't know how to harness my power, but one day, my birth parents—who of course must also have superpowers because everyone knows it's genetic—would appear and teach me everything I needed to know. He would become my handy sidekick, and we would run off together and fight crime.

The condition made it hard to be around large groups of people. The more people in close proximity, the greater likelihood of an episode. Needless to say, college was not my cup of tea. I enjoyed learning, but it was nearly impossible to decide on a degree that would lead to the right career for someone with my limitations. I wanted to help people, but I couldn't be there in person or near large groups of people. There was a stretch of time during freshman year that everyone thought Hollis and I were together because his arms were around me all the time, just so I wouldn't freeze to death in public. I was repulsed by these allegations, but Hollis just egged them on to aggravate me. He and my roommate Nina would humor me and stay in most weekends to play drinking games in our dorm room, so I wouldn't lose my mind.

Eventually, my comp professor brought it to my attention that I had good writing skills, and with my father's background, I might make a great medical transcriptionist. He was right. I know that language all too well because I've grown up translating it. I'm not passionate about my job, but I'm good at it, and I can do it from home. Sure, it can get a little isolating, but that's why I go for my coffee walk every day, and spy on the neighbors from our window nook. There is a little girl who lives on the third floor of the building across from us. She's not too creative, but occasionally she throws some goofy faces my way. The old man on the first floor spends his entire morning reading the paper on his tablet while his wife dusts her china cabinet or scrubs the floors. When we go out, it's usually to the same little dive bars that are 80 percent empty any day of the week. I don't have a social media page. If I did, I would have to deal with rejecting invitations to events that I can't handle sitting through. I keep my world small, and I'm just fine with it.

4

BRUNCH

It's Sunday morning, and that means it's Brunch, Hidden Bible Day with my parents. Hollis and I get our shit together and hit the road for the suburbs. It has been years since the abolishment, but it's still so bizarre to think reading the Bible is this rebellious act; let alone one that could land you in prison. Hollis reaches for the radio panel—

"I don't think so, buddy. You got choose the station last week, so today we ride to the soothing sounds of Coffeehouse."

He slaps his hand on his forehead. "Ugh, I'm going to fall asleep. An entire hour of this is not good for anyone's health."

"As opposed to the mish mash of noises and digital garbage that you listen to?"

"There's just no arguing with you. Wake me when we get there," he caves.

We pull into the driveway where a massive, shiny Harley-Davidson Road King bike is parked front and center. My mother would lose her shit if my father brought that home. No way it's his. Hollis waltzes through my parents' door ahead of me.

"Honey, I'm home! Who bought the new hog?!," he asks.

Following behind him, I stop dead in my tracks. There is a terrifying-looking man standing in our dining room devouring mouthfuls of bacon. His dark, scraggly hair is long enough to pull back into a ponytail, his muscles are rippling through the worn, dirty white t-shirt he's wearing and there is a deep scar above his right eye, running straight through his eyebrow. He approaches us with an extended hand, and I can't stop staring at the grease running down his beard.

"Leo and Hollis," he says. "It's so great to finally meet you. I have been waiting for this day for some time." His eyes are beaming with joy and excitement.

We stare back at him, dumbfounded, until my father bolts into the room, and Michael heads into the kitchen to help my mother set the table. I hear the stereo turn on and they start singing while they work.

"I see you guys have met Michael. He's an old friend of ours and will be joining us for brunch today," my father explains.

"What did he mean he's been waiting for this day for some time?" I whisper.

"We'll explain everything. Come dish up a plate."

Everything is set up buffet-style on our kitchen island. I move along, blindly scooping items onto my plate. There is a strange feeling in the room. My eyes are set on this friend of my parents. He must be at least six foot four, maybe five. My parents don't associate with anyone so rough around the edges. He's definitely not one of my father's colleagues. Is he my biological father? It could explain my darker features, but how could they be so nonchalant about it? If so, he has some nerve thinking he can just come in here all smiles, without even taking a shower, to meet me for the first time. Anger starts to burn inside me. My mother sits down next to me, reaches over and grabs my hand.

"Leo, there is no easy way to tell you this, so I'm going to ask that you remember how much your father and I love you. Your adoption wasn't an accident—"

"I knew it, you're a freaking superhero!" Hollis interrupts.

"From the general definition, no. Sorry to disappoint you, Hollis. However, your father and I are archangels. I am the angel Jophiel, the angel of beauty and wisdom. Your father is the angel Raphael, the angel of healing. The world as you know it will be coming to an end very soon. We were sent here to raise you with all the knowledge you will need to know in order to fulfill your purpose. Majority of the population will be destroyed, and there is nothing you or I can do about that. We are not here to save as many people as possible. Your assignment is to find the individuals that you will need in order to build the new society. Your purpose is to scout some of these individuals."

I place my fork back down. "Yeah, sure. So why is he here then? Is he my biological father and you are just trying to soften the blow with an even worse story? If so, you've greatly underestimated my instincts."

"Metaphorically maybe, but not literally," Michael laughs.

My mother clears her throat. "Your biological parents are not aware of your purpose, and they are not relevant to this conversation. Their purpose was making you. You know we are serious. Michael is the Commander of Angels and the Protector of Faith. He is here to train you. This is going to consume all your focus moving forward, so you will need to quit your job. We will take care of your bills, food, and anything else you need to accomplish this task."

The same buzzing noise I heard the day of the abolishment fills my ears. I can't accept this. This is a mistake. The hash browns in my stomach have mixed with acid and are starting to slide back up my esophagus. "This is ridiculous. There is no way that I am meant to or designed to recruit people for a new civilization. I can't even be in a room with more than a dozen people! God wouldn't assign someone like me to do this. He just wouldn't."

"This is where you could say you have somewhat of a superpower. Your body only runs cold when you are near a demonic presence, Leo. That is why you feel frozen in those moments. We did our best all these years to keep you from feeling abnormal because of it. We knew it would serve you well in the task at hand, and we didn't want to scare you at a young age, so we had to mislead you. For that, we are so sorry. If there had been a better solution, we would have been made aware of it. Abba designed you as a living demon barometer, and that is no accident."

"Who is Abba?" I ask.

"That is how we refer to God. It is another way of saying father," Michael says, as he continues eating his brunch.

My father pulls my chair toward him. "Michael will give you the address where your training will take place. He will walk you through your assignment and prepare you for the upcoming months. It's important that you follow his every instruction exactly as he states. I'm sure you will come up with more questions once the shock of all this wears off. We understand this is a lot to take in, but just know that you were built for this, Leo. You will have all the support you need. Hollis, that includes you."

"Yes, sir," says Hollis.

Michael hands me a piece of paper with an address, date and time written on it. I can't think, and they are all staring at me. Anticipating my reaction. I head for the door, dragging Hollis out with me. They don't try to stop me. I'm sure they don't have to ask what I'm thinking. They can probably read my mind. Do they know everything I did growing up? All the stories I came up with for making it home late. They knew the truth, and just let me think otherwise.

I tossed Hollis the keys. No way I am about to drive after taking that in. Hollis bounces down the front porch stairs and flings his body into the driver's seat. I could feel the excitement about to burst inside him, but he held it in. He would look over periodically, with a half grin. Only Hollis would be excited about the end of the world. Finally, he let it out.

"Leo, you have to say something. This is insane! You get to select who makes it through the end of the world! Come on!"

I crumple my face into a scowl. He is like a giddy schoolgirl who just found out she won class president. He badgers me to stay up with him and research every apocalypse series we can find. He finally conks out on the couch, and I make my way to my bed. I lay awake, staring at the old popcorn ceiling, and the questions start rolling through my mind one after another. How will everyone die? Where will we go to be safe when this all goes down? How do I explain this to a total stranger and convince them I'm not bat shit crazy? What is going to be left after? How soon is this going to happen? Why didn't I just stay at my parents' house and ask all these questions earlier today? I need to write this down.

Appointment Card

Address: 1247 2nd Street Fillmore, FL. 33523

Date: January 4th

Time: 13:00

I don't recognize the small town just 47 miles north of the suburb I grew up in. The town of Fillmore now has a whopping population of 16 people. The address takes us to what appears to be an abandoned library. I look the streets up and down. Not a single person in sight. Just a few small houses with some boarded-up windows. Hollis is looking around, too. "I don't see the Harley. Think we beat him here?"

"Maybe he has wings and legit flew here."

We decide to get settled in. There are cobwebs draped in every corner, shelf and window. I flick the light switch up and down. It's good there is a lot of natural light, because none of the lights work. We maneuver through aisles of large, wooden tables and chairs. The towering shelves of books have ladders on wheels to reach the top rows.

Suddenly, there is popping sound, followed by a loud BEEP!

What makes a sound like that? No, not an old oven. I think it's one of those metal boxes called a microwave. I'm pretty sure it caused cancer for thousands of people, but damn, that smells amazing.

Michael saunters into the room holding a massive bowl of popcorn.

"Thank Abba for Orville Redenbacher," he chuckles.

I look to Hollis and whisper, "Who's Orville Redenbacher?"

He shrugs his shoulders. Michael sets the bowl down on one of the tables and pulls out a dusty, old school chalk board. "Who's ready to get down to business?"

"I don't think I really have a choice, so let's get this over with," I reply.

"Everything's a choice, and you're here, so let's start at the root of this. Years ago, the hearts and minds of society moved into a negative meditation. You might recognize this as anxiety. Believers were bombarded with the message that religion is the source of everyone's pain and suffering. The pressure that this caused stirred up panic in their hearts, and eventually it extinguished any remnants of their passion for the Lord. Basically, anxiety is where faith goes to die. A pursuit of perfection defined by evil entities then became priority above all else. It took keeping up with the Jones' to a new level. As you navigate this journey, it is important that you remember who instigated this. If God doesn't exist anymore, then who is dictating the only set of moral standards?"

Hollis and I remain silent.

"Come on, anyone? You don't have to raise your hands."

"The humans in legislature?" I ask.

"Right. Gold star for you, Leo. Don't forget about all the people in power who influence them. Avoid finding yourself in their presence, unless you are dying to experience hypothermia. The best thing you have going for you at this point is your anonymity. Keep it that way. If you feel a demonic presence and it is not crucial to your mission, avoid it at all costs."

He walks back to the chalk board, places his hands behind his back and paces back and forth like a drill sergeant.

"The groups necessary to build a new society are law enforcement, teachers, physicians, nurses, judges, lawyers, scientists, engineers, farmers and environmentalists. You will be specifically responsible for recruiting a neurosurgeon, a police detective and an environmental scientist."

He picks up a piece of chalk and writes:

"Character traits must uphold:

They are honest.—Treats others with love and respect.

They are humble.—Open to learning and growing.

They are brave.— At times, may make unpopular choices if it is the right thing to do.

Above all, they must profess their belief in God, the Father Above All, Creator of Heaven and Earth!

Helpful tips

*Look for those who walk in love. Look for glimpses of compassion; may be a little rusty in the faith department. Do not let that deter you.

*Abba uses sinners. The New society must remember this dark time. If every recruit is perfect and pure, no one will be able to testify to the way things were before.

*Light is attracted to light. Let yours shine, see who responds. Keep your eyes open, use the instincts you have been blessed with. In order to determine these traits, you will perform surveillance."

I interrupt. "Can we rewind a little? How will everyone die? How many of us will be left?"

He rolls his eyes. "The earth's population will be well under 1 percent of what it is now. There will be a series of exterminations. Massive earthquakes, fires, floods and disease.

All that Mother Nature has to offer. There will be creatures you could only imagine in your wildest nightmares. Basically, Hell will be able to unleash itself onto Earth. Ultimately, this isn't your concern. You and all of those chosen to be a part of the new world will be safe, so no worries."

Hollis is sitting next to me munching on popcorn like we are at the movies. I continue along my list of questions. "Where will the chosen survivors go?"

"There will be a designated underground safe haven for the new society. You will not know its location until the time is near. Now, back to the job at hand. You have approximately one year to recruit one individual within each role. You must stay inside the provided map boundary, as there are others completing the same task outside your area. Your first step will be research. Find the best of the best in their profession. That's the easy part. Once you've narrowed the list down, you can start surveillance. You will have allies available. These archangels will be there to assist you at the right time. Any instructions they provide are to be followed. They are experts in their arena, and if you need them, it probably means our mission is in jeopardy. There will also be one more human, other than Hollis, to assist you. Just like the archangels, they will arrive at the right time."

Hollis's wheels were turning. "Don't you think these professionals are going to question our sanity when we approach them with this?"

"We will cross that bridge when we get there. Let's just get a worthy candidate first."

"How am I supposed to help in all this?" Hollis asks.

"You're Leo's wing man." Michael slaps Hollis on the arm. "You are going to be her second set of eyes and ears. When she needs you on a stakeout, be there."

Hollis puffs up his chest. "On it, Captain. So, are you like Raph's and Jo's boss?"

Michael laughs. "Outside of Abba, we don't really put a label on leadership. That's pretty much how Lucifer fell. Raphael and Jophiel have their gifts and I have mine. I know there will be more questions, and we will have more time together to discuss them. You can choose what profession you want to start with. You have one month to choose your first candidate."

They might be up and ready to take this on, but I need to know more. "All those people will die horrible deaths. I knew the abolishment was a huge, terrible step in the wrong direction, but do all those people deserve this?"

Michael takes a deep breath and places his hands on my shoulders. "You can sit in a stupor, mourning for those who made their bed, or you can rise to the occasion and build a world worth living in. Those people were given ample opportunity to make the right decisions, and they chose evil. If you believe in good, you best know that evil also exists. To believe anything different is naive. This is your moment to make a difference. Be the defender of the new world."

I see a glimmer in his eye. He knows that pep talk was top notch. I extend my hand into his massive palm and shake on it. He lets out a thunderous belly laugh, and then he is gone. Hollis and I spin around in circles, looking for any trace of him, only to find ourselves alone in the grubby, old library. Hollis points toward the chalkboard. It has been wiped clean. All the notes, gone. I guess that explains the empty parking lot.

5

WELCOME TO HATES, SIR

We arrive back at the condo and I feel an intense pressure building in my head. I rummage through the medicine cabinet and pop a couple ibuprofen in my mouth. Hollis needs to decompress and decides to take a shower. I lean onto the door frame, staring at my disastrous bedroom. The laundry basket is overflowing with dirty clothes from the last couple weeks, the blankets on my bed are crumpled, and there is an empty bag of chips sitting on top of my dresser. I bend down and lift the laundry basket with the intentions to bring it to the laundry room, but as soon as my hands grip the wicker handles, I toss it across the room. Normally, when I'm stressed out, cleaning burns off all the nervous energy, and my problems seem less worrisome after. I can't pretend this is a normal problem. I grab my jacket, pull it over my shoulders and set out to get some fresh air. Three blocks away from our building, I take a seat on a public bench.

I pull my legs up to my chest and wrap my arms around my knees for comfort. There is a man on the sidewalk across the street. He picks up his pace behind a young woman wearing a bulky brace on her left foot. She is hobbling around on crutches as everyone else on foot passes her by. I almost miss it, it happens so fast. He rips her purse right off her shoulder, throwing her down onto the hard concrete. Her chest slams down with a thud as he makes a run for it. There are other pedestrians, but they just look the other way. The thief makes it to the next block and slows to a casual jaunt. *Welcome to Hates, Sir.*

Across the street from them, a woman in a shiny, new Tahoe pulls into a handicap parking spot. She hops out and heads straight into the adjacent nail salon. I glance at her rearview mirror and check out her license plates to find she doesn't have a handicap permit. *Eternal damnation for you, ma'am.*

Two business doors down, a small group of college-aged guys and girls clean their plates. They look around the restaurant suspiciously, nod to one another, and dash out the front door before their waiter can bring them their check. If only they knew the torment that quesadilla would earn them.

There is a police officer sitting in his patrol car on the same block. His head is facing down, so I guess he is either looking at his phone or has dozed off. Regardless, unless someone is bleeding out on the concrete, it's doubtful he will look twice. I look at my phone. This all happened within half an hour in plain sight.

My parents have told me stories about how different moral standards were back in the late 1900s to early 2000s. Apparently, grocery stores used to employ people to facilitate the checkout process and some of the other employees would even bag your groceries for you. The doors on public buildings often had to be opened manually, and total strangers would occasionally stop and hold the door open for others. At coffee drive-through windows, one person would pay for the individual's drink in line behind them, and then that person would do the same for the people behind them, and so on. They got the idea from this super old novel, In the Garden of

Delight, that then became a movie called Pay It Forward. I can't even remember the last time I spoke to a stranger, let alone pay for their coffee. The thought wouldn't even occur to me. There is never a reason to. How could I be their best option to stalk and approach these candidates? Based on my observations, most others appear to have sold their souls a long time ago. I suppose avoiding human contact is a minor infraction. At least I'm not mugging crippled people.

The walk home isn't proving to be more encouraging. I raise my eyes to look at the passersby faces just to see if anyone will look at me. Most of them avoid eye contact, none of them smile and some of them actually scowl at me. They all race by, darting away as to avoid having to brush up against another human being. Now that the world is facing the largest genocide of all time, I just can't see them as people. Because thinking of them as people would mean that they have feelings and opinions. It would trigger empathy, and empathy would make it difficult for me to do my job. I prefer to think of them as a species. They are all simply Homo sapiens. Their opposable thumbs, hairless skin and bipedalism are what define them.

Once they are all gone, the species is going to be endangered. I guess I don't really know if that's entirely accurate. Maybe the environmental scientist I need to recruit will know those qualifications. I turn the corner next to my building, my shoulders slumped, and trudge up the stairs. I reach out to the pad next to the door with my key card and nearly slam my face into a man's chest. I look up to find he is just staring back at me, and he is holding the door open. He's tall, his hair is dark and wavy, and his eyes show the marks that crow's feet would leave had he been smiling.

"Are you waiting for me to go?" I reluctantly ask.

"Yes. That's why I'm still standing here, holding the door for you like a jackass," he replies.

"I guess they do exist," I mutter to myself as we make our way to the elevator. A perplexing energy fills the space as we climb to the third floor. If we hadn't interacted, I wouldn't feel the need to say something. This is his fault for holding the door for me. I may not like making direct contact with strangers, but it's odd to find someone else who is comfortable with complete silence, in an enclosed space with only one other person. He isn't even looking at his phone. Maybe he's an alien. We glance at each other, as if calling one another's bluff, and then quickly turn back to facing the elevator door.

Hold on, what if he is a serial killer? White American male, check. Emotionally manipulating? I would say holding the door for me counts as superficial charm at the very least, so check. After witnessing the utter garbage the world has become, I wouldn't be shocked. It could explain his odd behavior. The rickety doors shutter open and I march down the hall trying my best not to move as if I'm onto him. I glance back and see that he is still behind me, moving in the same direction. I walk faster and almost break into a run, whispering to myself, "Please be open, please be open, please be open." I turn the door handle and fall into Lorenzo's condo. He is sitting in his underwear, looking at his phone on the sofa.

"I knew it was only a matter of time before you came knocking down my door, Leo."

I brace myself on his kitchen counter in an effort to catch my breath. "Shut...up...I thought I was being followed by a serial killer and I didn't want to bring him right to my place where he could cut me up into a million pieces," I stammer.

"So, you thought you should bring the serial killer to my place, where he can cut us both up into a million pieces instead? Not your brightest moment."

"Now that I'm thinking more clearly, I can see how that was a bad idea. I'm sorry. Can I just hang here for a few minutes until I know that the coast is clear?"

"I guess so. I could see how a girl like you would find safety in strong, protective hands like mine," he smirked.

After thoroughly explaining how this visit was in no way sexual, I make my way back down the hall to my condo. I let out a sigh after closing the door behind me, only to look up and see the tall, dark wavy hair guy swigging down a beer with Hollis in our kitchen. I do a double take as Hollis wraps his arm around my shoulder. He pulls me toward tall, dark wavy hair serial killer guy. "Leo, this is my new coworker, Amos. Amos, meet the infamous Leo."

"Ahh, the strong silent type from the elevator," he smiles.

A wave of embarrassment washes over me. I have one training session with the Commander of Angels and I go full blown conspiracy theorist on my roommate's coworker.

"I could say the same for you," I said, warily returning the smile.

There is something about him that feels familiar, like déjà vu, but just the subconscious memory of him. It's the way he smells. That's it. It's the weird microwave popcorn. Orville

Rubenspaker or whatever. He's the one. He notices that I am staring at him, but instead of looking away, he holds my gaze.

Hollis breaks the silence. "Well, this has been awkward. We are heading to Rosco's for a drink. Care to join us, Leo?"

"Not tonight. I can't. Lots of laundry to catch up on. You guys have fun though."

They chuck their empty beer bottles into the trash and head to the bar. I don't dare join them. I need to collect my thoughts before I say something that blows my cover.

***

It's 9 a.m., and I've been up since 6 contemplating waking Hollis. I pace up and down the hall in front of his room. I pried his door open so I can watch for any signs of life. He finally rolls out of bed, and I practically pounce on him. He staggers into the kitchen and I scurry behind him like an excited puppy.

"That was him. The other helper person!"

Hollis rubs his eyes and holds his hand in front of my face. "What? Who? Can I have a cup of coffee before we do this? And can you turn the volume down a notch?"

"Didn't you smell him?" I ask.

He shakes his head. "Smell him? Did I smell my new colleague? Nope. Pretty sure I didn't smell him. What has gotten into you?"

I slam a cup of coffee in front of him to keep his interest. It nearly scorches the top of his mouth upon his first sip, which he illustrates with a jolt.

"He reeked of that delicious microwave popcorn that Michael made in the library!"

"Have you even thought to consider that just maybe he had made a different kind of popcorn yesterday and you're just losing your mind? Think about it. He is the network's new audio technician. I'm pretty sure that doesn't set him up to assist you in scouting the last living souls on earth. He doesn't even work in human resources."

"Why don't we make a bet of it, then? You call him and line up a night for us to get together. All three of us, and I'll prove it to you. If I'm wrong, the drinks are on me," I offer.

"Using my love of gambling against me are you?" he says, eyebrow raised. "Fine, but only because it's my job to be your wing man."

I know he's the one, and I am certain he knows who I am, too. Strangers don't just radiate that kind of intensity. I've heard of eye-gazing workshops in which a host pairs up complete strangers, sounds a gong and each pair is meant to stare into each other's eyes, no talking, for one entire hour. Some say they experienced a wide range of emotions, but always starting with a deep discomfort. It's so uncommon to look into each other's eyes, and often we are taught that staring at someone is rude. Attempting to connect with a stranger is a risk most people are terrified to make. That is what I should have felt here tonight, but I didn't. There was an understanding in his eyes, and I didn't want to look away. I need to know why he was chosen to be one of my allies.

6

ICE BREAKER

Maybe the floral romper? No, that's too casual. I chuck it onto my bed with the others, and pull a red maxi dress out of the closet. No, makes me look like a tourist. I need something more...serious. It's the night I'm going to gather the information I need about Amos. It won't hurt to look like a female that understands the value of appearances for one night. Half of my closet is strewn about the room. I hold up my usual little black dress. It's fitted, but not too tight. We have a winner. It has just the right amount of class, with a side of I didn't try too hard. A little concealer and mascara to seal the deal. I slip on my strappy black wedges and head out to round up Hollis. He's perched on the sofa watching football with a beer in hand. I do a quick spin to show off the new, improved me. He nearly chokes on his beer. "Look at you, getting all dolled up for our new friend Amos!"

"Alright, when we get to the bar, you need to suggest we play an ice breaker. Then I'll get us started with a game, and you just follow my lead. Make sure you bring your wallet for those drinks."

Hollis shakes his head. "You are going to feel like a moron when he has no connection to this."

He slips on his shoes and holds the door for me. Such chivalry when I'm in a dress. I wonder what else I could get accomplished in this get up. We pull up to Andy's Bar & Grill. It's the largest of the establishments I'll agree to frequent. Hollis and I spent a few months combing the area for restaurants and bars that I could manage to spend a couple hours in. He made a list on the marker board hanging next to the fridge as a reminder that I can do some normal things.

The food is subpar, but they have my favorite scotch, and tonight they run their best deal on bar pours so the place should be busy enough that Amos won't question why we chose such a dive. As we walk through the door, I hold my breath in anticipation of any possible cold fronts. I let out a sigh of relief once I know the coast is clear. The smell of floor cleaner mixed with the deep fryer oil fills my nose. We snag the round booth in the back corner. It's a perfect view for people watching, but far enough away from everyone that I can typically avoid discomfort. The bar is to our right. There is an older man with a baseball cap bellied up next to a woman, maybe ten years younger than him. They have had at least a couple rounds of whiskey based on the empty shot glasses in front of them. She is tapping her fingertips on the bar and pretending to be interested in the football game he is watching. I can almost feel the sticky wood beneath their hands. I order my usual scotch immediately, asking for two right away. I'm going to need the liquid courage. Hollis is taking his sweet time asking the server about all the specials. Once he feels his inquiries have been charming enough, he allows her to put our order in.

"While we are playing the odds, I would like to bet that she will most likely give me her number before the night is over," Hollis brags.

"No chance, she—" The bell from the entrance dings and the front door slides open to reveal our real conquest. He's wearing dark denim jeans, a faded grey t-shirt and a pair of casual, white tennis shoes. Not the kind of tennis shoes you would wear to workout in, but the kind that are comfortable and stylish. He sees our booth and doesn't skip a beat. He moves with confidence, each step with a purpose. Hollis hops up and goes in for the hand grip, half hug that men do to show care for one another without risking their masculinity. Like, hey bro. How endearing. He turns toward my side of the booth. "Mind if I take a seat?"

"No, get in here. Hollis has had only good things to say about you since your last night out. However, He's fairly easy to impress, so I figured I better decide for myself."

I respond with all the extra charm I can muster. He doesn't laugh, but his eyes smile back. They are chestnut brown in the center and surrounded by a halo of green. The gesture isn't lost on me, but it is dulled by the sense that he is hiding some sadness. It's a haunted expression. Lucky for me, I'm not the girl who is interested in fixing a broken man. We are here on a mission.

Our server approaches to take his order. She puts on a first-class show presenting the specials of the evening, as though we were at a Michelin star restaurant. Once she finishes, he immediately tosses the menu her way and orders an old fashioned. He clearly doesn't live and die for attention the way some men do. I glance at Hollis and raise my eyebrows in an attempt to take his focus off the waitress and stick with the plan.

"Why don't we make this fun with a little ice breaker," Hollis encourages with an animated grin.

I throw my hands up in excitement. "Great idea! I know just the one. I will ask you questions for three minutes and then you can ask me questions about myself for three minutes. Think of it as speed dating for friends."

Amos agrees with a hand gesture to move the game along.

"Alright, here we go. Where did you grow up and what is your family like?"

"I grew up in the small town of Springfield, Oregon. I have one sibling, a sister, named Olive. My parents, Grant and Sibley, own and operate a marijuana farm. They devote most of their time to that. I don't really keep in touch with any of them."

"How old are you?"

"Thirty-nine."

"Did you earn a bachelor's degree?"

"Yes."

"What was it in?"

"Philosophy."

"That's interesting that you would end up an audio tech."

"I ended up with a lot of experience with my first profession. I followed my bachelors with a seminary."

"You were a priest?"

"Bingo."

"How do you get audio experience as a priest? Did you perform exorcisms?!," Hollis asked.

"Shut up, Hollis," I say, holding my hand over his mouth.

"As you probably remember, churches typically put on quite a production that required audio expertise. Yes, I performed a few exorcisms. My favorite color is red, I enjoy reading, and long walks on the beach, blah, blah, blah. I think that was two minutes. Now, is it my turn to ask the questions?"

"Your two minutes are up, Leo. The floor is all yours, Amos," Hollis says in his best game show host voice.

"Hollis has already given me a pretty clear description of you, so I'm going to get hypothetical. If you could build a perfect world, what would it look like?"

His mouth is in a flat line, and his eyes don't waiver from mine. His hands stay folded together on top of the table. Is this a coincidence, or does he know? He definitely knows, but I need to see this out as if he knows nothing.

"Well, that's easy. Everyone takes their part in caring for the planet and each other. There is no war or hunger. Everything else should just take care of itself," I respond.

He looks me dead in the eye and asks, "Did Michael make that weird popcorn in the microwave when he met with you, too?"

I turn to Hollis grinning ear to ear. We have our guy.

AMOS
AUGUST 2028

7

THE BOY WHO HAUNTS ME

I spring up, gasping for air and my arms are flailing. It feels like an elephant was sitting on my chest, and the drumming sound of my heart pounding fills my head. The sheets are drenched in sweat, and chills run through my body. It is the same nightmare every single time. I'm standing on a street in the middle of the night. The streetlight shines down on me. There is a man wearing a trench coat and a hat standing in the shadows, maybe fifty feet away from me. He slowly starts walking in my direction and then, as if we are in a movie being fast forwarded, he comes at me like a freight train until he is right in front of my face. He looks like any average man, other than his yellow, bloodshot eyes. Then he opens his mouth to speak and reveals his rotting, foul teeth. They are sharp and skinny, like fat toothpicks jammed into his black gums. His breath smells like vermin had crawled inside of his mouth and died.

He grins ear to ear. "Faith is dead. Just like he is now. You killed him, and we are coming for you next."

The concrete below me starts to melt and swallow me whole.

I can go on for months without disruption, only to find the next several months are filled with the same vision night after night. I can't say that I've been spared the scarring of traumatic events. I watched my mother bury an 18-year-old boy beneath the row of maple trees south of our fields when I was nine years old. His name was Crew. The seed driller needed repair, so my father had jacked it up and asked Crew to get underneath to repair it. The jack he used didn't hold and the drill came crashing down onto his abdomen His eyes splayed wide open as the blood pooled out from underneath him onto the concrete garage floor. It was an honest farm equipment accident, but they didn't want the bad press. When I suggested that we call the police, my mother slapped me so hard across the face that it left the red outline of her hand for days.

"You speak a word of this to anyone and you'll end up in a foster home! You know what those people are like, don't you?" she threatened.

I knew well enough to fear ending up in the system. Those kids were given just enough to survive, and most of them were suicidal by the time they hit puberty. The year I turned 12 I told her that I was going be a priest one day, so I could help people before they became like them. She laughed in my face and told my father of my "pathetic plans." Begrudgingly, I hauled the containers full of food scraps to the compost pile, watered the crops, and kept my mouth shut for six more years. My senior year of high school, I kept a calendar and a permanent marker in the drawer of my nightstand. Just before bed, I would cross that day off. It was one day less until I could pack my things and never look back.

It's always the same boy who haunts me. I remember every minuscule detail of that night. Connor Reynolds is only 12 when the Catholic church's investigative team shows up at his family's doorstep. It is the same drill every time. A representative of the church is accompanied by an appointed psychologist and a medical professional. The church's first ambition has always been to prove this was not possession of a demonic entity. It received thousands of requests for exorcism every year, the majority of which were proven unnecessary. Too often, it was someone looking for something else to blame, other than their ill family member. It was a service that put the church at risk, so it should only be performed when someone's behavior could not be explained by any other medical means.

Connor's family went through the same investigation that every family goes through. A series of questions to determine his mental state, followed by days of observation. The team witnesses the boy trying to poison his little sister with anticoagulants. He hadn't realized that they had placed cameras in the kitchen where he was mixing them into her sippy cup. A few days later, he nearly suffocates his mother with her pillow in the middle of the night. His father put locks on his doors after that evening. They had tried numerous medications and burned through six therapists that specialized in the violent type of behavior Connor was exhibiting. The family wants to place him in foster care to protect their daughter, but they can't live with the guilt associated with the torment he would bring unsuspecting families. He would go for weeks refusing to eat.

His teachers express concerns and child protective services paid them many visits. They are not Catholic. In fact, they aren't of any religious affiliation. The mother explains how she spent years trying to convince herself that there was a logical explanation to his behavior. That was until the day she sees him talking to himself in their bathroom mirror.

"The voice coming out of his little body was not his own. I knew then, that something evil was inside of my baby."

After exhausting every possibility, the church decides that the Rite of Major Exorcism is necessary, and that I am to execute it. It is my second exorcism. The first went just as planned, no complications. This feels different, and I should have requested that another priest perform the exorcism. I proceed with an assistant from the church. The room upstairs has been prepared ahead of time. All the wall decor and personal defects are removed to prevent injury. We bind his limbs using the same equipment a mental institution would use on their patients. Over the years, this proved to prevent accidents. Once everything is in place, we begin. I am going through the appropriate prayers and scriptures until my mind starts drawing a blank. It's pertinent that we use the exact words from the Bible. The procedure cannot be improvised. I look down to my book and start to search for the words when the boy lets out the guttural laugh of a haggard old man. He spews words in a language I don't understand. The temperature in the room plummets at least thirty degrees, and his hatred filled the room like a thick fog.

A gravel-filled voice inside me, so loud it drowns out the demonic noise, feeds me my next prayer. "Hearken, therefore, and tremble in fear, Satan, you enemy of the faith, you foe of the human race, you begetter of death, you robber of life, you corrupter of justice, you root of all evil and vice; seducer of men, betrayer of the nations, instigator of envy, font of avarice, fermenter of discord, author of pain and sorrow."

I am able to continue through the rite, but Connor's body is weak. The binding is strong and keeps him from breaking free, but his head is not held down. He continually throws his head back, shifting the bed closer and closer to the wall behind him, until he can smash his head into the wall, over and over. We scramble to pin it down, but it is too late. The damage is too great, and eventually, Connor's body gives in. I can still see his mother's body crumple to the floor at the foot of the bed, shaking in grief. She forces herself to stand up and lays across his body, holding onto him one last time. Her husband has to pry her off him when the ambulance arrives.

I am given a leave of absence to fast and rebuild myself spiritually. I continue in my role to perform two more exorcisms before the abolishment. I don't know if I was under attack or if Connor's death stunted me, but my mind goes blank when I need those words, and it's the same each time. That same, gravel-filled voice was there to feed me the words, and those demonic entities were expelled from those they possessed.

When the abolishment comes, I feel the deep despair that comes with your very purpose being ripped from you. I try thinking of athletes who have lost limbs and can no longer compete, or soldiers who are injured in combat and have to start a new life. Conflictingly, I feel a sense of relief that I would not have to fear a repeat of that night with Connor. I feel guilt daily for that sense of relief, and I wonder if Connor's mother felt that same shameful relief at her own son's death. *Lord, I pray for courage. I pray for the forgiveness of everyone who has inflicted this repression on to our world. Have mercy on them, Lord.*

LEO

8

DUELING DOCTORS

Things are finally starting to fall into place. Michael all at once, out of thin air, to let me know that he took Amos through the same crash course, The End of the World and Your Role in It, taught by the Commander of Angels. That said, he still doesn't know when he will be needed. According to Michael, it will be obvious. One would think that as the apocalypse approaches, they would be a little more forthcoming with the details. Riddle me this, Michael.

The condo is quiet and empty. Hollis went to work an hour ago and I imagine he will be curious to learn what I've uncovered by the end of the day. I have less than a year to hunt down and convince the top neurosurgeon, police detective and environmental scientist in this region that the end of the world is near, and they need to jump on our underground railroad bandwagon in order to survive. Piece of cake.

First things first, get online and read reviews. Look for accolades and awards. Once I know who my best in the business are, I can dig into their shade.

Let's start with the neurosurgeon. Doctors, I understand.

I grab my laptop and flop onto my bed. The map outline gives me five counties to scour. It will take too long if I need to investigate several different neurosurgeons. I will need weeks to follow them and determine if they will even be receptive to this.

Think like a recruiter.

Aha! Two of my counties are in more highly populated areas and therefore, draw more impressive candidates. I start on a website called Healthgrades and make my way through the other health portals.

Candidate number one is Dr. Felicia Rudolf. She is smiling but not showing teeth in her profile picture. Her black hair is tied back in a slick ponytail. Her skin is a beautiful, deep caramel shade. I don't see a trace of makeup. How very clinical of you, Felicia. Her profile reads the same on every health portal online.

"Dr. Rudolf strives to deliver a comprehensive evaluation and treatment plan for the patient's neurological issues with a compassionate approach. She places the patient at the focal point of her strategy to achieve the best neurological outcome and fastest functional recovery."

Nothing about this woman appears to be compassionate, but she has earned more five-star ratings than any other neurosurgeon in her county. If I ever experienced a brain aneurysm, I would want her in charge of my treatment. I'll run her background check and start surveillance on her first.

Multiple reviews later, I come across candidate number two, Dr. Isaac Kershaw. He was neck-in-neck with Dr. Martin Coan for top reviews and accolades, but his biography stands out to me. He's a dead ringer for a believer.

"Dr. Kershaw believes that medicine is a calling and he is dedicated to providing the highest quality medical to his patients."

He said it's a "calling." If that isn't biblical, I don't know what is. I'm surprised that their CEO allows him to use that language publicly. It looks like he has a family.

If you have children, you have to put someone else before yourself. Well—that's how it's supposed to work. He has a daughter named Eve. It might be a stretch, but I'm following my gut. Once I give Rudolf a once over, I'll be stalking you next, sir.

I find Dr. Rudolf's address via the county assessor website. She lives on Kylemont Blvd. and she paid a cool $6 million for her humble abode. I guess all those years of medical school really paid off. I can't find any indication that she is married or has children.

That's a lot of square footage for one person.

Not that I should judge. The longest relationship I've kept was two months long, during my freshman year of college. Just long enough to warrant giving up my virginity. Nina was the only reason we ended up together. We had nothing in common. He was a sophomore business student who was friends with Nina's boyfriend. I was angry with God, myself and the world. I had kept myself locked away for so long, I just wanted physical contact with someone. Anger was the only way I could justify it.

I look back to my screen at Felicia's face. What hurt her so badly that she is all alone? Maybe she just spent so much time studying that she forgot basic social skills.

At least these stakeouts will take place in the land of the rich and richer. If there's security in this neighborhood, I'm making Hollis get into his best burglar costume and practice ninja moves. The bedroom door creaks open, and I nearly jump out of my own skin. Hollis stands there, questioning my reaction.

"Is it really past five already?" I ask.

"Almost, I took off a half an hour early today. I figured you could use a little help, and to be honest, I couldn't focus. Being your assistant pro bono is no laughing matter."

"Well, you best be taking this job serious, because I have no freaking idea what I'm doing."

Hollis drops his gear on our kitchen counter, grabs a bottle of water from the fridge and looks over my shoulder. "Let's see what you've got so far."

"These are the top two candidates. Take a look at their ratings on the health portals. Here are some of their awards and accolades. I keep second-guessing myself about Dr. Rudolf. I'm not sure if I'm just giving her a shot because I can relate to her loaner status."

He pulls the health portal up and scrolls through her ratings, "These reviews speak for themselves. She's clearly the best at what she does in her area, so you can't go wrong looking into her." He continues reading her biography. "You realize this woman is a good 20 years older than you? Just because you haven't gotten married yet does not mean you're going to be alone forever. I mean, you'll probably always be completely infuriating, but that's a whole different issue."

I slam the laptop shut. "You're a dumbass."

"I'll have you know, that some have referred to my simplistic nature as genius, little lady. So, when will our stalking commence?"

"As badly as I would like to put this off, I think we need to start tonight before dark. Just an old-fashioned stakeout from my car. Nothing to get too excited about. It's a gated community, but I don't think the gates are closed before eight o'clock." I re-open my laptop and map the address.

"There is a community park, right here. I was thinking we could park the car off street and do some research on the picnic tables until it's almost dark. Then, we could move the car adjacent to her house and wait for the action to unfold."

"I'm game. I just need to make one stop on the way to pick up all the junk food. Every good cop stakeout scene in the movies includes a boatload of snacks. I have no idea how those guys go for hours without using a restroom, but we have to do this right. I was thinking cheese puffs pair nicely with the apocalypse. Maybe some jerky for protein? What are your thoughts?"

"Get it all. I'll be a stress-eating machine."

Two convenience stores later, we pull through the shiny gates of the Waldorf Community. There is a tiny building attached for security staff, but no one is there now. I notice a small camera at the top corner of the gate structure. The signs state that the gates will be locked every evening at 8 p.m. Each home is larger than our entire condo complex, and their yards have bushes trimmed in sphere or spiral shapes. Some entrances have large arches that I imagine lead to courtyards filled with palm trees and patio furniture. Others have circular drives. I'm sure that makes valet parking easier when they host large parties.

The outskirts of the street have a separate lane just for their golf carts. I'm relieved that I upgraded my car this year. I would have looked pretty suspicious in my sad 10-year-old sedan from the college years. At least now we could appear as some less fortunate guests, or as a couple of hired hands here to trim the lawn. There are a few cars parked off street, so we shouldn't look too suspicious when we get into position later.

The street leads us to the entrance of the community park. There are four tennis courts, two basketball courts, a playground, a separate dog park, and a fully landscaped seating area with bronze benches and picnic tables under a gorgeous gazebo. I can't even imagine what their homeowner association fees are. I'm sure more than our rent.

Hollis clears his throat. "At the very least, they should have four tennis courts. It reminds me of my father's pretentious neighborhood. He would fit right in," he says.

"It's definitely not too shabby. That doesn't exactly bode well for Dr. Rudolf in this case. I guess she's allowed to spend her money how she pleases."

I check my phone for the time.

"It's approximately 6:24 p.m. I say we bust out some of those snacks and dig up Dr. Kershaw's address. Sunset is at

6:50 tonight. Right around that time, let's find a good parking spot and get our surveillance on," I suggest.

"Let's do this," he replies.

We pull into the perfect spot just under a magnolia tree, across the street from her mansion. Hollis busts out the binoculars. There is a light on in what appears to be the kitchen. A cat jumps up onto the quartz countertop and moves toward the dining area.

There she is, leaning over her kitchen island and reading her mail.

"I have her in my sights. I repeat, she's in my sights. Over," Hollis said, doing his best covert mission impression.

"You realize we don't have walkie talkies, right? I need you to keep a lookout for any cars coming, or anyone else who might notice us. You never know what kind of bored, rich, snoopy neighbors this lady has."

The countertops are barren. The only item in sight is a coffee machine. Not even a toaster. She probably doesn't eat toast. Too many carbs. The gaping crevices under her cheekbones and between her thighs don't disagree with me.

Either she has very modern taste, or the people who owned the home prior to her did. Every wall in plain view is a basic grey shade. The furniture is white with the occasional black throw pillow. She leans down looking through her freezer and pulls out a small boxed meal. She places it into the oven and takes a seat back at the kitchen island.

Beep! Dinner is served. She places the contents onto into her cat's food dish and places it on the ground. Of course…how foolish of me to think she would eat a frozen meal.

Hollis breaks the silence by opening a bag of chips, and he starts crunching away. I reach over to grab one and he glares. "Don't you dare touch my chips, eat your own." He sighs. "This is worse than watching paint dry. How can we learn anything about someone who has no one to interact with?"

He hands me the bag of chips.

"You make a valid point. If she doesn't bust out a bible or Satan worship material tonight, I may just have to do my best following her around when she goes to work tomorrow."

I polish off our last bag of chips and decide to call it. "This isn't getting us anywhere. Let's pack up. I'll see what she does around other people tomorrow."

***

Hollis is still fast asleep, so I sneak out quietly. I need to get in front of her neighborhood before 4 a.m. so I don't miss her. Most doctors work wild hours, and if she is going in today, it might be this early.

The streets are quiet. There is something particularly gratifying about accomplishing things before the rest of the world has gotten up for the day.

I pull into a spot just outside the gated entrance. *Keep your eyes open.* I start nodding off, and right at that moment, bright headlights flood across my face and move into the street.

There she is.

I keep a healthy distance, but I have to park in the visitor lot when we arrive at the hospital. I ask the welcome desk for directions to the neurology office, and head in that direction. There's a small waiting room just outside, and two vertical windows on either side of the doorway leading into their offices. That might be my only view. She must be taking consultations today, because she isn't dressed in scrubs. One of her nurses keeps looking in my direction. *Don't get curious, lady. I'm just here for the ambiance.* I head out to the main lobby before she can ask any questions.

It's just past noon, and I see Dr. Rudolf heading into the cafeteria. I notice she has changed into her scrubs. She picks up a salad, and I follow her back as far as the hospital will let me. I stop at the family waiting room just outside of the operating area. Don't look suspicious. I take out my laptop and pretend that I'm working. A half hour goes by, and an older woman holding a wad of tissues takes a seat just a couple rows down from me. Her shaking fingers thumb through a home improvement magazine. I'm sure she's trying to distract herself while waiting for a family member to come out of surgery. I want to make conversation to help her out, but I can't risk her asking questions. Just keep to yourself. *You are only a fly on the wall.*

I've nearly bitten my nails right through to my skin when Dr. Rudolf comes through the double doors with a nurse at her side. She sits in the seat across from the old woman and starts to talk. The old woman's face pulls in between her brow, her eyes close and tears start pouring down her face. Dr. Rudolf looks as though she just explained how the procedure works. There are no movements to console the old woman. No facial expressions that could imply empathy. Based on my temperature, she may not be pure evil, but she is definitely ice-cold.

She stands up, turns to speak with her nurse and heads right back through the double doors. The nurse sits down next to the woman to further explain and console her.

I don't care how good she is in this profession. She's a garbage human.

9

BLESS YOU

Hollis is not going to be happy about this, but he has to work, and knowing how the last stakeout went, I'll learn more from watching Dr. Kershaw at work than at home. He lives in a more modest $1 million home that happens to be in a non-gated community. I'm immediately fonder of him for that fact alone. I pull into the neighborhood and park across from his house at 4 a.m. It reminds me of a castle. There is a small brick tower to the left of the main door, and I am sure there is some kind of grand, spiral staircase behind it. When their daughter's prom date knocks on their door to pick her up, they will escort him inside so they can climb up a few stairs and snap the classic rich kid prom photos.

Most of their windows are covered by blinds or curtains. His alarm must have sounded, because a light turns on in a room at the top, center of the home. It must be the master bedroom, where the curtains have been left with a gap between them just big enough to allow me to catch a glimpse of some activity. Dr. Kershaw is awake, but I don't see anyone else moving about. Rightfully so. No one should wake up this early or follow a neurosurgeon's erratic schedule. He grabs a pair of black gym shorts and a blue dry fit t-shirt that is neatly draped on the bench at the foot of their bed, heads into the bathroom and shuts the door behind him. I guess there are some things better kept private. He emerges dressed in the gym attire with a toothbrush hanging out of his mouth. The master light goes out and another, I imagine in the staircase, turns on. Don't forget to put your toothbrush back in the bathroom. A light downstairs turns on. Grabbing a cup of coffee, maybe? Seems probable, but he probably has the superhuman energy that overachievers are born with. The garage door sounds and lifts open. The doctor has left the building. Surprisingly, you drive a Tesla that appears to be at least five years old. Hmm, how humble of you.

I follow at a safe distance until we arrive at a small gym a few blocks from the hospital called The Facility. There are maybe seven other people there for the class. It's a mix of men and women, all of whom I have the utmost respect for. Crushing a workout this early in the morning is no small feat. I can barely manage to throw on my clothes before 7 a.m. They warm up with a sequence of exhausting movements followed by the most intense workout I can imagine enduring. The coach or trainer, whatever he is called, follows them up and down the gym, barking orders at them. Dr. Kershaw is keeping pace with everyone there, and at times he is finishing the set first. They cool down with some stretches and he says goodbye to his fellow survivors. The parking lot is small, so I duck down to avoid detection.

We head straight to the hospital. He pulls into a front row parking spot designated for the doctors on duty. A few feet away, a small group of sex workers is trolling for any devastated visitors who might get on board with anything to numb the pain of losing a loved one, or simply having to live with an ill spouse. Their restless legs wobble and shake on top of their six-inch platform shoes or inside their thigh-high boots, no doubt from withdrawal. All it will take is one quickie in the parking lot to get that next opioid fix from one of the local nurse/freelance drug dealers.

I find the quickest spot in the regular visitor section so I can stay with him. I make it to a waiting area just outside of the neurology department and he goes back into what I suspect must be a doctors' lounge, to shower and get into his scrubs.

I sit and wait.

The walls of the waiting area are slathered in hideous commercial wallpaper and it smells like harsh cleaning supplies and death. I get glimpses of him popping out to meet with clients from the pre-op area of the surgical center and in between trips to his office in another wing of the hospital. It takes all my effort to remain calm when he does appear. I'm guessing he performs two to three surgeries a morning and spends the rest of his day in the office or in consultations.

It's 1 p.m. and he comes out of the office. I follow him to the cafeteria and find a place in line just a couple people behind him. A woman comes screaming through the hallway and I see two hospital security officers chasing after her. She's only wearing one of the hospital gowns you are given when you are admitted. The visitors in the cafeteria are startled. She gets within a few feet, and I feel it coming over me. My veins harden and it takes everything in me to keep my teeth from chattering. She dodges the security guards, flashing her white backside to the crowd with every turn. Dr. Kershaw tries to take control of the situation and demands that security return her to her room upstairs before she scares his patients in the waiting room. The nurse behind him whispers, "I'm pretty sure it's one of the regular schizophrenia patients that Dr. Carrol sees. Sarah Dalton, that's her name. She's gotten out before. They have placed her in St. Joseph's Psychiatric Care Center, but every so often they send her back here for further evaluation."

He makes his way to the front of the line and orders a Cobb salad with the dressing on the side. I know how to test him. My parents said that people used to routinely say "bless you" to someone after they sneezed. Way back, during times of plague, the Pope suggested people say God bless you anytime someone sneezed with the hope that it would protect them from death. It has been awhile, but I've heard people say it. I have to try.

I let it rip. "Aaaah-Chuu!"

Crickets. No one says a word. These were the habits of faith that had died hard. Even people who didn't believe anymore still said things like this.

Instead of sitting down at a table with colleagues, he takes his lunch back to his office. I decide to spend the afternoon researching facial expressions and their indications online. Apparently, those with narrow faces and prominent noses are assumed to be more intelligent. My heart-shaped face and small, slightly turned up nose is not fitting that bill. However, those with a happier expression were assumed to be intelligent verses those with more of an angry expression. So, all I have to do is smile more often. I hear men telling me, "You should smile more often," enough as is. I don't need to hear I from the voice inside my head, too. If using my face to express confusion, frustration or anger makes me stupid, then I don't want to be smart.

I have finally warmed back to a normal, human temperature, and Dr. Kershaw packs up his things and heads back home. This is my life now. I spend most of the day engrossed in my own thoughts while pretending to be working on my laptop, until the person that I'm spying on makes a move. The drive home is too quiet. I actually miss Hollis' banter, but I'm not calling it a day yet. This is what I've been waiting to see, and tonight the blinds are open. He has a family, so now I get to see a glimpse of his interaction with them. I pull back into my parking spot across from their house. His wife, Marin, walks into the foyer. Her hair is on the border between brunette and black. It's stick straight and stops just below her chin in a sleek bob. She is beautiful, but her eyes look tired and her shoulders are slumped over in defeat. She doesn't appear to be excited to see him, but she meets him halfway into the entrance with a hug. They exchange what I would guess to be mundane details from their days. His daughter, Eve, races into the room and bolts for his arms. She's the spitting image of her mother with a little added baby fat. He lifts her into the air and spins her in circles. She's beaming with excitement. In her right hand is a stuffed alligator that she is attacking him with. Chasing him around the living room and chomping with delight. Their lighthearted games put a smile on Marin's face. It lifts her tired eyes and brightens her complexion. He peers over and catches her in the brief moment of happiness. They make eye contact, and his eyes start to water. He breaks the connection and blinks back the tears.

So, there is a heart in there.

***

Hollis joins me every other evening for weeks to ensure what I saw the first day with the doctor was not just a fluke. Some evenings are spent parked in front of his house and others at the hospital, but I prefer watching him at home.

At least once a week, they have family game night. Eve doesn't quite grasp the concept of Monopoly yet, but they are patient with her. Isaac lets her sit in her own chair and he lays her money out by denomination in front of her. Every roll of the dice is followed by a celebration. She is a happy kid, and Isaac is much more involved than most fathers today.

I know I've uncovered what I need. In the general sense of what makes a dedicated surgeon, he most certainly ticks all the boxes. He expresses empathy for the families of deceased patients. When there are difficult decisions, he digs deep before making suggestions. He cares, and it was written all over him—in the way he moves and through his facial expressions. Sure, his wife had her rough days. But wouldn't those who believe, struggle through this life more than those who didn't believe in the first place or those who have simply given up the faith? His daughter brings the joy back to them with her smile and wonder at everything around them. They have shown me a family dynamic that I would want as an example for the new world. When I sit in my car watching them, I feel a sense of hope. I want to know them personally, and that's proof enough for me. I don't want to burst this bubble I've put them in. The story I've framed around Isaac, Marin and Eve. What if I approach him and find that he is nothing like the man I thought he was?

***

Hollis is still laying there, his mouth wide open and a strand of drool runs from his mouth to his pillow. He is so quiet and peaceful when he's asleep, but I've been up for hours. I can't wait anymore. It's only 20 minutes until his alarm would normally go off. That's it. I grab his shoulder and shake it. He groans.

"Good morning, sunshine. I know waking you up is a repeated offense on my part, but I have something important to tell you."

Without opening his eyes, he grabs the pillow from beneath his head, rolls over onto his stomach and pulls the pillow down onto the back of his head to block out the sound of my voice.

"It's him. I'm certain of it. I'm going to reach out to Michael today for more guidance. I thought you would need to know, wingman!" I yell into the pillow.

Keeping his head under the pillow, he lifts his arm to give me a thumbs up.

"That's great. Can we agree that these conversations could wait until I've at least had my coffee?"

I race to the kitchen, pour him a cup and wait outside the bathroom for him.

"Can you come with me if he can meet me today?" I shout into the bathroom.

The door opens, he takes the coffee mug out of my hand and takes a drink immediately.

"Yes. I can call into work and tell them I need a personal day. Are you sure I shouldn't just quit my job?" he asks.

My parents made it very clear that he needed to stay at his job for the sake of keeping a sense of normalcy around our home. I don't want to know who or what would be watching us closely enough to notice, but we don't need any enemies getting in the way.

"No. We have to follow their instructions. Just keep your job for now. We can always ask again once we get further into the process."

I call the phone number that Michael wrote down on the piece of paper with the library address. A woman's high pitch voice picks up. "Hello, how can I help you?"

Did I dial the wrong number? I look down at the number on cell phone and then at the piece of paper. *No, I got it right. Just roll with it.*

"Hi, this is Leora Smith. I am looking for Michael. Sorry, I don't really know his last name...or if he has a last name. Do I have the right number?" I ask.

She giggles. "Of course, I'll connect you. Please hold."

She clicks off and elevator music begins playing on the other end.

"Leo! Hey girl, did you land one yet?" Michael asks.

"I didn't land him yet, but I know who I'm going after. Do you have time to meet with Hollis and I today?"

"For you, of course, see you at your place around 15:00 hours."

I turn to Hollis. "What should we get to host the Archangel of War?"

He bursts into laughter. "Michael seems like a beer guy. Maybe some chicken wings? We know he likes bacon."

I run my fingers into my hair and clench my fists, "How can you be so nonchalant about this? I can't even sleep most nights. You do realize that this isn't a movie, right?"

His face goes straight, and he reaches for my hand. "My role in all of this is to support you. Of course, I'm freaking out inside, but that isn't going to change anything."

He points out of our window, "Ninety-nine percent of the people out there are total trash. The people in my studio at work, they only care about one thing—getting ahead of everyone else. If it doesn't serve them, they don't care. Just in our lifetime alone, mankind has had every opportunity to make a change for the better."

He throws his hands in the air. "Maybe it's not healthy, but I choose to see this like one big spring-cleaning job. God is taking out the trash. You're in this position because you are compassionate, and you'll know who the right people are. So, stop freaking out."

"Alright, I'll lay off the doom and gloom. But at the very least, we are picking up the good beer for Michael's visit, and if it turns out that consuming alcohol and animal products is not permitted in the new world, I don't know if these are my people."

Hollis wraps his arms around me, lifts me up and spins me in a circle. "That's my girl."

***

What time is it? 2:50, okay. He's going to be here any minute now. We have beer, chicken wings and a vegetable platter for a healthy option, just to be on the safe side. Hollis scrubbed the bathroom and I detailed the rest of the condo. My hands are shaking. I feel as if we invited God himself into our home. I know all the nerves are pointless because he probably knows our place is typically a mess. Just as expected, 3:00 on the dot and he walks through the front door. He looks down at us, turns back out and closes the door. Hollis and I look at one another in confusion.

Ding-Dong! The doorbell rings. I open the door and Michael comes in again. "I had completely forgotten about the whole doorbell or knocking practice that you people abide by. My apologies."

He looks over my shoulder. "Oh, look at this! You made me food?! You shouldn't have." He grabs a chicken wing, submerges it into ranch dressing and goes to town. He nearly takes up half our kitchen. It makes our place look so small.

"We weren't sure what your diet typically consists of, but Hollis thought you would be a beer and wings kind of guy."

"I'm really a connoisseur of anything delicious. I enjoy the taste of beer, but it doesn't have the intoxicating effect on me that it has on you humans. Angels have the whole balanced, steady metabolism that can't be rocked thing going for us. Also, you realize that you both already have a ticket into the new world, so you don't need to try and impress me. Just do your job. Speaking of, who's our first contestant?"

I clear my throat, "His name is Dr. Isaac Kershaw. I have been following him for two weeks. His credentials are off the charts, and he displays compassion both at the hospital and at home. If I were going under the knife, I would want him to perform my surgery. Morally speaking, he sets a great example. I just can't wrap my head around approaching him. I spoke with my father and he knows the chief resident at his hospital. He could line up a meeting with Dr. Kershaw, explaining that I am a student who is interested in learning about a career in medicine. That gets me face-to-face with him, but what do I say when I sit down with him?"

"Once you are there with him, don't waste his time by pretending to be a prospective student at all. Explain who you are, and why it is important that he join you and the others who will make up our new world."

"Oh sure, so just dive in with 'Hi, I'm not really here to learn about your career, but I am here to tell you the end of the world is here and we need you to come hide in this cave until the world is destroyed and we can come out to rebuild.' That won't raise a giant culty red flag in his face at all."

"Never lose eye contact. You will know the right words. Do whatever it takes to win him over. What's the saying you humans use? Oh yeah, Rome wasn't built in a day. Nothing that good will come easy, but it makes it that much better when you get there. Go with complete confidence. Abba believes in you and he's the ultimate recruiter."

"I can do that. I can do this." I realize I'm talking to myself aloud.

Michael finishes the last wing in the bowl.

"Well, the wings were great, and it was a good pep talk, but if that's all you needed, I've got other Heaven war things to attend to."

"Thank yo—"and…he's gone. He always has to get the last word.

10

BUTTERED RUM RECRUITMENT

It's recruitment day. My father confirmed that he was able to line up a fake interview with Dr. Kershaw. I stand in front of my barren closet contemplating my best prospective medical student disguise. I don't know why I fuss; it doesn't really matter. He is not the type of man to take one look at me and walk away prior to giving me the benefit of the doubt. I want to play the part anyway, so I pull on a pair of black slacks, a blue button-up collared shirt and a pair of black ballerina flats. I feel the nerves humming under my skin, so let's avoid a catastrophic tumble in high heels. Thank God he has agreed to meet me for coffee at a small local place near the hospital. I don't think I can stomach the long process that comes with ordering a meal at a restaurant. It's 20 minutes earlier than necessary to head out, but I want to have time to get my drink and find us a table far enough away from others before he arrives. He will no doubt be on time, if not early.

The coffee shop is small, but in a pleasant, cozy way. The wooden chairs and tables all look like they were carved by hand out of the same piece of wood. I order my buttered rum latte and select a small, two-person table in the back of the room. Ouch! A tiny bit of blood seeps out of my nail bed. I need to stop chewing on my nails. Usually, I don't actually bite them, just nibble on the ends. A soothing mechanism. It explains the fixation I had with my pacifier when my parents adopted me. Up until that year, I was the four-year-old still walking around with a binky in her mouth. That's when they decided to trust me with the pearl necklace my mother had left for me and here I sit, chewing the nails on one hand and rolling the pearl between my fingers of the other. I dab the injury with my napkin and crumple it into my purse.

Just as I expected, Dr. Kershaw walks in three minutes prior to our scheduled meeting time. Today must be a consultation day, as he has opted to wear a baby blue pinstripe button up shirt with khaki slacks versus wearing his surgical scrubs. He makes his way to the counter and orders his typical americano, black. The barista is surprised that he doesn't want cream and double checks with him to make sure she got the order correct. He patiently repeats his order adding "no cream." He embodies the cool, calm and collected professional that one would expect a surgeon to be. When he places an order or asks for assistance, people stand at his attention and hang onto his every word. I wonder if he has always had this confident, entitled way about him, or if he didn't start to develop those tendencies until after he had finished his residency. The barista hands him his order and I approach him.

"Dr. Kershaw, Leora Franklin. Pleasure to meet you."

He smiles and reaches out to shake my hand.

"Leora, the pleasure's all mine. My chief resident had great things to say about your father."

I return his smile and direct him to the table I've commandeered. Before he has a chance to say anything related to the implied reason for our meeting, I dive in.

"That is so kind of him to say. Thank you for taking the time to meet with me. As I discussed with your secretary, I am

Raphael Franklin's daughter. However, I am not here to talk to you about medicine."

He places his cup of espresso back down and tilts his head.

"When religion was abolished 19 years ago, it set the apocalyptic process in motion. I'm not here to help save the world because we are beyond that. I'm here because you demonstrate the morals that we should uphold daily, and you are simply the best at what you do. There will be a mass destruction in about 11 months. Everything as you could imagine will be gone, aside from the planet we stand on and the people that are chosen by scouts like me to remain here."

I give a moment of pause to allow him to let this sink in and ask any questions. I am met with silence. His facial expression is a cross between confusion and a desire to maintain a professional appearance. I decide to continue.

"Those who are needed, like you, must profess their belief in God, the Father Above All, Creator of Heaven and Earth. This will not be revealed to the public, and your identity with us will be protected."

My hands are shaking under the table. I clasp them together to steady my nerves. He takes in a deep breath and lifts his voice to a higher octave, as if to be delicate with me.

"Leora, I am not sure who you have been spending time with who has convinced you of this, but you are aware that this conversation is punishable by law. All legalities aside, I am an atheist and always have been. I believe in science," he replies.

His expression reminds me of a father who has been forced to tell his child that the Easter bunny doesn't exist. He feels pity for me, the sad girl who must have lost her mind. *Unbridled confidence. Stop second guessing yourself. You can't falter.*

"Isaac, this might sound strange, but I've been watching you for weeks. I've witnessed your character and how you make decisions. They are not fully based on science or simply facts. You feel—or better yet, allow yourself—to feel empathy where other surgeons of your stature do not. I do not believe that you ONLY believe in science. Think about the reasons you wanted to study all those hours to become a doctor. This is your chance to do something big. We need you, and this IS your calling."

He shakes his head, "I am so sorry, but you are mistaken. I am a man of science, and honestly this sounds like a conspiracy theory that you heard. It might seem real to you. They might have been very convincing, but it's just not reality.

Have you told your father or mother about this, Leo? Maybe they can help you."

His voice is teetering on the edge of annoyance now. He thinks I am insane. The "schizophrenic" woman's scream echoes in my mind. Sarah Dalton, that's her name. The chill that ran through my body, and Amos—this is why I need him. I know what we need to do.

"What if I can prove it to you? The schizophrenic patient that disturbed you while you were waiting in line in the cafeteria a couple weeks ago. She is not schizophrenic. She is possessed by a demonic entity, and that is why none of the medications they keep trying will work for her. They never will, because there isn't a medical explanation for what is wrong with her. A member of our team was a Catholic priest before the abolishment. He has experience with removing evil entities like this. Come to her exorcism and you can see for yourself."

He hesitates. "I can't risk losing my family and career to attend an illegal practice because a young woman tells me a scary story." He follows with a nervous smile. I can see the curiosity in his eyes. I push harder.

"If you're right, then all you have lost is a couple hours of your time. It will be a secure location and completely confidential. But if you decide NOT to give us those couple hours of your time, you will be condemning your family to hell on Earth, Dr. Kershaw. At the very least, do it for Marin and Eve. If you are not convinced, I will move on and choose another neurosurgeon. You have my word."

He wraps his hand around the width of his burrowed brow, deep in thought. I can hear every whoosh of the espresso machine, the glasses clanking onto tables and chattering voices at all different octaves around us. I sit in a tornado of blurred activity, bracing for his next words. He removes his hand and looks at me with a dead, stoic face.

"I'll agree to witness this so-called exorcism, but I need to know everyone who is involved and the location ahead of time."

I realize I had been holding my breath, and with its release my body melts down into my chair.

We got him.

***

I'm tapping my toes on the base of the table and stringing the pearl back and forth in a soothing rhythm along its chain as I wait for him to arrive. The metal seating offers much to be desired, and the unkept grounds are a clear indication of neglect. I'm starting to think I've made a mistake by not including Hollis in this conversation. Although often offbeat, he can bring an element of humor that can offset fear. He makes people feel comfortable.

An odd couple—the man stands maybe five foot six inches tall on a good day and she has to be at least five ten—walk past me with their corgi. Along the path they pass a more "normal" looking couple. The normal couple burst into laughter once they cross paths, in reflection of the odd couple's arrangement. I feel a twinge of guilt for thinking the same thing, but then relief that they didn't directly insult them. Two little boys playing swords in the grassy area are yelling, "Die, you freak!" And "Not until I've stolen your treasure, you scum!"

They really don't get props from me for their creativity. Too close to reality, kids. Then I see him strolling around the bend, heading my way. He's donning the same effortless demeanor. As he passes the other people, his expressions remain full of grace and sincerity. He passes the odd couple, and it's obvious he has no negative, or even curious, thoughts about their union. A walking, talking saint. He takes a seat and removes his hat.

"You realize there are other parks in the area with a little better reputation," he says, raising an eyebrow.

"Let's be real—not that much better," I reply, fully aware I chose this scene as a reminder of the sad world we are living in. I remove my sunglasses so I can look him in the eye again. "You know how you had mentioned having experience performing an exorcism?"

He reluctantly replies, "Yes."

"Well, it's time to get your priest pants back on. We are exercising the gross out of a schizophrenic patient to win a neurosurgeon by the name of Dr. Isaac Kershaw," I respond enthusiastically.

The color in his face washes away leaving a blank, pale slate. His mouth is parted, and it remains open like his eyes staring at the leaves in the tree behind me. I've lost him.

Suddenly, they peer back at me. "This wasn't a part of the deal. I'm not ready to go back there."

"It's the only way he will even consider it, and he is the best neurosurgeon in this boundary."

"This isn't something you can just throw together in a day. I'll need a private, soundproof space, preferably in a padded room, zip ties, a holy cross, holy water, blessed salt and at least one other person must be willing to help physically detain her if need be. I still have my Bible and rosary beads." He stands up and begins pacing. "You need to understand this will be very messy and things can go very wrong. No one is ever the same after, and if we get caught, we will not be able to fulfill our promise from prison." His eyes narrow in disbelief. "You are positive a demonic presence resides in her?"

"She's possessed. I am positive of that. I can take care of your catalog of inventory. You give me the list, and I will find it. Those things are simply logistical. We already know her name, and my father has dug up details from the hospital's incident reporting system. Before committing to this, I had no idea how I would know who the right people were or how to gain their trust. Michael told me that words would just come to me, that I would be in the moment and just know." I grab both of his arms. "He was right. When I was sitting in that hospital chair, watching that woman screaming, it was as if everything slowed down. As if everything around me was in slow motion, in addition to the chills she gave me. Look around us, Amos. This isn't going away. There isn't another option. I wouldn't ask you to do this if there was."

His gaze lowers back to me and I grab hold of the eye contact and pull on that lifeline.

"Alright. When are we doing this?" he asks.

I take out my laptop and we map the area surrounding the hospital to determine the closest option. I don't want Dr. Kershaw to find any excuses, like an inconvenient location, and back out last minute. There is an abandoned house two blocks away, in a rough part of town with boarded up windows and most likely a rodent problem. The idea of performing the most terrifying procedure imaginable in the most disgusting dwelling doesn't thrill me, but this is not a neighborhood that the police will show up quickly to if things go south. We decide that it would be best if my mother contacts the psychiatric unit ahead of time to send them the appropriate documentation. It will say that her remaining family would like her moved to a mental institute up the coast and will arrange for her pickup. Both her parents died in a car crash years ago. The only family I could dig up was her aunt in New Hampshire. It appears that she has been unresponsive when the hospital reached out to her. I can't image she will have a change of heart this time.

111

It's nearly dark and the park has thinned out. Well, the normal population base has, which means the people you don't want to run into are going to be here soon enough to do "business." I close my laptop and place it back into my bag. Amos places his hand on my forearm and turns to face me. "I need you to promise me that you won't be attending the exorcism."

"I have to be there, Amos. Kershaw won't feel safe if I'm not there. I can handle it. Don't worry about me."

He starts to respond and stops himself. I widen my eyes, waiting to hear his rebuttal. He purses his lips and starts again. "I'm concerned because I have some feelings for you, and there's always a chance the demon will pick up on that. If you or I waiver, this could end badly."

He looks away.

I feel my face start to flush, but I reign it in immediately. *You can't get distracted. Make him feel confident. Find the words. Give me the words.* I grab his shoulders pulling his attention back. "You are human, and you have not broken your relationship with God. Anything that demon says to you will wash off you like water on oil. If it wants to fight dirty, you have a whole book full of weapons. This is war, Amos. Get it together."

He nods in agreement and we make our way back to the parking lot together but trapped in our own thoughts. Just as we are about to go our separate ways, he asks, "Can we keep the last part of that conversation between us? I would prefer if Hollis didn't know about that."

I laugh. "You have my word; we both know he would have a hay day with that kind of information." Alone and belted into my seat on the way home, a warmth fills my chest. I let the feeling sink in for a second.

11

BRUNCH II

I return from my daily coffee run to the sweet, buttery scent of pancakes wafting in the air. I glide my way to the kitchen like a cartoon character whose nose led them right off the ground to the source of that delicious scent. Hollis is dancing around in what appears to be a pair of pineapple printed onesie pajamas that he has cut the legs off to make them into shorts. He grabs a plate, spins around to hand it to me. Then he slides a spatula under one of the cakes, flips it out of the pan and onto my plate. He roars in his own celebratory applause. "And the crowd goes wild!"

"Bravo, chef master onesie, but you do realize it's Sunday Brunch day, right?"

"But of course, I do, Madame. I have had the honor of conversing with the parentals and they will be joining us in our lovely chateau for Sunday Brunch this morning," he coyly responds with the most atrocious French accent.

I bow to his extraordinary show. "Oooo la la. In that case, let me shower so I'm ready. Thanks for the heads up, by the way!" I race to the bathroom and slam the door behind me.

My mind is running a mile a minute under the stream of hot water. I need my mother's assistance, but I know they will drill me about the procedure. Will Michael be here, too? I should have asked Hollis. But seriously, why didn't he tell me sooner? They must know so much about me that I've thought was kept secret. Images from college run through my mind. All the booze and first-time sexual encounters. I realize I have been lathering my hair in shampoo the whole time and my scalp feels raw. The doorbell rings as I'm drying off. I come out to greet them, my hair still wet, but I'm fully clothed. Michael is nowhere to be found, just my parents. They are just your parents. Sure, they might know every thought you've had, but they are still just your parents. We exchange the usual hugs, and like vomit, the words fly out of my mouth. "Do you know everything I've ever done or thought? Because, if you do, it's so wrong."

My mother wraps her arm around my waist and guides me to the dining room table.

"Sweetie, we are not omniscient. If Abba wanted us to know your every thought, we would. He did not find that pertinent to your calling, so don't worry, your secrets are only between you and him. There are times that angels are assigned as guardians from afar, in which they would have access to thoughts, but we have been here with you, physically, since they day you were adopted. Abba has given us the information we need to know in order to keep you on the right path. Nothing more," she replies with a reassuring smile.

"Do you know the status of my virginity?" I ask accusingly. Hollis bursts into laughter behind them. My father rolls his eyes.

"No, and we don't care. Let me clear something up. You humans like to put certain levels on sin, but the truth is one sin is no different from another. All humans sin. You all have free will and you're all loved the same by Abba. So, it's time to get over your broken hymen and talk about the very important topic of recruiting Isaac Kershaw," he responds.

My shoulders fall in relief. I may have overreacted. We all grab plates and dish up our food. Hollis keeps throwing me glances and silently laughing. I throw a dish towel at his face in retaliation. My mother delicately spears her fork into a piece of melon and slices it with the knife in her other hand. She looks like she would if we were going to church. She's wearing a floral print mid-length dress and matching pastel pumps. I wonder if she and my father are truly a couple in real life. An angel couple? Angel spouses? I've already embarrassed myself enough today, so I'll ask that one another time.

"I hate to continue making assumptions, but I must assume you know we are having quite the challenge recruiting Kershaw?" I ask.

"Yes. Michael is kept up to date on the status of your mission, and he has made us aware. I will be reaching out to her psychiatrist this week with documentation for her transfer. Michael will not be there for the exorcism, but he is sending an expert to assist Amos. You will be in charge of making sure Kershaw gets there, and Amos will ensure that the house is set up properly. In the meantime, you need to do more research on Sarah. Kershaw will need to know her life story. It's the best way to ensure he feels empathy, and that he finds value in the procedure," she explains with a somber face.

"You know I didn't have a choice. He is an atheist," I reply.

I'm not sure if they are disappointed that I couldn't recruit him without the exorcism show, but regardless, I feel the need to defend myself. No matter how many years go by, I still need her approval.

"Honey, atheists are really just confused supporters. Think about all the effort they have put into researching this topic to come to that conclusion. They have been deceived by a notion that non-belief and freedom are a package deal, and sometimes, that belief and disappointment are a package deal. He is afraid to relinquish control. Imagine the comfort and liberty he will be able to experience with faith. Don't judge him for being human, Leo." She reaches over to move the hair out of my face. I sit back and nod in agreement.

Hollis is clearly uncomfortable with the silence. "So, what do we need to know?"

My father takes the last bite of his omelet and sets down his fork.

"Amos will be performing the Rite of Exorcism to rid her of one or many diabolical entities. You must enter that space as if you are shielded with amour. She will know things that you believe there is no way she could. She will have physical strength far beyond what could normally be. She will have violent aversions to anything Christ related, and she will very likely come after you physically and verbally. First steps will be uncovering the demon's name or names. She will deny any possession and attempt to bring doubt to you all. Amos will demand, in the name of the Lord, that the demon leave her body. There will be a series of prayers and scriptures. She will tell you things that only you may know or have thought, to throw you off. The demon may attempt to "play dead" to give you the impression it has left her body when in fact, they lay waiting. There will be a breakpoint in which the demon will reveal its name or names. Followed by a war between the demon and Amos, and finally the expulsion. It will be ingrained in Kershaw to believe she is having a seizure, hallucinations or delusions. Do not let him interfere. He will have no doubts by the end. In your experience watching him, did you come across any indiscretions?"

I search my memory. Every stake out replaying like a movie reel in my mind.

"I didn't find anything in my research or witness anything that stands out." The image of Marin's sullen face when he would return home each day washes over me.

"His wife often looked unhappy, but that doesn't mean anything, right?"

He looks to my mother and back to me. "Probably not. Just keep him in arms reach while Amos is working on the possessed. His ignorance could make him a target, and most people have some skeletons in their closet."

Hollis, with an obnoxious throat clearing, grabs my father's attention. "I would like to be there and make sure that Leo is okay. Am I allowed? I wasn't sure if I needed an invite."

"Yes, of course. Amos may need you. If he needs someone to help physically detain her, you are his guy. Can you handle that?" He extends his hand to Hollis.

It takes a split second, but he grabs his hand and shakes in agreement.

In just two days, I get to experience my first exorcism.

12

THE PROOF IS IN THE PUDDING

It's nearly 2 p.m. and the rain is still not letting up. As if we didn't need more foreshadowing of the pure evil we are to encounter tonight. Hollis called in sick to work so he could better prepare himself. It turns out that his preparation is the same kind that he exudes prior to a big date. He has vacuumed the living room twice, deep cleaned his bathroom and mine, alphabetized the spice rack, and is now currently picking lint off the bottom of our sofa. Our condo is one mean, clean waiting cell of nerves. I, on the other hand, have prepared via a marathon of horror films with an emphasis on demonic possession in hopes that the over exposure will dull my reaction to the real deal. It has been a day filled with spinning heads, green, chunky vomit and rapidly decaying bodies.

Another hour of scrubbing therapy and foul, body contortion movie scenes have gone by when Hollis gears up in his athletic gear and grabs his keys. Without warning, he wraps his arms around me in a death grip hug to whisper. "Don't look her in the eye or get too close."

I roll my eyes. "Who died and made you the demon expert? You spent your valuable research time scrubbing the condo, so I'm pretty sure I'm more educated in this area than you. Don't worry about me. You go help Amos pick her up from the hospital. He should have the rental transport van by now."

I grab my keys and head out behind him to get Kershaw. He asked that I pick him up from home today. Which means he must have taken the day off. Why would he take the day off if he didn't think this could be real? I guess he could have reason to believe he might not make it back. Or he might be concerned I'm a serial killer. Great minds think alike. I can't imagine he told Marin what he is actually up to. She probably just thinks he is being a good husband and father. Taking the day off to spend quality time with them and running a few errands for her. *Brownie points for you, Isaac.*

As I pull into the pristine community, I notice that they have upgraded their entrance with a fountain. The storm overhead cloaks the neighborhood in a shade of gloom that makes the mansions seem haunted. The stone statues are guarding the manors in an omniscient way. They might as well be gargoyles. Kershaw asked that I text him when I reach the neighborhood. His garage opens, he backs out the Tesla next to my car and rolls his window down. "I'll follow you."

The deep circles under eyes tell of the sleepless nights he has had. He rolls his window back up and waits for me to pull ahead. Marin pulls the curtains from their foyer window to see him off. She doesn't look concerned, but the act itself means she must be curious.

The abandoned house looks more intimidating in person. Amos and Hollis have parked the transport van on the street corner so they could move her in quickly through the side entrance that's closest to the room that Amos has prepared. I get out of my car and glance down the block to see a desolate street. Let's hope the neighbors work late. Kershaw parks behind my car and meets me on the sidewalk.

"So this is it. I guess it's fitting for the task at hand, right?" He smirks. I can't tell if he really thinks this is a joke or if he's one of those people that uses humor to calm his nerves. "I promised we would be discrete, and our odds of fussy neighbors are not exactly high in this part of town. Her name is Sarah Dalton. The—," I hold up air quotes, "—'schizophrenic patient' from your hospital. She was an A student in high school, an active player on the volleyball team, and a soprano in the school choir. Her only living family is an aunt in New Hampshire. Both of her parents died in a car crash when she was only 11. She was placed in foster care. She was moved to new houses three times before she turned 18. She didn't exhibit any signs of 'mental issues' until she was 16. The records indicate she has gone through six different psychiatrists, all of which have tried different medications with the same results. The first incident involved declawing her foster mother's cat with a pliers. The cat tore up her arms and chest, but she continued anyway. Her 8-year-old foster brother was the witness."

He interrupts. "Many schizophrenic patients have difficulty finding the right treatment." I hold up my hand to stop him. "I understand that you are conditioned to find logic in this, but do not be reckless in there. You are here as a witness, and that means you do not leave my side. Regardless of what she says or does. Can you agree to these terms?" His smile slowly fades away and he nods in agreement. We make our way into the side door per Amos's instructions. I hold in my breath as I open and close the door behind us as quietly as possible. The hallway is lit by emergency LED lanterns hanging on hooks along the ceiling. The walls are lined with old paneling, and the smell of moldy laundry fills my nostrils. Hollis greets us, holding his index finger in front of his mouth to make sure we keep quiet. He guides us back out of the house.

"She is sleeping…or pretending to sleep. When we picked her up at the hospital she didn't even react. It was like she was in a comatose state but with her eyes open. We moved her in and strapped her into position and she hasn't said a word since."

"Is Amos alright? The house smells like the previous owners left wet laundry sitting out."

"He is laser focused. He's setting up a stand with holy water, his books, extra towels and other exorcismish items I'm not familiar with." He looks to me and then Kershaw, wide-eyed. "You should know the house didn't smell like that when we arrived." Kershaw lifts an eyebrow in disbelief. My stomach turns at the thought.

We wait patiently outside of the house for Amos to let us know when it is time. The sun is starting to set, and I hear a roving engine blaring down the street. An old stark white corvette pulls up and parks behind the transport van. An older man, maybe in his seventies, with a slim build and smile from ear to ear approaches, "Well, if this isn't the dream team, I don't know who is!"

He extends his hand to Kershaw. "Selaphiel, but my friends call me Sully. Also known as the Archangel of Prayer. Lucky for you all, it's my job to preside over exorcisms on Earth."

Thank God. Not that I didn't have faith in Amos, but I'm pretty sure even he would be relieved to have some back up. I happily extend my hand in greeting and he pulls me in for a hug.

"Leo, just look at you all grown up. Raph and Jo just go on and on about you." I suddenly feel like I'm chatting up a distant relative. He looks to Kershaw. "And you, sir, are about to find that missing piece. Don't worry, it will all make sense," he says with a wink.

"We are just waiting for Amos to—," I try to explain but Sully interrupts, "Oh boy, it's time to get in there. Sarah has waited long enough to get her life back." He grins again, his eyes beaming with love.

I put on my armor—a fleece jacket, a stalking cap and pair of wool gloves. Kershaw is watching the process and is clearly confused as to why I would be bundling up when it's nearly 80 degrees outside. I let him know that I will explain once we are done, and we follow Sully into the house. He leads us through the lantern-lit hallway until we reach a door on the left. Sully doesn't skip a beat. He flings the door open, and goes stomping in. The room is lit by the same LED lanterns we saw in the hallway. I feel my body temperature take a dive.

"Amos, Amos, Amos." He extends his arms to him for an embrace. "You are such a blessing. Let's do this, shall we?" Amos's eyes are as wide as if he has seen a ghost. "It's you…the voice. I wasn't imagining it. You were feeding me the scriptures all that time!" His eyes start to well up with tears.

Sully takes a bow. "The one and only. Call me Sully. No time for tears. Save those for later."

Amos wipes his eyes and drapes his sash across his body like a shield.

The walls are padded with some type of thick, white foam and the window is sealed up with boards. Across the room, strapped with cushioned hand cuffs and zip ties for reinforcement to a four-post bed, is Sarah. She isn't speaking, but with every breath she takes there is a loud wheezing. She looks much worse than the last time I saw her in the hospital. Her face is covered in welts and her scalp is covered with nickel-sized wounds where her hair is missing. Kershaw is clenching his jaw and fidgeting with the pocket on his shorts. I imagine it is taking all discipline within in him not to put a stop to this. To take out his cell and call the authorities. Amos traces the sign of the cross over himself, and moving across the room, he does the same to each of us. He also takes the holy water and expels it out of the bottle onto each of us.

He begins by reciting the Litany of the Saints, followed by a prayer. Just as he starts to pray, Sarah bursts into rattling laughter. Her voice is shrewd. Like a woman many years older than her with a bad smoking habit. Then she speaks in a condescending tone, "Sully! Sully! Help me." More laughter.

She stops abruptly and turns her head sharply at Amos. "You know that you are not strong enough for this. You weren't then, and you're not now."

128

I catch Hollis's eye, a flash of concern in his expression. We continue to pray along with Amos. Sully is leaning in the corner to the right of her bed. He isn't praying, but intently watching Amos with a slight smile. He is not worried, but relaxed.

Amos pauses, then begins again with a stronger voice. "I command you, unclean spirit, whoever you are, along with all your minions now attacking this servant of God, by the mysteries of the incarnation, passion, resurrection and ascension of our Lord Jesus Christ, by the descent of the Holy Spirit, by the coming of our Lord for judgment, that you tell me by some sign your name, and the day and hour of your departure. I command you, moreover, to obey me to the letter, I who am a minister of God despite my unworthiness; nor shall you be emboldened to harm in any way this creature of God, or the bystanders, or any of their possessions."

She is writhing in pain, rolling her head back and forth. She extends her neck and spits in Amos's direction. He comes closer and lays his hand on her forehead to continue, "They shall lay their hands upon the sick and all will be well with them. May Jesus, Son of Mary, Lord and Savior of the world, through the merits and intercession of His holy apostles Peter and Paul and all His saints, show you favor and mercy."

She heaves up a heavy vomit, coughing it out and gasping to catch her breathe. As Amos continues in prayer with his hand remaining on her, she roars "NABIUS!" The sound shakes the house. It feels as though she screamed into a microphone at an amplified concert. Kershaw's mouth drops and he reaches to cover his ears.

Amos, shaking, grabs his book and continues to read from the gospel. The smell heightens and nearly makes me gag. Hollis and Kershaw have pulled their shirts up to breathe through like a filter.

Sarah is no longer laughing. She's thrusting with her entire body as though she can break free of the binding, or the bed beneath her. Blood is dripping from her wrists and ankles. In one violent thrust, she lifts the bed and it slams back onto the ground. Kershaw, in a moment of panic, grabs my hand. His eyes widen in shock. "You're freezing. Why is your hand so cold?"

I hold onto his hand. "I'm okay. This happens to me in the presence of a demon." Sully saunters over casually to

Amos's side. Sarah shutters and pulls away from him. He points to the book and in unison they recite:

"I cast you out, unclean spirit, along with every satanic power of the enemy, every specter from hell, and all your fell companions; in the name of our Lord Jesus Christ. Begone and stay far from this creature of God. For it is He who commands you, He who flung you headlong from the heights of heaven into the depths of hell. It is He who commands you, He who once stilled the sea and the wind and the storm. Hearken, therefore, and tremble in fear, Satan, you enemy of the faith, you foe of the human race, you begetter of death, you robber of life, you corrupter of justice, you root of all evil and vice; seducer of men, betrayer of the nations, instigator of envy, font of avarice, fomentor of discord, author of pain and sorrow. Why, then, do you stand and resist, knowing as you must that Christ the Lord brings your plans to nothing? Fear Him, who in Isaac was offered in sacrifice, in Joseph sold into bondage, slain as the paschal lamb, crucified as man, yet triumphed over the powers of hell."

With a trembling hand, Amos quickly traces three signs of the cross on Sarah's brow, retracts his hand and continues. "Begone, then, in the name of the Father, and of the Son, and of the Holy Spirit. Give place to the Holy Spirit by this sign of the holy cross of our Lord Jesus Christ, who lives and reigns with the Father and the Holy Spirit, God, forever and ever."

The storm of roaring, thumping pain that rattled the whole house stopped all at once. Sarah's body appears to have deflated and melted into the bed in exhaustion. Her eyes slowly flutter open, and she shakes with tears. Amos and Sully gently remove her restraints and move her to a clean bed in the room across the hall. I look to Kershaw and let him know I have a first aid kit in the back of my car. He jumps at the chance to take care of her. As he is cleaning her wounds, he turns to me. "When will we know where to go when the time comes?"

"There will be a haven in place for all of us, and the details will be shared once we are closer to that time. There will be less than one percent of the population left when all is said and done. That is all I know as of now, but I will update you as I learn more."

He cleans his hands, places them in mine and professes his belief. The rest of the group gives him a round of applause and welcome him to the family.

13

WHEN IT FALLS IN YOUR LAP

It was nine months and 14 days from the deadline when Constance Evans appeared out of nowhere. Actually, it was five days prior to the date I had planned to start looking for her. Hollis and I had scheduled a few days off to recharge after the exorcism. It dawned on us that the beaches may not be habitable after everything is said and done, so we opted to pay them one last visit. Packing my bag felt different this time. Being concerned with sunscreen is so futile at this point. I know skin cancer will still be a thing in the new world, but I just want to throw caution to the wind. Maybe we will be given a cure for cancer after everyone else is gone.

Hollis has no problem basking in the simple joys we have always worked for. He went overkill with the beach supplies. A cooler is packed with every beach bum dream drink variety, a jumbo-sized umbrella, neon floaties and he arranged for a cheesy boat tour that locals like us don't usually partake in. We debated all the ways he will need to change his pickup game. Since such a small group of people will remain, he now needed to scope out women who exude goodness. Look for the ladies who do good deeds, volunteer and would help an old person across the street. I don't discourage him. Helping Hollis pick women for merit outside of their bra size could be entertaining.

It is a beautiful day. We make our way across the bridge and I can smell the salt in the breeze. There are at least a dozen boats visible to us out on the ocean, and a sprinkling of jet skis dancing around in the small waves. A family of dolphins is riding the wake of a large boat full of tourists sporting visors and fanny packs. I used to hate the tourists, but now I am glad they are here seeing the world. *Carpe that diem, people.*

Hollis changes the playlist from our usual Pop of the Forties to Island Jams and sings along with his best reggae accent. We decide to claim a spot on the beach since we can't check into our hotel until 4. Our favorite spot is just south of the pier. The sand is so fine it's like laying in powdered sugar. When we were kids, we would pretend that we were up in the mountains. I would lay down, face up toward the sun, and swipe my arms and legs up and down to make "snow angels" in the sand. Hollis would swim out a way on his boogie board, paddle in quickly to gain momentum, and jump up on his "snow board" to beat me to the bottom of the mountain. My parents were the ski patrol. They would allow us to play right up until dinner. We would beg and plea for just 10 more minutes. Our excuse was always that we were almost done building a snowman out of the sand. The carrot nose would never stay put, but those raisin eyes weren't going anywhere. Until the seagulls plucked them out.

Our jam session is interrupted by an incoming call. Hollis picks up and mouths to me that it's Amos.

"I'm sure Leo won't mind if you join us tonight. Just give us a call when you get here, and we can all grab dinner at the shack together," he says, moving his eyebrows up and down in a salacious gesture.

He ends the call and I punch him in the arm.

"Ouch! Easy with the violence. You'll thank me later. I mean, it is the end of the world, nearly."

I give him my most threatening glare. "You realize it's not actually the end of the world for us, Hollis."

He thinks about it for a second and shrugs his shoulders, "All the more reason to celebrate, then."

It has been months since we have taken a trip to the beach. There are fewer families than I remember. The sand is still the same soft powder but littered with garbage that people couldn't be bothered to throw in the trash. As the sun starts making its way down the afternoon sky, the homeless population starts commandeering the benches along the walkway. There aren't enough areas for them to set up camp, so they fight over territory. Runners who still brave the area for an early morning run often find them bleeding out or already dead along the beach.

A couple hours of people watching and basking in the sun on the beach go by. My stomach is growling, so we decide to pack up and make our way to the hotel. There is a large group of people around a podium on the boardwalk in front of the rescue aquarium. A woman with black- rimmed glasses and wild, curly, auburn hair is speaking. Before we have a chance to hear her, a man runs toward the stage yelling, "You hippie freaks! This is what I pay taxes for?! Go home!"

Just as security starts making their way toward him, he throws his cup of frozen yogurt right into her chest. She stands still, stunned. Security tackles him to the ground. He starts to fight back and one security guard starts wailing on him. The speaker realizes what is happening and reacts. "Stop! Stop hitting him! Let him up now!"

The crowd is taken aback by her reaction. This man was assaulting her, and she defended him? I look to the man next to me. "Do you know who that is?"

"That's Constance Evans," he responds. "She's an environmental scientist working with oceanographers to save our coral reefs."

Hollis looks at me. "Abba made this one easy."

She continues speaking, covered in frozen yogurt. Someone hands her some wipes and she cleans the sticky mess off her chest as if nothing happened. She doesn't wear a stitch of makeup or take time to do her hair. All signs of selflessness. I don't see a wedding ring...or any jewelry, for that matter. Maybe some things were simply coincidence, but this had to be fate. I smile. Abba is cutting me some slack.

We make our way to the hotel and check in. Our adjoining rooms have balconies overlooking the ocean, front and center. I'm not sparing any expense this time. Money will be irrelevant soon, and that means we are rich in any way that doesn't make us suspicious. I start unpacking my suitcase and I remember that Amos is joining us for dinner. I look at my options. A pair of white linen shorts and a basic navy cotton tank top, or a gray cotton sundress with sneakers? I wish I would have packed something more impressive, but why bother if I'm not comfortable. I'm not here to impress anyone. Amos might as well get used to that. Hollis certainly is. He wouldn't notice if I wore the same outfit for a week straight.

After showering off the sunscreen and sand, we meet up and go down to the hotel bar. Hollis invited Amos to meet us here so we could walk to the Grouper Shack together. I order us two margaritas. It's the only drink we have when we go to the beach. The tradition started on Hollis' 21st birthday. Being out in the sun all day zapped the energy out of us after a couple of drinks, but tequila was the only alcohol that wasn't a depressant, so it was decided. Another fun side effect was that it made me much more likely to find humor in his jokes, so it was a win-win for both of us. Just as the tequila was working its way into my bloodstream, Amos grabbed a barstool next to us. "What are we drinking?"

He is relaxed in a pair of salmon-colored shorts and a white v-neck with flip flops. The signature beach tourist look. When in Rome, I guess. I order him a margarita and explain the tradition. "Sorry, you don't have a choice. It's tradition, and you're one of us now." The bartender brings his drink and we move to a high-top table facing the ocean.

Amos takes a drink and clears his throat. "I need to apologize for being so resistant to the exorcism of Sarah Dalton. You were right on the money. Also, I was able to meet Sully, so thank you."

"No worries. It was a big ask. Now, you're going to need to walk us through how you know Sully."

He goes on to tell us of his past exorcism adventures with Sully's voice guiding the way. I catch myself hanging onto his every word and put the brakes on. He's just a regular guy, and I'm putting him on a pedestal because it's the end of times. It's likely a biological reaction for the need to reproduce, so cool it. Funny how my job is to convince scientific individuals that not everything has a logical reason for happening, but I force myself to put these thoughts in that same logical box. It's times like this I wish I could go to a therapist. I laugh at the thought of seeing their reaction.

The Grouper Shack is packed, but we brave the line to get some deep-fried fish to soak up the booze. We tell jokes and try to make up some of our own while waiting. "So, a camera man, a scout and a former priest walk into a bar…"

The best part: I only get struck with the chills once. I can't pinpoint who they came from due to the crowd, but the tequila quickly helps me warm back up. We finish our fish on the beach and make our way back to the hotel. The Three Musketeers of the apocalypse.

***

The sound of seagulls' "Huoh! Huoh! Huoh!" are ringing in my head. My mouth is so dry it's difficult to swallow. I remember why I don't drink often. The picture of us arm-in-arm marching back to the hotel flashes in my mind. Ha. It was worth it. The headache starts to dull after a couple huge glasses of water. It's still early and we are on vacation time, so I decide to let Hollis and Amos sleep longer. I power up my laptop and log into the hotel Wi-Fi. I know we said this is our time to decompress, but she showed up on our vacation for a reason.

I type "Constance Evans environmental scientist," into the search bar.

Jackpot, she is an easy find. *Thank you, Constance's parents, for choosing a unique name for your daughter.* She has completed research around numerous controversial pollution and human health issues and served as a host for many scientific panels. Nice. Her opinion is clearly respected. Unlike the neurosurgeon, this one is not as easily navigated in terms of determining how individuals are ranked in this field.

I return to my search bar. "Environmental science news, Pinellas County." Her name is mentioned in two forum articles on the first search page. I knew it, she's big time. Another scientist, Ansel Hemsworth, makes a couple top headlines for his research as well. Interestingly, it appears they work out of the same lab. My job just keeps getting easier and easier.

A sing-song knocking sounds at the adjoining door. "Are you decent, Leo?" I quickly close my laptop, shove it under the sofa pillow and let them in with a horrendous fake grin.

Hollis balks. "You were researching her, weren't you?"

I don't need to apologize for doing my job.

"Just until you guys woke up." I changed the subject. "Let's get some breakfast, boys!" Amos shakes his finger at me in a tisk-tisk scolding notion.

The day is full of more sun and sand, but I can't enjoy it anymore. The nagging questions about Constance come back around and around. They chase me all day until I finally give in. Before I have the chance to say it, Hollis leans in. "Just go pack up your things and we can head back. I know your head is somewhere else."

I cringe in remorse. "I'm sorry. I'll make it up to you after Constance, promise."

Amos helps load our things in the car. "Let me know if I can help you snag her, or even just a stakeout pal."

I catch myself smiling. "If it comes down to kidnapping, I'll definitely give you a call."

We arrive home and Hollis throws himself into bed to sleep off his hangover. I hide away in my bedroom digging for any dirt I can find on Ms. Evans. She doesn't appear to have any social media pages. Her parents, on the other hand, are out there and appear to be quite the socialites. Mrs. Susan Evans, a successful philanthropist, has a lot of wealthy friends. Mr. Denis Evans comes from a wealthy family and has made some good investments in pharmaceuticals. I find some old family photos that Susan posted online. They are very formal. Susan is beaming with joy. Denis giving just a slight distinguished smile, but Constance is straight-faced. I recall her wild, curly hair at the beach. That was definitely natural. No one was going to do that to their hair on purpose. In this family photo, her hair is slick straight and held back by a silk headband. I can feel the oppression just looking at it. Something tells me Susan and Denis didn't want this career for their daughter. The average salary of an environmental scientist in this area is only $87,000 a year. *Constance, you rebel.*

Scrolling down further, Susan also posted a photo of teenaged Constance with a large group of her peers. Hmm, they are all wearing construction helmets and working gloves, and they appear to be on a worksite. The caption reads, "We are so proud of our Constance for helping give back. Her church youth group helped rebuild an orphanage in Guatemala this year." Her mother clearly didn't have a problem with her daughter getting her hands dirty if it was for a good cause that they could socially benefit from. I zoom in on Constance. She is gripping her stomach in laughter. She is smiling ear to ear, eyes shut, chin pointing up toward the sun. It's clear she thrived in any environment that allowed her to make the world a better place, and at one point, she was a believer. If we can convince an atheist, this will be a cake walk.

Let's move on to real estate. According the county assessor's website, she owns a 1,300-square- foot, two-bedroom house and it's just a few minutes from the lab. That means I don't have to spend hours in traffic, following you back and forth from work to your house. Hallelujah! The assessed value is $246,000. Just a tiny shack in comparison to what she could probably have. Maybe her parents withhold their fortune from her. Or better yet, maybe she refuses to take money from them.

Let's move on to our other scientist, Ansel Hemsworth. Ah ha! He does have a social media account in his name. I click on the link, and…I don't understand. The profile picture is with our very own wild-haired Constance. Is it possible that they are just good friends like Hollis and me? I scroll through the photos that I am allowed to view. Constance and Ansel at the ribbon-cutting celebration for the new research center in Sarasota. Here they are volunteering at the homeless shelter on Thanksgiving Day, and here is Constance sitting on Ansel's lap with her arms wrapped around him on a patio. The caption reads, "Our new home." They are most definitely not just friends. Friends are renters together, not homeowners together. The thought occurs to me that I could get two for one with this deal! I needed this.

I think I have earned myself a little break and some snacks. The kitchen cabinets are barren, but I manage to find some potato chips. Hollis hears me rip the bag open and decides to join me. "Ugh, I'm never drinking again."

"Good idea...I have great news." I hand him the bag of chips. He crunches down on one and responds with a full mouth. "Well? I know you are dying to tell me all about your findings. Go on, do tell."

"Constance is the real deal. Top of her field. The other top scientist in our area just happens to be her freaking boyfriend! No joke. Get your things—we are doing a stakeout now."

We pull into their neighborhood, and I immediately feel more comfortable than sneaking around Kershaw's. Lower income means no fancy garages and plenty of other cars parked along the street. Landscaping consists of the occasional basic palm tree with a few shrubs. Mostly small, ranch-style homes. Hollis finds a spot to park just south of their house and across the street. I put my binoculars up to see Ansel and Constance cooking dinner together. He is manning the stove while she cuts up vegetables. Looks like some kind of stir fry. I don't see any meat. Probably vegetarians. Hey, it's better for the environment. Her hair is swept up in a messy bun. She is wearing sweatpants and a lightweight, long-sleeve shirt with a tribal-looking print. Ansel has thick black hair and a groomed beard. He matches her casual style in sweatpants and a graphic Volcom t-shirt. Their home is simple. The small living room has one sofa and an end table. There are a few potted plants hanging above the windows. They finish cooking and sit down together at the small cafe table in the nook to eat, taking their time and enjoying each other's company.

"They seem pleasant with one another," Hollis observes.

She finishes her food and heads up stairs. Ansel glances toward the stairs and grabs his phone typing away. He glances back up at the stairs again to see them empty and continues with his phone. It's all too easy to spot someone trying to hide something.

I shake my head. "MMMMM, it's all so pleasant until one of them is a dirty cheater."

It's possible he is just planning a surprise for her, but if this world has taught me anything, it's highly unlikely. Hollis, also looking through his binoculars, sees the same red flag I do. Ansel finishes up and makes his way up to the bedroom that she entered. He gives her a kiss on the cheek and the lights go out. It's certain they are a couple, and I need to find a way to get closer to Ansel. That's for another day.

***

Sure enough, Ansel is a piece of work. Constance and he drive separately to work, and he finds ways to leave the lab to "run errands" or pick up "lunch." Reality is that he meets up with other women. Three other women to be exact. They all swoon over him. The weird part is that he actually takes them out for meals and goes shopping with them. Last week, he attended a funeral with the red head. It's like clockwork—he runs off for a couple hours to entertain one of them and returns to Constance with a bouquet of roses or a bottle of champagne in hand. What a consolation prize. They don't stand a chance.

He lets Constance do the hard work to bring them success. I know what the result will be, but I decided to test my intuition anyway and get behind him in a grocery checkout line. He is spine- chilling, and he is the most charming man I have ever encountered. Every person who comes into contact with him is smitten. Even the men. They all sway to the beat of his sick drum. They agree with all his ideas and seem to get a high off of his approval. There really is nothing more manipulative in this world than a six-foot-two handsome man full of pure evil. Constance only sees the charm.

I can't spend all my time stalking him, though. I turn my focus on her to make sure she is the right fit. It's easy to assume when the only comparison I have is her demon boyfriend. She continually exhibits the selfless nature we witnessed at the beach. When they run out of supplies in the lab, she volunteers to put the order in. A turtle trying to cross a busy street? She is the one pulling over, getting out of her car and stopping traffic so it can make it across safely. We are going to need someone with her passion to save the planet. I should just let that be enough, but I know Ansel will be an issue and we can't risk him figuring out what we are up to. I'll need proof. Something to keep her from confiding in him about our plan.

Hiding behind the shrubs in the park for hours wasn't fun, but it was worth the effort to capture him "running his errands" with mistress number two. He leans in and shoves his disgusting tongue down her throat. Snap, Snap. Got it. I feel more like a private investigator for the wife of a cheating husband than a recruiter for the surviving society of the Apocalypse. It pains me, but I need to show her. She isn't safe with him, and it's the best tactic to keep this under wraps. For once, Ansel is going to be the one getting nailed to the wall.

14

LIFE'S A MYSTERY, KITTEN

Michael's secretary lines up a meeting for me to catch up on our newest recruit at the abandoned library in the booming metropolis of Fillmore, Florida. I walk in to find the wood floors, book shelving, tables and chairs have all been polished to a rich, mahogany gloss. The large chalk board on wheels is still wiped cleaned to a blank state. I hear a "Whoosh!" Is that a toilet flushing? Michael flings the bathroom door open to reveal his shiny, athletic tracksuit. I am sure it is the largest size he could find, but it is still much too short and clinging to his unnaturally large muscles.

"Look at you. Did you run out of your usual biker threads?" I ask.

He does a spin. "Oh, no. I can have anything I want here. These are my cleaning clothes," he shrugs, and takes a couple shallow squats to show off the stretch of the material.

He reminds me of the shiny, metal guy that would top a trophy, but on a giant level.

"Stylish and functional. It's looking good in here. Maybe you can clean up the mess I'm finding myself in, too."

He smiles. "Oh darling, this is not a mess. This is the fun part! Remember how we wanted Hollis to keep his job?"

"Yes," I respond.

"You are going to get set up with a new job title. Reporter for the Channel 6 News, and Hollis, your camera man, will be joining you to interview Constance. Before you get all worked up, just know that she will gladly oblige you with an interview. Anything to give the cause a louder voice, right? Put on a pantsuit and line everything up with Constance directly so she clears you with the security staff at the lab. Upon arrival, you will give her the same speech you gave Kershaw with the added exclusion of her garbage boyfriend. This could make her defensive, but that's why you have video footage of him. You will ask her for her cell number and send it directly to her. Give her a little time to let it sink in and hash things out with Ansel. If she doesn't contact you within a few days, call her and ask if you can prove it to her through science. Make sure she knows it will be worth her time. Remember not to use words on a call that could bring trouble our way. I will arrange for assistance to further persuade her."

"How am I going to show her through science?" I ask.

"Just wait and see. Let yourself be surprised. You can have a little fun with this. It's the easy part. Rebuilding the world? Now, that is going to throw you so many more challenges."

He gives me a fist bump and walks me to the door.

Hollis is thrilled at the idea of getting to play my camera man, and even more excited to see me in full makeup and a pantsuit. He starts searching online for the perfect news anchor themes.

"I know, you need one of the high-waisted pantsuits with the skinny legs from the 2020s. We can straight iron your hair and fill in your eyebrows until they look like caterpillars, like this girl! Look at this!" He laughs.

I make my call to Constance's lab in full character, Grace Olson from the Channel 6 News. She is caught off-guard at first, but just like Michael predicted, she is happy to oblige. We have a full-on makeover party with Amos and my mom to turn me into a news anchor. I shot down Hollis' retro theme idea for the sake of actually getting me through security. However, I look so ridiculous that he quickly gets over the disappointment. I'm 100 percent over the top. My hair is sky-high, and the red lips and eye shadow are just too much. The pantsuit fits snug over every tiny curve my boyish figure has to offer. My mother is loving life. Hollis knew that this was one of those life moments she would die to witness. She showers him with love for the invite, folds her hands on her chest and gasps at the sight of me.

"This is the day I've been waiting for, honey. You look gorgeous! Why have you been hiding behind all those big t-shirts and yoga pants all these years?"

I tilt my head as to say, *Really? We're doing this again?*

Hollis props his hand up under his chin. "You don't need all of this, but you really do look..." he stops himself. I slap him before he can go on. "Knock it off, perv. I look like a brain-dead barbie who doesn't know how to apply eyeliner." I clip the fake lanyard we made onto my suit pocket, Hollis loads up the camera and we make our way to the lab.

153

The security guards, wearing their company polo shirts and khaki pants, look more like cell phone company salespeople. We make our way through their metal detectors and they escort us to Ms. Evan's office. Unlike her home, the room is very cluttered. On her desk there is a sandwich with one bite taken, a bag of salted pretzels and random piles of small glass tubes I assume are used in the lab. I see that she has cleared an area on the other side of the room and has placed two chairs across from each other. In the corner, I see two framed pictures of the beach leaning against the wall. She's like a crazy genius who works better in chaos. Odd that she would live in such a different space at home. Maybe that's Ansel's doing.

She greets me with an airy, frazzled energy. "Hi Grace! Welcome, come on in. I cleared some space for us here or we can do this out in the lobby area where there is more natural light. I'm just so excited to get the opportunity to share our research."

I offer my hand to shake hers and hopefully calm her nerves.

"Constance, thank you for taking the time to meet with me. I—"

"Please, call me Stassi," she interrupts. "My parents are the only people who call me Constance."

I continue. "Well, Stassi, thank you for taking the time to chat. I am so impressed with the work that you are doing, and grateful that people like you exist. But I have to admit, I am not here to interview you. When religion was abolished 19 years ago, it set the apocalyptic process in motion. I'm not here to help save the rest of the world, because we are beyond that. I'm here because you demonstrate the morals that we should uphold daily, and you are simply the best at what you do. There will be a mass destruction in 11 months. You've been fighting against the destruction of our planet for years, and humankind is to blame for the damage that has been done. Everything as you could imagine will be gone aside from the planet we stand on and the people that are chosen by scouts like me."

I give a moment of pause to allow her to let this sink in and ask questions.

She responds dumbfounded. "What?" She doesn't try to keep up appearances. Her expression is sheer shock and awe. I decide to continue. "Let me explain the requirements. First, those who are needed, like you, must profess your belief in God, the Father Above All, Creator of Heaven and Earth. This will not be revealed to the public, and your identity with us will be protected. Until the time comes, you will go on living your life mostly as you do now. Secondly, none of this can be revealed to Ansel. He can't be a part of this."

"If you would have told me this a decade ago, I may have actually considered the idea, but humankind has wreaked havoc on this planet for centuries and it's not going to go downhill that fast."

"Why would you have considered it a decade ago, but not today?" I ask.

"I—I don't know," she stutters. "I had lots of ideas about how things worked a long time ago. I was young and naive. Who do you really work for?"

"I guess you could say I work for God. I know it sounds crazy. It's a long story, but I can prove it to you." She looks from me to Hollis. He nods in agreement.

"Sure, okay. If this theory of yours is accurate, why couldn't Ansel be involved? He is also a top environmental scientist."

"Let's just say, Ansel won't be here when all is said and done. He is not who you think he is, and he certainly doesn't meet the requirements. I have a video that will explain it."

I hand her my cell. "Put your personal number in here and I will send it to you, so you can see for yourself."

She reluctantly types in her number and hands the phone back to me. I make eye contact with her. "Watch the video, and deal with that issue first. Once you have that sorted out, think about what I have asked of you and call me when you are ready to hear more. We need you, Stassi. Thank you again for your time."

Hollis lifts his camera equipment off the floor, and we see ourselves out.

We wait for three days. I lay awake, pressing into prayer. *Let her come to her senses. Push her to learn more, God. Make the curiosity unbearable. Give her courage to leave Ansel and ask all the right questions.*

***

Two days go by, and still no response from Stassi. Come on, don't make me call you. On the bright side, I've picked up running to make the time pass. I find that when I'm crossing paths with something evil, it pushes me to run further and the cold fades away faster since I'm barely exposed. I'm halfway through my run when I feel my phone vibrating in my pocket.

A number I don't recognize. *Let it be her. Let it be her.* I pick up. "Hello."

I hear breathing right away, and then, "You were right about Ansel, but any investigator could have determined that. I'm still not convinced that you're not a part of some cult. You mentioned that you can prove it to me, so prove it. I won't do this at my place of work, but you can meet me at my house this Thursday, at 6 p.m."

I don't skip a beat. "I'm sorry about Ansel, and I would be happy to prove it. I'll see you Thursday at 6." Before I can say goodbye, she hangs up. My heart is thumping into my ribcage. I jump up and throw my fist in the air. Mid-celebration, I notice the man with the salt and pepper hair who I usually see sitting in the corner at the HQ Workit. He is peering at me from an alleyway between neighborhoods. He sees that I've caught him spying and darts back down the alley in the other direction. *Who or what are you?* Maybe all this good work is getting too loud. If someone knows what I'm up to, that means I have a target on my back. I rein it in and run back to the condo faster than I ever have.

I am toweling my hair dry and making my way to the fridge for some water when I nearly jump out of my skin.

Michael is sitting on my sofa. "Hey there, padna! Get dressed. We are going to meet your next expert. And wear something you can move easily in." He laughs.

I shake my head. "You enjoy this far too much."

I throw on a pair of running shorts and a dry fit tank top. He leads me out to his jacked-up Army vehicle. "Feast your eyes on the beautiful Conquest Knight XV. There are only 12 in the world. She weighs 6,400 kilograms. Each ballistic steel door weighs 160 kilograms, or about the size of two small men, and her windows are bulletproof."

He shrugs and looks from the enormous vehicle to me. "We have a little rough terrain to get through."

The ride is surprisingly relaxing. Apparently, it's easier to put your life in the hands of an angel. He turns on some classic rock and proceeds to drum along to the beat with his hands on the steering wheel, singing along. "There goes my hero! Watch him as he goooes."

Occasionally, he holds out a fake microphone for me to join in. I respond, "I'm too young to know the words to these songs."

"Oh, come on! I know you've heard it!"

A couple hours in, we take a turn down an unpaved road surrounded by jungle. So, we are heading deep into the everglades. Great. He stops abruptly at a small clearing in front of swamp. Well, in all fairness, the everglades are just one massive swamp. Or as some might say, one huge, slow-moving river. I can't imagine navigating this land on my own. The thick marshes extend for hundreds of miles. Every inch of it looks the same, so one wrong turn and it will eat you alive. I've lived here long enough to know what's in those waters. It's thick with alligators and water moccasins. If you survive them, you still have to worry about a Florida Panther stalking you from the trees above. *Calm down. Take a breath. He won't let you die.*

We step out and head closer to the water. I follow his lead just through the clearing to find a woman with long wavy, blonde hair prancing barefoot along a huge fallen tree stretched across the water. She reminds me of a nymph in a fairy tale. Maybe 15 feet from her an alligator is working its way slowly through the waters. It doesn't even flinch at her presence. She is humming a song and twirling her white dress to the rhythm. Michael waves his hand. "I thought I might find you here!"

She turns on a dime to face us, skipping along the log in our direction, with open arms. She reaches the end of the log, leaps into the air, grabs hold of a hanging branch and swings over the water to us. She wraps her arms around me. "Leo, our beautiful lioness with the gift of discernment. I am at your service."

She continues to play with the leaves in the tree above us and grazes her toes along the shallow water beside us. I am sure she is perfectly safe—angel protection and all, but I can't help myself. "You really should be careful. The gators don't mess around. Maybe step a few feet away from the water?"

She giggles and looks to Michael. "And it's good to see you as well, my captain."

He places his hand on my shoulder. "Leo, this is Ariel. She is the angel of nature. And that gator over there," he points to the murky water, "bows to her, so don't worry for her safety. She will be the expert to help you win over Constance."

That was embarrassing.

"Pleased to meet you, Ariel. Sorry about that. I forget how capable you angels are."

I take a closer look to see she is dripping in beaded bracelets and crystal necklaces. They run the gamut of her forearms and drape from her neck in all different lengths. "Leo's recruit is in denial and we need to give her a little scientific nudge in the right direction," Michael continues. "You're cleared to enlighten her with something they have yet to discover."

Arial grins from ear to ear and slides her palms together in plotting. "Get me my lab coat."

***

Thursday evening arrives and Ariel agrees to meet me at Stassi's home. She steps out of a black Audi wearing a fitted, black business casual dress and an oversized white lab coat. Her long, wavy blonde hair is swept up into a tight bun. She must have left all the crystals and beads in the everglades. I ring the doorbell, and Stassi answers the door in a split second. I glance at my watch. We are three minutes early. Someone is excited to hear what we have to say. I hold my palm up toward Ariel. "Stassi, this is Ariel. She is also an environmental scientist and she is going to help clear some things up for you."

She leads us toward her dining table. "Alright then, please take a seat."

Ariel looks around the room. "Can you get me a pen and paper, Stassi?"

She opens a drawer in the kitchen and places the pen and paper in front of Ariel. We sit around the table patiently watching Ariel calmly jot down a series of a formulas and a small paragraph. A few awkward minutes pass, and she hands the paper to Stassi.

"This should solve the pollution issue you have been facing, and not just here in Florida. Everywhere."

Stassi snatches it from her hand and her eyes race across the page. She slams it down on the table. "That could actually work—you figured it out. The formula adds up. How did you do this? Has anyone else seen this?" she asks, her eyes wide in wonder.

Ariel places her hand on Stassi's shoulder. "No honey, only you know. I know this because I am the angel of nature. You're welcome to take credit for the solution, but you should know it really won't do you any good. Soon you will be working with a blank slate." Stassi bursts into laughter and quickly covers her mouth as to not offend Ariel.

"You clearly have a gifted mind, but I'm sorry, I don't believe you are an angel."

Ariel leans in closer to her, wraps her hand around her ear, pulls out a quarter and whispers, "Life's a mystery, Kitten."

Stassi frowns, and her eyes well up with tears.

"How could you know that? He didn't say that to anyone but me. How did you know him?"

Ariel wipes away a tear from her cheek. "I didn't, but Abba did."

I don't know if it's out of loneliness or acceptance, but she invites us to stay and have a glass of wine with her. We listen to her tell the story of confronting Ansel with the video I sent her. He didn't even try to save face. She asks him to explain and he rambled on about how pathetic she is. The following morning, she left for work and he hung back to pack up his things. When she returned home, he was gone along with any trace of him. She thanked us for informing her of his transgressions.

"I always knew something wasn't right about him, but I didn't want to believe that," she sighed. "He always had an excuse to leave, and I made a good door mat."

It was getting late, and Ariel had other things to tend to. I reached out to shake Stassi's hand. "It sounds like you have made your mind up, but we need to hear you say it. Will you join us?"

She nods. "Yes. I'm in."

I explain that all the details will come her way once I know more, and she repeats the profession of her belief. I wait until she has closed the door behind us and stop Ariel before she gets in her car.

"So, what did you whisper in her ear?" I ask.

She pulls the bobby pins out of her hair, bends over to shake it out and lets it cascade down her back.

"It was a secret thing her deceased grandfather would always tell her right after pulling a quarter out of her ear. If you want a tip from me, just remember that it's the memories that tug at their hearts, every time."

15

SNACKS, CONDOMS AND STALKERS

I'm one step closer to my goal. I should be proud. I've already won over two of the three recruits I need, but my mind wanders. I'm staring at my ceiling fan rotating on the slowest speed. Fast enough to keep the air fresh, but not too fast that my nose dries out. When all of this is over, there will be less than 140 million people left on the planet. When I say it out loud, that actually sounds like a lot of people.

I pull my laptop open to help put it into perspective. Currently, the population of the United States is 322 million people. I know the new world will still have groups of people all over the world. I can't help but wonder how many of us will be in the United States. The type A personality in me wants so badly to start planning for this, but every time I put effort into preparing for something I know nothing about, it ends up being a waste of my time. I wonder what Amos has been up to. He hasn't brought up the "feelings" conversation we had at the park. I don't think I can deal with that right now anyway.

I realize it's Saturday, and that means that Hollis has the day off. I crack his bedroom door open. "You decent?"

He mumbles something to the effect that I'm stupid and I shouldn't be up this early. I take it as my cue to jump up and down on his bed until he rolls out and makes us some espresso.

I let the caffeine work its way into my blood and propose a plan for our day, "What do you think about going for a morning run with me, restocking our groceries so we can live like normal people for at least a week, and then meeting Amos out for a cocktail tonight?"

"Sans the morning run, as I don't run unless something is chasing me, I am game. Can we please try a new dive tonight? I need a change of scenery. There has got to be some newer, small spots in the Blue-gull District. Pleeeease?"

"I'll allow it under one condition...that we eat breakfast for dinner tonight."

"You have a deal, and I'll even make it for us."

In the spirit of trying new things, I take advantage of my newfound bravery and chose a different route for my run. The first mile or two always hurts. About one mile in, my legs feel weak and it's hard to breathe. Once I break that barrier, a burst of energy starts pumping through me and I can go on for miles. Today, I only make it four blocks and I start to feel tiny raindrops hitting my face. I pick up the pace. As I expected, within seconds I am in a down pour. I know it won't last long so I decide to ride it out. The rain is so heavy I am swimming in my capris and tank top within seconds. I stop in a round-a-bout, throw my hands up to the sky and spin around in circles. Once I've stopped spinning, I spot a bobcat watching me from the edge of the nature preserve to my right. I hold perfectly still as not to startle him. He doesn't turn away. His piercing green eyes lock onto mine. Maybe we will find a little spot for you when it comes time to hunker down, buddy. Almost as quickly as it came, the rain starts to let up. He turns back into his forest and I back to mine.

***

Hollis is in his element, flipping pancakes and dancing across the kitchen tile while I stare at today's New York Times crossword puzzle. Twenty-five across, a popular chutney ingredient. Seriously? I don't even know one ingredient in chutney. Hollis's grandmother, his father's mother, used to visit him once a year, and every time, she would bring a book of crossword puzzles to do with us. Eventually, we outgrew the easy level books and she started bringing the New York Times. I'll never forget her last visit. We were racking our brains to figure out the theme of the puzzle for hours. Finally, I figured out one of the long answers that would lead us to the theme—Coriolis Force, or as we were taught in high school, a deflection of air that results in the rotation of the earth. She threw the paper up in the air in celebration and made Hollis and I ice cream sundaes with whipped cream, sprinkles and tiny, chopped nuts. We didn't even finish the puzzle.

"When the moon hits your eye, like a big pizza pie...that's amore!" he sings.

"You do know that pancakes don't really constitute as an Italian food, right?" I interrupt.

He points the spatula at me. "I'm pretty sure that Italians eat pancakes too, smart ass."

In an attempt avoid an hour-long debate, I tell him the tales of rain and bobcats from my run.

He laughs. "And before she could save the world, she was eaten by a bobcat. Maybe you do need me along on these journeys."

I try to think of a snide comment but smile in defeat. *I'll give you this one.* He cuts each piece of pancake and egg into a precise triangle and places the egg piece on top of the pancake for each bite.

I reach in and quickly cut a piece with my fork. "Oh no, what are you going to do now? You can't eat a square piece of pancake!"

He silently stabs a large pancake dripping in syrup, raises it slowly and flings it in my face. The sticky syrup is running down my forehead, over my eyebrow and dripping onto my cheeks. This is war. The room becomes a blur of flying egg bits and pancake until we make a truce, dropping our food weapons. He reaches over and wipes some butter off my chin. "I would make a butter face joke, but I'm afraid of the retaliation."

I point my finger into his chest. "You're a smart man, Hollis. I have dibs on the shower first."

***

The Blue-gull District does not disappoint with its retro street signage and hidden taverns. This is the land of replicated speakeasies. We try to imagine what the secret pass phrases are. Amos and Hollis come up with their own. "Holy velvet furniture batman, perms and parachute pants, tinsel hair extensions for the win!" They find themselves quite clever. One bar is disguised as massage parlor. Another's facade is a candy shop. Maybe they are legitimate businesses. I'm not really sure how all of this works. The sidewalks are full of groups hopping from bar to bar.

As we walk from the car, I tell them all about Ariel, her swamp haven and how we won Constance, who we should all refer to as Stassi because she's not a fan of her parents. Their excitement could be heard from blocks away. Hollis especially enjoyed the concept of a "fairy angel" dancing around an alligator on a slimy, slick log.

While looking for a less a less "chilly" spot, we stop a group of twenty-somethings passing and ask them which bar might be less busy. They reluctantly point over to a small, brick building with a Frank's Convenience sign out front. Before we can ask for the pass phrase, they bolt. They probably don't want to be scene with a bunch of old has-beens like us. Frank's is a small store front with a few shelves stocked with individually packaged snacks and condoms. The man behind the checkout counter doesn't say anything when we walk through the doors.

Hollis gives it a go. "Jo sent me."

No response. This guy is good.

I glance at a vintage sign on the door. "Dandy Shandy?"

He moves toward the back of the store. "Right this way."

"Just leave it to me, boys," I gloat.

The man holds opens a door disguised as shelving. "We let anyone in after their second try."

He just had to put me in my place. A small hallway leads us into a cozy, dim lit seating area. The bar is maybe five feet across, and there are six small tables. There are only two other people sitting in the far-right corner. I make my way to a table on the left and feel a chill grabbing hold of me. I glance back at the other patrons. It is a man and a woman. I don't recognize her, but it is hard to make out their features in the dark corner. The man looks in our direction and I look away immediately.

This is not a coincidence. I take my seat and lean into the guys. "Don't make it obvious, but that man sitting in the corner." They casually look around the bar. "I have seen him before at the HQ Workit on our block. He sits in the high-top by the window and gives me the chills every time I walk by to get my morning coffee. A few days ago, I was on my run. I had stopped to catch my breath and I noticed he was watching me from an alleyway."

Amos puts his hand on his head in distress. "Have you told Michael about this?"

"No. He knows what is going on all the time anyway, right? I figured if he hasn't mentioned it, then it probably isn't an issue. Every time I'm concerned about something and let him know, I just end up feeling like an idiot. Also, they were here before us. Maybe it's just a coincidence. I'm probably just being paranoid, you guys."

Hollis grabs my arm. "If they are good at what they do, they would have had plenty of time to beat us here between our interaction with those strangers and arriving at the bar. This area is crawling with people. Your mother said that Michael keeps up on what is going on with the mission. That doesn't mean that he is aware of everything—or everyone—that comes near you. You need to bring this to his attention."

I wrap my hoodie around my shoulders and take a deep breath. "Alright. I'll contact him, but we can't just get up and leave. We just got here. What if they suspect something but don't know for sure? I don't want to tip them off. I say we order one drink, finish it and leave."

They both nod in agreement, and Hollis snaps a picture of him with his phone when he's not looking. It would blow our cover if he were to use a flash, so the dim, grainy image will have to do. The bartender takes our order and we do our best to drink at a normal pace. I can feel their eyes on me, but I don't dare look in their direction and give them an invitation to approach us. We casually finish our drinks and leave a larger bill than we knew we needed to save time, and we make our way out.

On the ride home, I take Hollis' phone to study the photo. Something about him looks familiar. The way the bridge of his nose is a narrow line that turns up just at the tip. His eyebrows laid softly around his eyes. The composition of his facial features are that of a kind person. In nature, babies are designed with cute features to encourage the others to take care of them. Maybe Lucifer was smart and trained his demons to only target cute humans for possession. If that is his tactic, he wants nothing more than to destroy me.

I help Hollis clean up the tornado of breakfast food strung about the condo. He heads to bed just before I step out into the hallway to throw the trash down the shoot. Just as I am letting go of the trash bag, an arm wraps around my shoulders and a hand covers my mouth. My heart is beating in rapid succession. My breaths become short and sharp, and my body is filled to the brim with a piercing cold. *This is it. I'm going to die before they even reach the end.*

A soft, calming male voice says, "This is going to take some time for you to absorb, Leo. I need you to take this photo." As he hands the photo to me, he turns my body to face him. The salt and pepper hair, narrow nose and soft eyebrows stand on display, right in front of me. I force my eyes to look down at the photo. It can't be. It has to be fabricated. It's a picture of him, a woman with golden wavy hair and there I am in her arms. My dark ringlets and chubby cheeks. I can't be more than one year old.

He softens his hold on me and starts to explain. "I know that you must be confused as you feel the darkness that has taken over me, but I have never stopped loving you, Leo. You deserve to know the truth. Your mother died in a car crash just two days after your first birthday. She was struck by a drunk driver. He didn't stop and help her…he just kept driving. I sat in court and watched the judge sentence him to only 10 years in prison with the opportunity for early parole. I was devastated. I couldn't wake up in the morning. Your mother loved you and I deeply, and the thought of her never returning was unbearable," he wipes a tear from his eye and continues.

"Eventually, I lost my job. I just couldn't focus. I interviewed everywhere, and no one would hire me. I prayed, and none of my prayers were answered. An opportunity to make a living laundering money came my way. You were so little, and we were running out of food. I needed to make a better life for you, so I went through with it. A few months in, the operation was busted, and I was sentenced to 20 years. The man who murdered your mother got half that sentence. I was incarcerated for 15 years and released early on good behavior. It was in those years that I discovered so much about all of those that God has abandoned. His own children, left to fend for themselves. After all this suffering, he is going to murder over

99 percent of humankind. Millions of mothers, children, and fathers."

He releases my shoulders and takes his hand off my mouth. "I have watched you all these years, Leo. I would never hurt you. Please, think about what I have told you. I love you."

He turns around and walks to the end of the hallway, down the stairs and out of the building. I will myself to move one foot in front of the other, back into the condo. I've waited my whole life for this moment. In hopes that they would find me, and we would be reunited. I place the photo under my pillow and lay awake staring at the ceiling until my body gives in and my eyes close.

16

DADDY ISSUES

I wake in the middle of night, over and over to the same face. Her pronounced chin and hazel eyes. My eyes. Staring back at me. I try taking sleep medications, but nothing works. I am running away from a storm. Its dark clouds are galloping on top of each other in a race to swallow me. I shutter at the rolling thunder shaking the ground beneath me. I am alone. I think I'm alone until I turn a corner around an old building. Just as I can feel the storm catching me, she wraps me up in a white, sponge-like cocoon. She holds my face in her hands. "It will be alright." I want to stay there in that safe place with my mother, but it never lasts. If she haunts me, why can't she tell me what to do. Isn't that the point? Maybe there is a message in there I don't understand.

Hollis presses me for an update on our next recruit, but I insist on taking my time researching the possible candidates for this profession. I trust Hollis with my life, but I know he will err on the side of caution regarding my father. I can't tell him yet. Just a few more days. I also can't focus on the task at hand when I know my father is out there, watching me. It has been weeks since our discussion. I've relied on delivery services for anything and everything to avoid leaving the condo. It really is amazing the things you can have delivered.

I could simply put this in Michael's hands. Sell my own father out to his perceived enemy. Watch as they detain him until he soon meets his death along with majority of the world, or maybe he is supposed to be a part of the one percent. Who am I to say that he should be excluded? He hasn't made a direct threat to my mission. That I know of. If Amos could save Sarah Dalton, he might be able to save him. I know Amos won't perform an exorcism without Michael's consent. I lock my door and sit in prayer for hours. The image of Michael standing over me in the library keeps coming back to me. I can't find comfort in planning without him, and it becomes apparent that I'm reaching for something out of my control. I grab my phone and arrange a meeting with Michael and Amos that evening.

***

Michael and Amos, the prompt creatures they are, arrive at the same time. I ask them to pull up a stool to sit with me at the kitchen island. Amos sits to my left and Michael to my right. I imagine the weight of him crushing the bar stool as he crashes to the ground, and probably through the floor and everyone beneath us. I place my phone in front of us on the island and the photo of myself with my biological parents beside it. I open the photo app on my phone and show them both the photo of my father and the other woman at the bar.

"Michael, a man—who has been possessed—has been following me. This week, he appeared with another woman at the bar Hollis, Amos and I were at. I have seen him numerous times at a local communal workshop and once in an alleyway while I was out run—"

Michael interrupts, "And I'm just hearing about this now?!"

"Let me explain. The same night that we saw him at the bar, I had planned on telling you about him immediately, but he stopped me in the hall of my building. This," I slide the family photo closer, "is a photo of him, my biological mother and myself roughly 29 years ago."

Amos' jaw is clenched tight and his mouth pursed in tension. Michael is shaking his head in disappointment. I talk them down enough to hear me out. I tell them about his struggles and letting me go freely with the photo.

"He is clearly hurting. Amos was able to help Sarah Dalton. She was possessed, just like my father. Isn't it possible that he is meant to be one of the one percent?" I plea.

Michael turns to face me. "No. That man is not your father, Leo, and he hasn't been for many years. Most people who have become possessed have been attacked, and they are too weak to fight it off. That man—Collin Draper is his name—sold his soul to Lucifer. How do you think he is able to conduct himself so easily? He isn't rejecting what is inside of him. He welcomed the darkness that he has become. His hatred of Abba is his own, just as his hatred of himself is. You in no way should identify with him because of your genetics. Every human is given free will, and your choices have followed the exact path that Abba created for you. Collin's choices followed the path that Lucifer built. Just as you give your heart to Abba, he gives his heart to Lucifer. Do you understand?"

Amos places his hand on my back with sympathy. I stare at the photos in front of us. Michael picks up my phone and deletes the photo. He grabs the family photo and starts rummaging through our kitchen drawers. He pulls out a lighter and burns it. It begins withering and contorting in the flame. I try to reach out and stop him.

He pulls away and looks up at me. "These images can impact you spiritually. I know it would be too hard for you to destroy them on your own. I can't always be by your side as there is a lot on my plate in the coming days. My men will follow him and find a way to obstruct him from hindering the mission." He looks to Hollis. "Since your cover is already compromised, I need you and Amos to quit your jobs and accompany this one anywhere she goes. Think of your new jobs as bodyguards incognito." They agree in unison.

Hollis seems excited at the concept. "What do we do if Collin approaches us?"

"If Collin is anywhere near you, my men will be too. Rest assured, you won't be seeing Collin again unless it's a front row seat to his arrest."

Michael's expression takes on the solid sternness of a warrior statue. His usual jolly, nonchalant aura is gone. He plants his huge hand on my shoulder, "You have less than seven months to make your final recruit and make arrangements for the final days. Don't leave this one to chance. They won't always present themselves in your path like Constance did. Give yourself some cushion. You will be responsible for getting some of your recruits to the safe spot along with all the necessary supplies needed to sustain you all for a minimum of four months. I would pack for six because you don't know what will be left when you come out of hiding. Stick with nonperishables and each of you should bring a few emergency survival packs. Some water will be provided for the masses, but everyone needs to pull their own weight. You will all be getting lists with specific items to bring, but I want to be transparent with what I currently know."

He pats each of us on the back and shows himself out. I can see the excitement of being assigned my bodyguard seeping out of Hollis' expression as reality settles in. He is pacing around the condo reiterating the plan. Regardless, he excuses himself to start gathering the items necessary to protect me.

I look at Amos, reaching for his attention. He responds without returning my glance. "I won't disregard the orders we have been given to fill a void that shouldn't exist in your heart. You have been given so much, Leo. The gift you have is not a burden."

The comment reeks of condensation and betrayal. "What makes you think that I would ask you to?" I respond, offended.

"The same way that you knew I wouldn't perform an exorcism without Michael's consent. I've spent days in fasting with God. Prayer is my life force and the only way I make decisions. He loves you deeply. No worldly father could amount to the father you have in him. Don't be blind to what's right in front of you." He smiles in my direction.

Every part of me wants to fight back, but I know he is right. Tears start welling up in my eyes. I wipe them away before they can fall and return the smile. I feel ashamed and manipulated, like a child. My sympathy for Collin turns to distaste.

This is war, and he is a terrorist.

17

SPY VS. SPY

If there is something I can do to distract from the pending capture of Collin, it's hitting the ground running to find our next recruit. It has been over 24 hours since the images of my mother appeared, and I can't say I'm disappointed. The impending doom it left me with wasn't worth the comfort. I've lived 29 years without her—I can move on. I grind my coffee beans and pack them into the espresso machine. Slowly stirring cream into my cup, the search engine firing on my laptop stares back at me. I type in 'local police department' and search the site for detective personnel. Great, there they are. How does one decide who is the best police detective amongst their peers? I type in the search bar, "Do police detectives earn awards?"

Yes, they most certainly do. They call them awards and commendations. Any awards they have earned make them more decorated. I like that, to be decorated. Well, we want our police detective to be lit up like a damn Christmas tree.

Alec Wilson, their Deputy Chief of Investigations, oversees the police detectives. How much actual investigatory work could he be doing? His photo is front in center on their webpage. He is beaming in an esteemed way that says, "I'm in charge here." I'm not here to recruit a trainer or manager who spends most of their days behind a desk barking orders. I decide to place him on my list of backups, just in case.

Lucas Robinson, Detective II, also a supervisory position. His photo does very little for him. The uniform hat shades his acne scars, but it can't take away from the stoic expression on his face. I picture 15-year-old Lucas. A face full of blemishes and much more scrawny than present day Lucas. It might be presumptuous, but I'm betting he wasn't Mr. Popular. Now, in a place of power, he feels more in control. If that is true, let's hope we will luck out and find that he has dealt with those demons. I find his name more directly connected to local investigations. He earned a silver star for moving a fellow officer out of the line of fire. He is a Florida native, born March 11, 2024, in Sarasota, Florida. So, that makes him 32 years old. His father, Nathan Robinson, was also a police officer. I guess it runs in the family. He was arrested two months after the abolishment for public acts of religion. *Bingo. Let's hope that your son doesn't share the police department's affinity for keeping religious beliefs at bay.* No social media profiles. He's received the highest award in his precinct. I move him to the list of candidates.

Henri Davis, Detective I, is our guy on the pavement. I see a glimpse of jet-black hair under his hat. He's in no way beaming with glee, but I see the slightest smile. He's handsome in the classic definition. His eyes are spaced just the right amount and his perfect jaw line leads to the just right prominent chin. Henri was probably Mr. Popular at 15 years old, but did he use his popularity for good? There is a long list of recent investigations he has played a part in, but it doesn't appear that he gets a lot of the glory. The news reports tend to congratulate Deputy Chief Wilson most often. He did earn a Merit Award for Excellent Arrest. He took down a sex trafficker. He was born on January 2, 2029, in Beckley, West

Virginia. That makes him 27 years old. Again, no social media profiles. Maybe they are encouraged to avoid too much online exposure. Either way, he fits the profile. *I'm starting with you, Mr. Popular.*

Let's start with the county records to see if any marriage certificates have been filed under his name. There she is. I knew he was too good looking to be single, but he married young. Molly Davis and Henri Davis were married July 10, 2053. He was 24 and Holly was 22. No one gets married that young anymore. Before the abolition, people got married young if they were pregnant to spare their family shame, or if they just wanted to have sex without breaking their religious beliefs. The average age people get married today is 37. Most don't care to have children, but about one in every few couples have a child. Maybe two, if they are up for a big family.

Let's see what I can find about Mrs. Davis. She does have social media accounts. She has all the features of a beautiful Asian woman. Her dark hair is straight and shiny. Her facial features are delicate. In each photo, she has just the slightest closed mouth smile. She either doesn't like to show her teeth or maybe she's not so happy with Mr. Popular. Last summer, she posted a photo of Henri holding a massive, dead python around his shoulders. The caption read, "Henri supporting the Florida Python Elimination Program." Other than that, there are only photos of them at the beach, on vacation with friends, and award banquets for the precinct.

They clearly don't have a baby, and I don't see any photos of extended family from his or her side. She has only posted four times and just to add these photos. Oddly enough, she doesn't list a career or have any professional media profiles. *What do you do all day, lady?* According to the county assessor website, they have a modest two-bedroom house just blocks from the art district downtown. The house is tiny, but it appears to have had some updates. A mere 900 square feet with a carport. It's interesting they wouldn't want a garage in that neighborhood. *How very fearless of you, Mr. Popular.*

I can start surveillance by camping out by their house. That way, we can figure out what hours this guy works. He's probably all over the place depending on the assignments he is working on. I will need to be careful this time. They are professionals at this game, and I'm just a baby spy. I remember Amos's offer to join me if I needed a stakeout partner. Our last interaction felt cold. It was a reminder of how little experience I have in this world in comparison to him. My small, sheltered view through archangel protective lenses hasn't been reality. He sees the world from a mountain of trials and tribulation that he has battled and at times overcome. This gift I have was necessary for my survival. He was right about that. I may have taken it for granted. There are some snake species here that are born with the markings of a venomous snake. Eventually, they mature and those markings fade away, but they did their job. They gave the baby time to grow and survive. God knew I needed this advantage to survive. I want to be the person who never needed a crutch in the first place. Amos wasn't given anything because of his grit. He fought his way to this place just to watch it burn to the ground so we can start over. I might be in over my head this time, but I do my best work when I'm being observed by someone I respect. I pull up Henri's photo again. It's time to do a little spy verses spy.

***

Amos agrees to join me at the entrance to Henri and Holly's neighborhood that evening. Hoping that it will give him purpose, I ask Hollis to keep watch on our condo in the meantime. He's not thrilled, so I promise he is my sidekick on the next shift. I don't want to exclude him, and I do feel safe with him by my side. I just need to clear whatever muddied up the slate between Amos and I.

The neighborhood feels busy. Most homes have the lights on and people buzzing around inside. The lots are small. Each house comes and goes in an instant as we drive through. It's a mix of poorly cared for shells of what once were decent homes, and those that have been dusted off and made new again. I hand Amos an energy drink. "Why don't we make this a drinking game? For every flipped house we drink." He laughs, "Ahh, the things I missed out on in my journey to priesthood." I turn onto McCullen Street and there it is in all its renovated glory. The Davis residence. Just like the homes around them, the lights are on and things are happening. I pull in across the street and hand Amos a set of binoculars. Mr. Popular is wearing athletic shorts and a dry fit shirt. Molly, on the other hand, is wearing a simple white cotton shirt and jeans. While he sits in a recliner attached to his phone, she is slaving away in the kitchen making their dinner. It's like watching paint dry.

"They are 27 and 25 years old. Can you believe that?" I ask.

"It's definitely abnormal, but not a crime to be married young," he responds.

"True, but I'm concerned they don't remember much of anything prior to the abolishment. I had archangels as parents conducting secret Bible studies all throughout my childhood to ensure I didn't forget, but they were only 10 and 12 when everything changed. At that point, majority of people were no longer believers."

He takes a deep breath and moves his seat back. "It must burn through a lot of that energy to exhaust all possibilities before conducting the surveillance." He pauses for dramatic effect and nudges my arm to lighten the mood. He's right, but I'll be damned if I admit it. Finally, they finish their dinner and make their way to bed. They said maybe two words to one another and it's clear that his home life isn't going to be the key to my discovery. I drop Amos off at his car a few blocks away. "Thanks for the backup." He smiles and stands holding the car door open. "Don't second guess yourself. I have dedicated my whole life to serving the Lord. He is the ultimate recruiter. Follow your instincts." He closes the door and makes his way back to his car. I am in a constant state of internal debates and he moves through this process like it's just another day. I place my foot on the break and turn on the facial recognition to head home. Tomorrow is another day.

HOLLIS

18

I KNOW MY GIRL

I remember when we had the whole world ahead of us. Time to explore and take our time figuring out what we wanted to do or who we wanted to be with. My, how things have changed. Running is the last thing I want to do, but it's the one thing she wants to do and that means I'll be there, making sure she is okay.

I'm impressed at the stamina she has built in just a couple months. I can barely keep up. We pass by other runners and people walking their dogs. Some stay focused on the path in front of them, and some acknowledge our presence. I wonder what they think we are. Just friends who have a mutual interest in exercise, a married couple, or a couple that just started dating?

But who cares? I really need to stop projecting my shit.

Here comes our building. Yes, we are finally done. I don't think I could go on for another mile. She chugs a glass of water, spreads her legs apart and bends over to reach her toes. Nope. I'm out.

"Don't forget to stretch!" she shouts as I walk toward the bathroom to take a long, cold shower.

I step into a pair of shorts and run a comb through my hair. It's getting way too long, but who has time to schedule a cut with the insane mess we are in.

She meets me at the door and runs her fingers through it. "Just because it's the end of the world, it doesn't mean you can run around looking like a greaseball."

I know it's not intentional, but please don't touch me unless you want something more.

"Thanks, mom," I retort.

We quietly take down our espresso on the way there. It's not the kind of quiet that would make most people uncomfortable. We are like an old married couple that still loves each other but doesn't need empty words to fill the space. Or from her perspective, a brother and sister.

I turn right onto officer Henri's street and pull behind a large white contractor van far enough away from his house. Leo fusses with her hair. She pulls a brush through it over and over again. She pulls it up into a ponytail. Just when I think she's finished, she pulls the hair tie out and starts over. "Couldn't they have given me straight hair if I was meant to live in this humidity?"

I laugh. "Even in the midst of this, you find a way to pick yourself apart."

She brushes through it one last time, settling on leaving it down after all that effort. She slaps the mirror back up. "You wouldn't know the half of it."

I tap the bottom of her chin and break into song. "You are so beautiful......to me. Can't you see?!" She fights to keep the steely frown on her face, but it eventually breaks into a smirk.

She's going to start asking questions if I don't start seeing someone soon. It's been months. I've had my fair share of one-night stands. If there is one thing that can scare a guy straight, it's seeing what you are waking up to. Most women really cake on the makeup, layer up the hair extensions, and don't get me started on the shape wear. One girl literally injured herself trying to get out of them. Pushing with all her might, her fingers slipped, and her elbow went flying into the wall. I understand their hungover faces don't do them justice, but Leo sits here without a stitch of makeup on and I can't imagine a more beautiful woman. Her skin looks like it was painted on by an artist, her black eyelashes curl up just at the ends, and she has the smallest dark freckles scattered along her arms and legs. Most women would die to wake up like that. For years, we told her parents that they owed her money because she never needed to get braces or glasses like most kids did. She catches me laughing to myself. "What's so funny?"

A light flicks on in the Davis house and I point in that direction. "Someone's awake."

Molly makes her way into the kitchen to make a pot of coffee. She's using one of those vintage machines that require you to fill the water and wait for it to brew for a ridiculously long time. I understand that some people are sentimental, but if they only knew how convenient the new ones are. The light is still on upstairs, but the curtains are pulled tight, so we will just have to wait for Henri to come down.

Leo is fixed to her binoculars as if they have become an extension of her eyes. She's leaning into the windshield willing him to come down. Her right leg is bent, with her foot tucked under her left thigh. She sits just like this every time we are playing cards or watching a game. When the stakes are high, that foot gets under the left thigh in a hurry. Then it drops to the car floor. He made his way down. Molly hands him a thermos of hot coffee, and he leaves without saying more than two words to her. Rude. She doesn't seem phased. He gets in his car and heads back out of the neighborhood. I leave a good distance between his car and ours. He pulls into the precinct parking lot and walks right in. Just south of the parking lot there is a neighborhood that we nestle into. We can't see the entrance to the building, but we have a good view of his car.

An hour goes by, and all we have to show for it are bellies full of dry cereal. Leo has been rambling on about all the possible scenarios we could find ourselves in following a police detective. Her imagination is bewildering. Just as I am about to ask if we can get out and stretch our legs, we see Henri and another man walking through the parking lot. They weave through the cars and get into one that isn't Henri's.

Leo's eyes are still glued to her binoculars. "You have got to be kidding. Well, this just got interesting." She lowers the binoculars. "That's Lucas. My other prospect."

I'm confused. "Are they partners?"

"I can't know for sure yet, but they are working together on something. Follow him."

We follow them to a three-story building with yellow caution tape roping off the northwest corner. There is a body lying on the sidewalk surrounded by chalk. Four other officers are already on the scene and reporters are barricaded on the other side of the street. It looks like a big man. There is a small pool of blood moving out from under his torso. They exit the car and make their way to the body. Lucas shakes hands with one of the officers, but Henri goes straight to the body to examine. After circling the scene a few times, he pulls his rubber gloves off, pats the other officer on the back and says something to Lucas. Lucas was just about to put a pair of gloves on but sets them down in response to whatever Henri had said. They get in their car and head back to the precinct.

Leo watches them walking back in. "Did you notice Lucas going in to examine him, and Henri stopping him?"

"Yes. I have a theory. Lucas is higher up than Henri, right?"

"Yeah," she responds.

"Maybe it's normal for Lucas to handle the politics involved; hence, him getting updated by the officer on the scene. That would leave the dirty work to Henri."

"That's possible, but why would he have started to put on the gloves, then?"

"Lazy cop?" I shrug.

She's probably on to something, but it's an unspoken rule that I be her voice of reason, so I play the part. We follow them back to the precinct and wait for any movement until nearly 6 in the evening when both Lucas and Henri exit the building. We watch as they get into their individual vehicles and drive out of the parking lot. It's tempting to follow Henri, but neither of us have eaten more than half a box of dry cereal all day, and hunger wins. She quietly stares out the window picking at the cuticles on her nails. I pull into our taco spot, the Grumpy Gringo. It's her comfort food.

She smiles. "How did you know?"

Keeping one hand on the wheel, I place my other hand on her knee. "I know my girl."

LEO

19

MOVING ON UP

This is the way I had originally imagined stakeouts to feel. The utter boredom of sitting in front of a man's house who has no conversation with his wife, and no company…ever. Then there's the utter boredom of sitting in front of a police precinct, watching officers who I'm not following come and go. Today has to be different. Please, God. There are only five months and 26 days until the end, and I need a breakthrough. Michael has decided he needs Amos for something today, and my other bodyguard has a 102-degree fever. I pick up the phone and call my mother. A small part of me questions if I should still refer to her as my mother or Jo. I decide I need the stability. "Mom, can you guys join me on a stakeout today?" That's a question I never thought I would ask my parents.

"On our way over, "she responds.

A mere two minutes later, they are knocking at the door.

I open the door. "That was freaky fast."

My mom reaches out her arms. "We were in the neighborhood." She wraps them around me and kisses my cheek.

"Sure, you were. So, today, we are going to get this investigator recruit figured out or I might hang myself from those rafters." I point out of my window.

Their faces both cringe in disgust from my choice of words.

"Just keeping you two on your toes," I respond.

We make our way to the precinct. My father calls shotgun to have a front row seat in this process. Come to think of it, he would probably make a great sleuth. He likes to hang back in a crowd and observe everything around him, and he has good instincts. He glances at my leg bobbing up and down in rapid succession.

"This is such a great practice in learning to be still with yourself, Leo. I know you have struggled with that," he laughs.

"Delighting in my torture? And they say you're an angel."
I snicker.

I peer through my rearview mirror to see my mother cleaning my back seat with antibacterial wipes from her purse. Typical.

"Speaking of our duties, why did Michael need to steal my bodyguard? I assume you two know."

"I'm sure he had his reasons. Remember, Amos is going through his own journey as well," my father responds.

Hours go by without Henri or Lucas leaving the building. My parents contently read news articles on their phones. I, on the other hand, am contemplating committing a crime just to get in front of these hermits. My father places his hand on my knee.

"You have time honey, let's get something to eat and we can make our way back after."

I tilt my head in a stern manor to suggest this is serious and we can't just up and go anytime we want.

He responds. "I know you are hungry, and you will think clearly on a full stomach."

I push the car into drive. "Alright, but just a quick lunch."

We come across a small diner just a few blocks away, and I pull in without giving them an option. It's the closest place, and we don't have time to waste. There are framed newspaper articles from years ago about old Hollywood stars, and pin up photos of actresses from old films hanging on the walls. We settle into a booth with cracked leather seats. The angel parents order their usual salads and I settle on a grilled cheese with tomato soup and loads of saltine crackers. I take the opportunity to use the restroom. On my way out of the bathroom, I feel a piercing cold hand wrap around my upper arm. It pulls me down the hallway, and out the back doors near the large garbage dump. I start to scream out, but his hand covers my mouth. It's the same hand. Then I hear his voice.

"I thought you were smarter than them, sweetheart."

Collin turns my head to face him. I watch as the pupils of his eyes grow to the extent of pushing all the color out of his iris. He stares back at me with his ominous, black eyes and searing expression. Thin, dark veins on his neck become darker and slowly extend into his face. Fear sets in. I feel a tingling throughout my body, but I can't move. I want to leap out of my own skin and vanish into thin air. He places a finger on my cheek.

"You chose wrong, and I can't do anything for you now. We are going to make this place inhabitable."

He starts to drag his sharp, yellow fingernail down my face when the metal doors behind us swing open. He drops me from his grip immediately. As if a bomb exploded in front of us, I feel a wave of light come off her. It's my mother, Jo. Her lean legs and arms tightened and flexed into weapons. Her delicate facial features clenched into the expression of a hardened warrior. He slowly takes a step back, cowering beneath her. She wraps her hand around the back of his neck and slams his face into the concrete below. Another voice echo from the hall. My father appears in the doorway talking causally on the phone. "Yes, right behind the diner."

Two men in hazard suits come running around the back of the building. "Thank you, Jo. We can take it from here. So sorry to have interrupted your day."

She morphs back into her soft, gentle self. "Thank you, gentleman. Let's not let this happen again."

They drag him around the diner and load him into a square prison transport vehicle. My blood starts to warm back to a normal temperature. My mother rubs her hands up and down my arms to warm me.

"I know you are so determined to find your recruit, but we really need to get you home after today's events," she says.

Staring at the back of the transport vehicle as they drive away, I nod in agreement. I feel like someone stuck a straw into my body and sucked all the life force out of me. I clasp my hands together to stop their shaking, my parents gather our food to go and drive me home.

***

I thought they had taken me home. I wake up on a plush sofa and find myself in a very art deco inspired living room. I hear a repeated *whoosh whoosh*. Did they buy a sound machine to reduce stress? I slowly sit up in front of a wall of floor-to-ceiling windows framing the ocean. The sun is setting, and the sky is a melting pot of deep orange to pink hues. It smells delicious. Hollis and my mother are chopping vegetables in the most gorgeous kitchen I have ever seen. The ceilings soar up to at least 12 feet and the appliances have beautiful chrome handles and dials. The island is the length of two king-sized beds.

Hollis catches my attention. "Good morning, sunshine. You've been asleep nearly two days."

I rub my eyes and approach them. My father is sitting at a dining table reading the paper. On the counter, there is cleaned stems of celery, chopped onion, garlic and carrots. Vegetable quinoa soup. It's my sick food, and Hollis's, too. I place my hand on his forehead and he slightly flinches.

"The fever is gone, but you, on the other hand, are a little jumpy." He changes the subject, "I'm doing great, but you had everyone pretty worried. I, of course, knew you were fine. It's about time you got some sleep."

I dip a spoon into the broth cooking on the stovetop and take a sip.

"So, is anyone going to tell me where the hell we are?"

"Language, honey," my father warns. "We are in your temporary home. The house has gated entry and we will be providing security until it's time to move. You are only 20 minutes from the precinct on the gulf."

I throw my hand up and twirl in a circle. "Now we're talking."

Hollis joins me in the fit of celebration. The image of Collin's black eyes comes barreling in.

"Is Collin dead?" I ask.

Mom stops chopping and places the knife back down on the countertop. "No, Collin is a demon, so he can't die in the terms a human can. However, he is being detained behind the gates of hell and you will never see him again."

I curl up on the sofa and tell Hollis the story of my mother's insane powers in the flesh. He sits at attention hanging on my every word. We turn on the tv and I lean in to rest my head on his shoulder. He violently shifts away.

"What's your problem? Did I do something to piss you off?"

He shakes his head. "No, I just don't want to risk getting you sick. I could still be contagious."

My father sighs, shakes his head and looks back down at his paper. Hollis continues to settle in on "his side" of the sofa, but I notice a sadness in his eyes. Is there something that he knows, that I don't? I can't take any more surprises. I grab the fancy throw pillow next to me and fling in his face.

He rolls his eyes. "You are a relentless child."

I see some comedic relief behind his serious exterior. That's more like it. I recognize it's only a band-aid, but I'm just too tired to poke around underneath to see what's festering. Instead, we play pretend for the evening. Dinner with the parents and the usual reality tv entertainment. It's almost like old times.

AMOS

20

ALWAYS A PRIEST, NEVER A GROOM

I can never figure this guy out. The last place I met him was a seedy bar in a rough neighborhood, and here I am at the Bel Air of beach neighborhoods. Not only is the community gated, but the house has its own gated entrance. I press the button on the gate call box and the doors slide open. There, in all its glory, stands a mammoth of a home right in front of the beach. It's near dark, so I can see that the lights are on inside. Someone is walking from the side yard toward the driveway where I am parked. I step out to find Michael soaking wet, only wearing a pair of palm tree printed board shorts.

"It's a beautiful night for a swim," he exclaims.

I follow him around the side of the house to the patio out back. He grabs the towel sitting on the bench in front of us and dries his face.

"You do know that shark attacks are most common this time of night, right?" I ask, knowing full well that he's not afraid.

He bends over holding his stomach in laughter. "You get me every time, Amos. Let's take a seat by the garden and chat."

I follow him around to a garden. A stone path leads us into a circular-shaped oasis surrounded by a ring of bright, fuchsia encore azaleas. In the center sits a fire pit surrounded by a royal blue patio sectional.

He gestures for me to sit with him. "I know you have been wondering if God has only prepared you to be of service to Leo." I nod in admittance. "Although, that has been a very important part of your calling, it is not your only purpose. In five months, you will still be in contact with Hollis and Leo, but not solely at their disposal." *What kind of bomb are you going to drop on me now?*

He clears his throat, "Your career as a priest was practice in the grand scheme of things. Amos, when the dust settles and you all crawl out of hiding, they will need someone to guide them, spiritually. Someone to monitor their faith and orchestrate the fellowship they will need to carry on."

I feel my chest tighten and my heart beats its way into my throat. I don't understand. "I thought my role as a priest was over. You have to understand...I've imagined my life differently now. Even when you assigned me to assist Leo. I thought the connection we had..."

"Your title will never be priest again, but you will continue to be married to Abba until you've fulfilled your mission." He reaches for my shoulders and pulls me toward him. "You are going to have a country of people looking to you for hope. Faith-driven people who love and live for Abba. It's every past priest's dream man! Your heart will be so full, you won't have room for a romantic relationship." He grins ear to ear and motions for me to follow him towards the mansion.

We walk a path lined with ferns and privet shrubs until we are a few feet from the patio closest to the entrance. The large windows peer into a lofty living area, and there I see Hollis unfolding a blanket. He makes his way to the sofa and I see her.

Leo. She's laying on the sofa, fast asleep. He gently lays the blanket over her and moves a piece of her hair out of her face.

Michael points in their direction. "He's Leo's soul mate. They were made for each other. What they have could stand the tests of time, and they need one another. You are destined to be their spiritual leader. Think of all the ways in which you are wise beyond her understanding. She needs you to fulfill your purpose. You were drawn to her because it is your job to look after her. It's easy to mistake a fondness for love."

I look out at the shoreline and listen to the waves lapping onto the sand. Michael nudges my arm and points at the window. "Hey, it's Raph and Jo." Raphi is standing at the window waving at us. I hold a hand up in acknowledgment as Michael enthusiastically waves back in their direction. Jo stands by his side and looks into my eyes. She places her hand over her heart and nods in understanding. They know what we are talking about. I imagine all the years they watched Leo and Hollis growing up, side by side. Helping them through childish fights, knowing one day they would be telling their love story. Everyone knew but me. Leo is fiercely protective with her heart. I can't imagine how long it would take someone new to come along and chisel away at the wall she has built up. But

Hollis, he has always been inside those walls. Keeping her safe. I hear my mother's laughter echoing in my mind. This is a test, and one I intend to pass. I'll never let them win.

Michael places his arm around my shoulders. I look up at him and force a smile. "I am honored. Even if I can't see how this is the way, I am committed to my purpose. I just need a moment to digest everything."

"Soak it in, brother. Oh, I should mention that there will be a few tweaks to the Holy Book. I've assigned an editor to remove and/or replace all misguiding information."

"Misguiding information? I thought that it was all testaments from God."

"That was the idea, but some of the disciples and translations got a little far-fetched. I mean, come on… 'Let a woman learn quietly with all submissiveness. I do not permit a woman to teach or to exercise authority over a man; rather, she is to remain quiet.' Talk about hearing what you want to hear!"

He walks me to my car and opens the door for me, and with a wink, he's gone.

LEO

21

DON'T LOOK SO NORMA

The drive from our new baby mansion to the precinct is surprisingly faster than I expected. There is a bridge that separates the mainland from the beach. When it glides back down into the city, I feel the forcefield of congestion swallow me. Everyone racing to make deadlines so they can afford to feed their addictions and get through another day. A vicious cycle of self-detriment. I stop at the first traffic light and see a man and woman both dressed in suits, nervously waiting at their walk signal to make their way to the courthouse across the street. He keeps twitching, clenching his jaw and pacing back and forth. She, however, stands very still. Both hands are on the handle of the briefcase she holds in front of her, and she avoids eye contact with him. I notice Hollis is observing them too.

"She is his attorney, and he is a crack addict who should be locked up, but probably won't get more than a few months because the dead-eyed jury has seen much more repulsive crimes than a quick street stabbing in a drug deal gone wrong," I wager.

He strokes his chin. "Fair assessment. I can't play against the crack addict notion as that's obvious, but just to shake things up, let's say that she is the attorney of the victim's family and they are both standing in the world's most uncomfortable stalling pattern." He stops to listen to the sound of the traffic direction, "Tik-tok, tik-tok. She's going, to put, you in, jail."

I cringe at the thought. "Ugh, just watching makes me want to crawl out of my skin."

The light turns green and we navigate through herds of desperate, sad people on foot and behind the wheel. The precinct is humming with traffic today and it sparks some hope. Our typical, sullen Lucas arrives with an unusual pep in his step. He speed walks into the building. Two minutes pass and Henri arrives with a new friend in cuffs. He yanks him out of the back of his car, slamming the top of his head on the way out. The man is tiny by most standards. He couldn't weigh more than 130 pounds. He has long, dark wavy hair down to his shoulders, a beard, and a wide smile on his face.

Hollis is perplexed. "I thought that Charles Manson died in prison years ago."

I couldn't deny him that. "Maybe they caught a copycat."

We wait for hours. Other officers come and go, but our guys are probably in there questioning Manson. I've tried thinking of ways to get in there an observe them, but they all involve committing a crime. My bladder is nearly bursting when they emerge. Lucas and Henri get into a car together. We follow them into the even less desirable part of town to see they've stopped in a bait shop parking lot. Hollis laughs. "If they go to the pier and hop on a boat, you are going to lose your mind."

"If that happens, you're going to be swimming after them," I reply. Clearly not amused.

They park and walk across the street to the Shucks Shakers Tacos food truck. I pull into a parking spot around the corner. They are the only people at the truck. It's now or never.

I throw my binoculars onto Hollis's lap. "Keep an eye out. I need to get closer."

I grab my purse and walk across the street. They are laughing with the chef as I approach. I'm a few feet away and my handy gift kicks in full force. I feel the wave of cold run from my head to my toes. Trying not to draw attention to the discomfort, I get my phone out and make myself appear busy. I'm just a normal disconnected asshole like everyone else, waiting to get my food. The chef moves back into the truck to make their order.

Henri turns to Lucas. "I'm telling you. We just need to go to Spill Up tonight. They will be there by 11. It's like clockwork every time."

The chef hands them their food in tin bowls and they head back to the car. I do my best to steady my jaw and order a couple of tacos. The heat starts to fill my body again.

It's not the taco man. It's one of them.

I have a view of their car from the truck. *Please don't pull away. Please don't pull away. Not until I know which one of you it is.* Lucas, who is in the driver's seat, takes a bite of his burrito. Henri does the same and pulls out some paperwork to show Lucas. *That's right, eat in your car. Don't drive and eat.* The man hands me my tacos and I try to walk back to my car as casually as possible.

Hollis is dumbfounded. "You could have blown your cover."

I interrupt. "One of them is evil. Bone-chilling, gross evil."

He slams his hands on the dashboard, "No way! You couldn't tell which one? How do you know it wasn't the food truck guy?"

"No, I couldn't tell which one! They were both two feet from me. I just know it's one of them because my blood started to thaw when they went back to their car. Henri told Lucas that they need to go to some place called Spill Up at 11 tonight. Do you know what that is?"

"I've heard about it. It's a club in St. Pete."

He pulls up their website to show me. A huge laser show showering hundreds of sweaty people grinding on each other and scantily clad dancers performing insane athletic feats inside of cages. Pretty much my worst nightmare. I give Hollis his phone back and pick up my binoculars. They are clearly in a heated discussion. Henri is holding the paper with his left hand and slapping it with his right in an effort to drill his point

223

home. Lucas retorts, his eyes wide, shoulders shrugged and his hands out in the air. He wipes his mouth with a napkin and the car starts to pull out of the parking lot. Five minutes into the drive I know we are heading back to the precinct. It's nearly 3:30, and traffic will be horrendous in an hour when everyone gets off work.

I can feel Hollis waiting for the go ahead. "Alright, let's figure out logistics for the club stakeout."

He smiles. "Lucky for me, guys don't have to do much from a wardrobe perspective. You, on the other hand, are going to need a club makeover. Any girl at a place like Spill Up is looking for attention, and you will stick out like a sore thumb in a boring little black dress."

I reluctantly agree to take his suggestion on the account that he will not take any photos of me and that we leave the club once we have what we need. The deal is struck, and I make my way to the nearest slut-you-up store.

***

I feel like I've been tarred and feathered. Hollis is probably becoming impatient. I make him go wait at the yogurt shop down the street while I figure out what to wear tonight. After an hour of doing hard time in a dressing room filled to the brim with sequins, leather and tassels of all kinds, I decide to settle on a pair of ultra-low black latex pants and a shiny, metallic gold tube top. It took me far too long to squeeze into, but that's probably user error. Of all the options, this one covered more of my body than any of the others. The salesgirl looks me up and down, popping her bubble gum. "Something is missing. Here, take this choker and make sure you wear some stilettos, so you don't look so Norma."

"Norma" is 20-something club queen for bland, or boring. "There's also a spray tan salon around the corner. You should probably make a stop there, too," she suggests.

You should probably rip the nasty, infected eyebrow ring out of your face and learn some manors. She saunters over to the counter to check me out. I bite my tongue. This is probably her only opportunity to talk down to someone, and I doubt we will be seeing much of one another in a few months. Hollis is waiting impatiently out front on a street bench.

"I knew it would be a major project, but over an hour?" he questions.

"I'm just getting into character. I figured taking zero consideration for others would fit the mold of an attention seeking bimbo." I get into the passenger seat. "To the beach cave, club boy!" Hollis rolls his eyes and peels out of the parking spot.

***

Never in my life have I had to put this much effort into trying to be something I'm not. I stand in front of the mirror, my brows knitted together and my mouth hanging open as I'm lining my eyelids with a black liquid makeup pen. It has taken four online cat eye and contouring makeup videos to muster the courage and apply it to my face. I gently flick my eyelashes with a mascara wand to finish the masterpiece. *Check.* My bare shoulders, arms and navel are adorned with body shimmer. *Check.* I spray my hair with a texture spray and pull up with a round bristle brush as I blow dry to create volume up top, pull the sides back with a bobby pin, and engulf my head in a cloud of toxic chemicals, also known as hairspray, for good measure. *Check.* One last look in the mirror. I'm a lean, mean, bombastic machine. I carefully step out into the living room where Hollis is waiting.

"Let's get to this dog and pony show, shall we?" I suggest.

He gasps. "Now, this is a side of you I have never seen. Are you sure we can't take any pictures?"

I grab my handbag, slip on my four-inch heels and walk out the door without responding. He runs after me, and we make our way to what must be one of the many realms of hell.

We approach the club entrance and get in line. It's only about 20 people deep, so the wait shouldn't be so horrific. I look at my phone. "It's 11:10. They might already be in."

Hollis shrugs, and two men approach the bouncer. It's them. The bouncer presses the laser security line to let them in. I impatiently tap my heel on the concrete. Hollis, in recognition, places his arm on the back of my waist to calm me. Easy there, buddy. Our turn finally comes, and we make our way in. There are dance floors on two levels. The first is a large, gaping mosh pit with cages hanging from the balconies above. In the cages are dancers wearing elaborate masks made of feathers and sequins, bikini tops barely big enough to cover their gigantic breasts and very cheeky, black leather bottoms. The stage has a large turn table that lights in different colors with each beat, but I don't see an actual DJ anywhere. I grab Hollis's attention. "Where's the DJ?"

"DJs do all the work from behind the scenes now. It's their way of gaining more publicity. Everyone has to try and guess who they are," he explains.

I laugh. "I guess when your audience needs to be inebriated to enjoy your talents, you have to get creative to keep them interested."

Hollis puts his finger to his mouth. "Shhhh, this is their temple and they are their Gods."

I scan the club, attempting to single out our detectives.

"Lucas was wearing a red t-shirt and Henri was wearing a bright blue tank top. Should we divide and conquer?" I ask.

Hollis grabs my hand. "No way. You are my responsibility and I'm not letting you out of my sight. They are clearly here on a mission, but they will want to fit in. Their most likely at one of the bars. They need to have a drink in hand to look normal, and so do we."

There are two bars on the first floor and another on the second. The mob of people slamming into each other to the rhythm of the music is not my cup of tea. Completely out of control. As we knock into random strangers, I am occasionally struck with cold. I won't be able to stay here long. Whoever they are looking for would be in some position of power. The second floor showed movement too, but off to the sides, there were lounge areas roped off for those with enough money to make it worthwhile to the club.

We make our way to the second-floor bar to get a closer view. Sure enough, Lucas and Henri had drinks and were making introductions with the gatekeeper of the bottle service area. I barge my way to the front of the bar, slam my money down and scream my order. The bartender with the gray mullet rushes to grab the order for me. I look down at my skimpy top. The little gold bandage that could, did. Nice work.

I grab the drinks and lean into Hollis. "I think it's dark enough in here that I can keep my face turned away and we can back into their area to listen in. If one of them separates from the other, I need to find a way to get close."

He agrees, and we make our move. Between the thumping base and humming of the crowds, I hear Henri. "He's clearly not our guy. I don't know why you insist on wasting our time here. I have wife to get home to."

Lucas mumbles something in disagreement, but I can't make it out. They make their way out of the lounge and walk right by us. Starting at the base of my tailbone and moving up it feels as if the fluid surrounding my spine is freezing. There is no way to distinguish which one. We allow them to get ahead far enough to safely follow. They move out of the club and right into their separate vehicles. I grab Hollis's arm. "We need to follow one. I started with Henri. Let's go with him."

We get into the car and follow behind him. Where we should be taking a right to head to his house, he continues straight. "Where is our guy heading?" Hollis questions.

Three turns later, he stops in a random neighborhood. We park down the street and turn our lights off immediately. We watch him get out of the car, knock on the door of one of the houses and walk in. I keep my lights off but pull up to a closer parking spot. I scan the house with binoculars, but I can't get a good view.

"I can't see any action inside," I say.

In frustration, I grab the zip up hoodie in the back seat and throw it on. "Keep your eyes out for me. I need to get a closer position if we are going to figure this out. That bush just south of the house should give me a view in that window." I point to the area.

"No, Leo. The answer is no. If he is the evil one, you're screwed. I am supposed to be here to make sure you stay safe. That is not a good idea."

I grab my phone. "Yes, your job is to protect me. Mine is to get my guy. Michael never said your job was going to be easy. Watch my back."

I run for the bush and get low. Pulling the binoculars up, I can see movement. There is a three-inch crack between the curtains of which appears to be a bedroom. I see a row of twin-size mattresses on the floor, and a group of women. A few of them are holding their round bellies and looking toward the bedroom door. They are as far back up against the wall as they can be, huddled together, shaking in fear. I take a closer look at one of them. She's pregnant. Then I realize…they are ALL pregnant. I pull my phone out of my pocket and take a photo of them. There is a second bush maybe five feet away further back in the side yard. It's the angle I need. I glance at the house next door. No lights on. Same of the houses across the street. I bolt for the second bush and nearly drop my phone on the way. Thank God for loopy cases. I nestle in tight, keeping out of sight, peering through the bush to avoid blowing my cover. Through the branches, I can see Henri at the room entrance speaking with another man. On the other side of the room there are more mattresses. At least another six, and I can see another group of women. Damnit. They are all pregnant, and they are all Asian. The image of Henri's wife grievously preparing his dinner flashes in my mind. I get my phone out and make a video. Henri reaches out to shake the man's hand, and on the release, I see a wad of cash slipped into his hand. Henri places the money in his pocket. *Oh, shit!* This is the end of their conversation. He's going to be leaving. I dart back to the car.

Grasping to catch my breath, I mutter, "It's some kind of illegal pregnancy ring. I was able to get photos and a video. It has to be him. The women were scared. They didn't sign up for this."

We wriggle down into the bottom of our seats as Henri passes us by to exit the neighborhood. Once the coast is clear, I hand my phone to Hollis and shift the car into drive.

He looks up from watching the video. "They're kids. Most of them look like they can't be older than 15."

I grip the steering wheel. "We are going to get them out of there. Make sure you take down the house number and street. We'll be back. "

22

SLITHERING SCANDAL

Molly's face is everywhere I look. After years of forced marriage, I would be sullen and indignant, too. He probably took her as his wife once she retired from being one of his cash cows. She's trapped there, making him meals and cleaning his house while he enslaves and impregnates more women like her every day. Maybe he isn't doing the impregnating himself, but he is definitely responsible for it, one way or another. There must be clues we could feed to Lucas to make him wonder what Henri is up to. To make this story come to life. I need to do more digging into Henri's personal life. There was nothing to be found online about his family.

Everyone has a family. Every mystery in the movies is solved by reading old newspaper articles, so I decide to start there. Luckily, the Library of Congress for American historical newspapers has a pretty extensive library online. I start with a basic search of his name, Henri Davis. A couple old articles surface. An obituary and a wedding announcement. I click on the obituary, and there staring back at me is the spitting image of our Henri, but the year reads June 9th, 2026. That is before our Henri was born. I read on. He had a daughter, Rose Berger, married to Allen Berger, and a grandson Henri Berger. Shit—he must have changed his last name to his mother's maiden name. He was Henri Berger, now Henri Davis. I search Henri Berger. A birth announcement. That's it. What the hell did you do that you needed to change your name, Mr. Berger? Or did you just hate your father? I decide to search his father's name. At least a dozen articles appear with photos of him with multiple snakes hanging around his shoulders. An article in The Parkersburg News and Sentinel reads:

Paster Allen Berger and his wife Rose Berger each bitten multiple times by poisonous snakes. The couple was found dead by their son Friday morning. His predecessor, Justin Coots, explains, "Paster Allen will be remembered for his conviction. It was their time." The church's way of showcasing their religious devotion is inspired by the biblical verse in Mark 16:18: "They will pick up serpents, and if they drink any deadly poison, it will not hurt them."

I scan through more photos. Most of them are taken in their snake church just outside Beckley, West Virginia, where Henri was born. In one photo, the congregation is lifting communion cups full of poison to their mouths. In another, they are dancing around, holding naked flames in their hands. I've heard of people taking things from the Bible too literal, but this goes to a whole new level. Read it from start to finish, people. Things evolve. One article included a photo of Allen, Rose and young Henri. He's peering out behind his mother's leg. His mouth is a straight line and his eyes are like sharp, angry daggers cursing the person behind the camera. Who could blame the kid? His parents were psychopaths. His childhood was a breeding ground for evil. It explains his passion for the Florida Python Elimination Program. I'm sure he pictures slaughtering his father with each python kill. He spent the rest of his childhood in foster homes. Very few couples want to have children at all, so it's not shocking that no one wanted to adopt a 10-year-old. I wonder how many times he heard the case worker explain that people usually want to adopt babies. They wouldn't want a child tarnished by abuse, especially coming from a scandal so public. Now, he's found a way to make that system pay for all the damage it's done to him.

I know we have all the ammo we need to convince Lucas. He doesn't seem particularly fond of his partner in the first place, so I'm hoping this is just what he needs to validate his feelings toward him. Regardless, I need to run the plan by my team. Hollis and I are catching up on everyday chores and waiting for Amos to arrive when the lights go out. The wind starts whipping into our building, and the alarms on our phones sound.

It's official, we are in a tropical storm watch. No big deal, this sort of thing happens all the time here. Every house is stocked with hurricane supplies. In the darkness, I'm feeling my way over to Hollis. "I think the emergency supplies are in the storage closet in the hall. I'll find some candles and a lighter."

Just as expected, there are multiple LED candles and a couple old-fashioned flame versions with lighters.

Hollis takes a handful. "Why pay a fortune for a mansion like this and not buy a generator?"

He makes a good point. We light up the main living room and create a path from the front door into the kitchen, and from there to a bathroom. There's a knock at the front door.

"Come in Amos, we are in the living room!" I yell.

Mr. Ferris, this evening's security guard, walks in. "Sorry miss, the entrance building didn't have any supplies. Do you have some extra candles?"

"Oh, no!" I almost invite him to stay with us here, but I catch myself before letting the words free. He can't hear our conversation, and Amos will be here any minute. "Please take some of ours. We have a newspaper and some books here that you can bring back with you as well to help pass the time."

Hollis shakes his hand. "We are expecting a guest soon. Can you let him in via the side door since the gates will be on lock down until power comes back?" Mr. Ferris agrees, and lets himself out.

Amos arrives and we all gather together in the warm, ember candlelight. I hand Amos a bottle of water. "Not going to lie, this feels extra ominous sitting in the dark tropical storm plotting for the apocalypse."

"You know, during my training for priesthood, I was told about the ceremonial use of candlelight during the first centuries of Christianity. There are many passages in the Bible that reference us as children of the light, in a perpetual war with darkness. In the book of Revelation, he says, 'And in the midst of the seven candlesticks one like unto the Son of man, clothed with a garment down to the foot, and girt about the paps with a golden girdle. His head and his hairs were white like wool, as white as snow; and his eyes were as a flame of fire.' I've never felt afraid in the dark since then. It comforts me." He shakes his head to snap himself out of the memory. "Anyway, tell me all about our detective."

"His name is Lucas Robinson, and I had pegged him as our second choice until a recent discovery that I'll get to in a minute. I have witnessed him questioning actions that go against moral code, and he isn't afraid to go against popular opinion. He is everything we need him to be, and I have full confidence that we can win him over." I explain the baby bump prison and its ringleader. "Now you can tell me if we are missing something. Do sons of snake pastors have any special powers we're not aware of?"

His eyes widen in interest. "No, snake pastor spawn are not gifted, per se. However, humans living in 'harmony' with a demon can have heightened senses and strength. Lucifer is their single source of power, and he is a very powerful angel. As you probably know, he is a fallen angel. Anytime he can manipulate the word of God in his favor, it proves to be more impactful. Think of all the terrorist attacks in the world. Those were driven by devotion to religion. He does have a plethora of celestial abilities, but he is in no way omniscient. Make sure that Lucas understands that Henri isn't to be taken lightly. They need to take all precautions when taking him down."

Hollis teaches Amos a card game we grew up playing and I spend the rest of the night writing my recruitment speech by candlelight while we wait out the storm. Just as I dot my very last period on the page, light fills the room and sounds of roaring laughter blare out of the tv. Startled at first, we all burst into laughter. I smile to myself. You just wanted me to carry out your work like an ancient church maiden, didn't you?

23

TAKE IT OR LEAVE IT

It might not be easy for a man in power to respect a young woman like me. I shuffle through my closet, looking for my best law-abiding citizen outfit. I don't dare wear a dress if I want to be taken seriously. I consider looking at my weather app, but I know that it's going to be scorching- hot today. It's September in Florida. No matter how badly I want to, I just can't recruit a police detective wearing shorts. I place them back in my closet and settle on a pair of black slacks and a white blouse. I've considered every possible reason for our meeting but keep coming back to the same one. If I want to gain his attention immediately and get him away from his partner, I will have to declare that I've witnessed a crime. The precinct is crawling with cameras, so I will wait for him to head home after his shift and approach him about it there.

I open my bedroom door. "Hollis, you're coming with me as backup! We leave at 4 this afternoon!"

He pokes his head around the corner, "Alright. No need for all the yelling cap-i-tan." With a salute, he heads back out to the kitchen.

This one feels good. It was more challenging to determine my target, but my confidence is through the roof. I've made prints of the articles from Davis's life in West Virginia, and of the photo I captured of the pregnant women. Hollis saved the video onto a memory card, so I slip that into my purse as well. He will have every piece of evidence he needs to bring him down. I sit on the edge of my bed in the unfamiliar room trying to bask in the nearing victory, but it's all very lackluster. I've just started to get good at this, and now it's all coming to an end. Literally. I can't be the only scout out there experiencing this. How do they deal with staying focused on the present when so much is about to happen? Once we've secured our recruits, all that's left is to gather them together and wait for an uncharted realm. Then what? We have been racing to the optimum standstill.

We watch as Lucas makes his way out of the building, and pray he heads straight home. I hand Hollis the bag of pretzels. "Even if you wanted to go out after work, you would want to get out of that uniform, right?"

He dusts the excess salt off his fingers. "Nah, he's single. That uniform probably comes in handy. You're better off hoping he's not feeling social."

We follow behind him from a safe two-car distance until we reach his house. I pull into a parking spot a few houses down and watch him pull into his garage.

"I'm going to give him a few minutes to get changed, maybe grab a beer. You know, get into a receptive mental state."

Hollis nods in agreement. "It couldn't hurt. Also, why don't you ever try that tactic with me?"

I roll my eyes. He makes his way toward the back of the ranch-style house and returns to the living area wearing a pair of green sweatpants and his white undershirt. That a boy. Get cozy and take a load off. I wait a few more minutes, grab my folder of evidence and make my way to his front door. Per my request, Hollis waits out front in the car to ensure Henri, or anyone else for that matter, doesn't make a random appearance. He answers the door and starts to explain that the neighborhood doesn't allow solicitation. I interrupt. "Mr. Robinson, my name is Leora Smith, and there is a crime I need to talk to you about."

He steps forward to stand on the front porch with me. "Umm Leora, you will need to come into the precinct office if you have a crime to report."

"I understand, I'm sure that is the standard procedure, but you will want to hear about this privately before making a decision on how to proceed." I hold up my folder. "I've brought all the evidence you will need, and you are free to take this with you. Can I please come in and explain?"

He hesitates for a moment, then opens his door for me to come inside. There are dirty dishes in the sink, a thin layer of dust on the furniture and the smell of day-old Chinese takeout wafting in the air. Like a real bachelor pad. He clears a chair and motions for me to take a seat at the dining table. I place my arms on top of the folder and look him dead in the eye.

"Thank you for letting me speak with you. Like I said, I do have a crime to report to you, but I will not be able to officially report it in the precinct office. Let me start at the beginning. When religion was abolished 19 years ago, it set the apocalyptic process in motion. I'm not here to help save the world, because we are beyond that. I'm here because you demonstrate the morals that we should uphold daily, and you are simply the best at what you do. There will be a mass destruction in less than three months. Everything you know will be gone, aside from the planet we stand on and the people that are chosen to remain here by scouts like me."

He stares back at me, laughs and shakes his head, and starts making his way back to the front door. He opens it, and motions for me to leave. "You need to leave ma'am. I spend hours daily fighting real crime, and you show up at my house to waste my time with a conspiracy theory?"

I stay seated. "Lucas, I know how this must sound, but quite frankly, we don't have time to waste convincing you of something you know deep in your bones is reality. There are thousands of other police detectives who would suffice for the job at hand, but we want you. God wants you. Your father is spending his life in prison because of the evil that is rotting our planet." He releases the doorknob and moves back to the table.

"So, what's the crime you want to report, then? Or was that just a ploy to pitch me this crazy apocalypse story?"

I open the folder, place the evidence on the table and motion for him to sit next to me. He takes a deep breath, walks around the table and sits across from me. I slide the first snake church article in his direction. He looks at the photo and throws his hands up in confusion.

"Is this supposed to mean anything to me?"

I hand him three more. The last includes a photo of Henri with his parents. He is nine years old, but it's clearly him.

"Do you recognize that little boy? You should. You spend hours with him daily." He narrows his eyes. "That's Henri? But it says Henri Berger. I don't understand."

"Berger was his surname. He took the name of his mother's father, Henri Davis. I'm guessing he changed his name initially to disconnect from his family's scandalous reputation." I slide the photo of the pregnant women cowering in the corner as Henri and his partner exchange words in the doorway.

"At some point, Henri has started dabbling in his own dirty work. He makes routine stops at this house where at least a dozen pregnant Asian women are being held. I watched him

245

accept money from this man." I toss him the memory card. "Catch, you can have a copy for yourself."

I move around to his side of the table and play the video on my phone for him to watch. The video stops, and he shakes his head. "I was right. He is dirty." He looks up from my phone. "This doesn't shock me." I take my phone out of his hand.

"I know. We've been following you. It's a part of the job. You understand. It's clear that you have a certain level of distrust with Henri, and rightfully so. Henri is possessed. By a demon. Don't look at me like I'm crazy. You need to know this because it makes him extremely dangerous. Demons allow humans to perform acts of strength that normally wouldn't be possible. Can you honestly say that you haven't witnessed Henri doing this?"

He takes a deep breath and sits back deep into his chair. "I may have thought that a time or two, but adrenaline could be the culprit. Let's say you are right, I'm clearly going to take Davis down, but why does it matter if the world is coming to an end in less than three months?"

"Honestly, it doesn't." I point to the articles. "This is all for you. You need to know what we know so you can remember

246

why you believed in the first place. Take Davis down, or don't. Either way, the world as we know it won't be here anymore. I am going to leave this in your hands because I trust you will do the right thing. Do not allow Davis to get wind of this. Any meeting around this topic needs to happen outside of the precinct, and only loop in those who you know you can trust. You don't know who else might be involved." I stand and start moving to the door. "I left my number on the folder. Take a few days to work through this and get back to me. Those who are chosen, like you, must profess their belief in God, the Father Above All, Creator of Heaven and Earth. This will not be revealed to the public, and your identity with us will be protected. If you choose not to move forward with us, we will appoint another detective." I reach out to shake his hand. "You are our first choice, Lucas. Don't take that lightly."

I walk out of the door vibrating with adrenaline. Each step toward the car cheering me on.

***

Now we play the waiting game again. It has been three days, and still no news of Henri's arrest. I relive the moment over and over with Hollis. "I know calling his bluff was the way to go. I'm sure of it."

He pours a cup of espresso and hands it to me. "I have to give it to you. It's a genius tactic. You boosted his ego by hitting him with the "chosen" title, and you left the ball in his court. He was never the kid picked for anything, his dad ended up in prison for believing in something all the other kids made fun of, and to top it off, he ended up with piss-poor skin. Now, he's being offered his shitty partner up on a silver platter and an invitation to an "exclusive club" in the after world."

So, I may be baiting the good guy with a little revenge and popularity. I'm alright with that. Lucas isn't poisoning the world with hatred, and no one is devoid of weakness. Speaking of, I pour a splash of whisky into my espresso.

After scouring the local news once again, I gear up for my third run this week. I applaud Hollis. "You know, I'm pretty impressed with your newfound vigor this week. You haven't cried about working out with me once yet."

He tilts his head to the side. "And I'm pretty impressed that you've only put whisky in your coffee twice this week."

I digress. "Touché. I thought that was one we both knew about but kept to ourselves." He reaches down and begins lacing up his tennis shoes.

"Honestly, I've had this urge to work out every day," he says.

I laugh at what must be a joke, but he really has been joining me for some pretty intense runs lately. He's always doing hundreds of pushups on the living room floor while we debate tactics. As long as I can remember, he has been in great shape without much effort, but he is a machine now.

"No, seriously. It's almost uncontrollable. Why do you think I've been so compliant? Have you considered why you suddenly started taking up running a few months ago? Not once, in all the years we've known each other, have you wanted to go for a run," he says.

I shrug. "It's probably just a desire to burn off nervous energy. Our bodies are probably trying to go into fight or flight or whatever. Let's go."

We hit the sand. He's right. I feel it, too. The urge to run faster every day. Just as we are about back to the house, my calves start to tighten up and I place my hands on my knees to catch my breath. I lift my head and there is Lucas, standing on our patio. Still out of breath, we make our way over to him.

"How did you get past security?" I ask.

"I think you forget. I'm a detective and I have a badge. It almost always works." He smirks.

"We will need to brush them up on that. Especially with Henri out there," Hollis replies.

We invite him into the house. Before I'm able to offer him something to drink, he blurts out, "Alright, I'm ready to join."

I want to jump for joy, but I keep a straight face. I pour each of us a glass of water in the kitchen. He professes his belief and we cheers to a new beginning. He explains that his team took Henri and his partner down this morning.

"His wife, 'Molly,' is actually Biyu Li. She was one of the original surrogates in their ring. Henri thought it would make him appear more respectable if he were a married man, so he threatened to eliminate her if she did not comply." That's why he married so young. He continues, "They were selling the babies to wealthy couples around the world. Anyone with clearance and a private jet, really. We are working to find the couples who invested, but it won't be easy."

I wince. "I wouldn't put too much effort into finding them, Lucas. We really only have two and a half months until they will pay the ultimate price anyway."

His eyes open wide. "I'll have to get used to that concept, and fast. So, when and where do we go now?"

I look to Hollis and back to him. "We haven't been informed yet, but you will be taken care of. You are one of us now."

24

ROLE EXAMINATION CONFERENCE

My parents are the last to arrive at the beach house. Hollis greets them and shows them to the roundtable of doom, as he has named it. Michael has removed the fancy art that hung in the grand dining room and replaced it with a projection screen. Once my parents take their seats, he hands out binders to each individual. I am sandwiched between Hollis and Michael's empty seat. Amos raises his eyebrows in curiosity as he pages through the binder. Hollis and I have been waiting for our instructions for two weeks now. He has spent hours with me in our gym and running on the beach, and Amos was thoughtful enough to check in on us a few times. We have barely two months until the day of the end. I really need to come up with a new name for that. The cover of my binder reads "Leora Smith, Viceroy SE NA." If he's signing me up for something new, I'm going to lose my damn mind. I got your recruits. Can't we just fast forward through the war and devastation? I've felt this restlessness. I lay awake and picture all those people that are not going to make it. How they would die? What our world will look like after all the destruction? I've read the book of Revelation at least a dozen times now.

Michael flicks on the projector to display a photo of a woman sitting in the rubble of a collapsed building. Her eyes are closed and her mouth is hanging open in mourning as she clasps onto a small, lifeless child. He clicks on to a bird's eye view of the coastline. It's littered with scattered wood and steel slabs.

He points to the image. "This is Mindanao, Philippines on August 16, 1976. A 7.9 magnitude earthquake hit the island and caused a tsunami that devastated their coastline. There were over 5,000 casualties. This is a tiny fraction of the destruction that will occur here."

He clicks through a series of images, all-encompassing natural disasters that have occurred over the last couple centuries. It's a marathon of cyclones, floods, fires and tornadoes. Some are so old the images are black and white.

He continues. "As it has been in the past, the Earth will also be struck with plagues. I'm sure you remember these from history class."

Images of plague victims light up the wall. A photo appears of patients lined up in rows. They are covered in blisters. A white man lays dead, his hands are black extending up into his arms.

"There are three forms of plague in humans that you may have heard of: bubonic plague, septicemic plague and pneumonic plague. The forms that will consume the Earth will be comprised of a unique bacterium. It is highly contagious and consumes its victims at a much more rapid rate than any other plague the world has experienced in the past. Meteorites will strike Earth. It will not touch anywhere near your asylum; however, this could result in earthquakes, tsunamis and an extended period of darkness. Temperatures will plummet." He gives the room a moment to react. Amos clasps his hands into a ball and presses his thumbs over his mouth.

"That's just great, so are you going to tell us a little bit more about that asylum?" Hollis asks.

Michael responds. "First things first, you will need the appropriate survival training and materials. Each of your binders includes a check list of items to procure for the dark days. Complete the appropriate trainings required and obtain the items listed by the date below." December 24th. I look to Michael, "Christmas Eve?"

"That's right. It will take you nearly 12 hours to arrive at your destination, which is between Pippa Passes and Pine Top in eastern Kentucky. The following day, Jesus's birthday, will also be day one of the apocalypse. There will be no confusion as to the cause of the unraveling that will begin. Sometimes Abba works in mysterious ways, and other times, a more direct approach is necessary. Not to worry though, December 25 will not only continue to be a celebrated day in the new world, but it will be the one of the few holidays celebrated as you continue forward. Bring on the Christmas trees!"

I glance over at Hollis to find him staring off into space deep in thought. I imagine he is reminiscing of the Christmas mornings he shared with us. The years prior to the abolishment were filled with Christmas trees brightly lit, a horde of presents to open, and a feast to devour. After the abolishment, we would close the blinds and huddle around in the den. My father would quietly say a prayer of thanks, we each opened one gift. My mother would light a candle and place it on top of a small cake. In unison, we would quietly whisper "Happy Birthday to You" to Jesus and blow out the candle. My parents encouraged us to be happy, but it just felt like a funeral. A reminder of what used to be. I would put a smile on my face just for my mother. I remember how her face would light up that morning, and I couldn't disappoint her.

"How many of us will be in our community? If that's what you would call it?" Amos asks.

"There will be 360 people in your asylum. The camp will be nestled in the Appalachian Mountains and protected from the destruction happening outside. There will be 12 bunkers that are mostly built into the base of the mountain, and the entrances camouflaged with forest debris for your safety. Each of you has a specific role and I would like to discuss these with you individually in the office at the assigned time on your binder." He points toward the office on the other side of the house.

I look to my binder. "Role Examination: 4 p.m." I glance at my watch. It's 3:45. Michael shuts down the projector and grabs a pastry from the basket on the table. "If there are no further questions until our individual meetings, I'm going to take five. Leo, I suggest you take a little peeksie at the role description before we chat."

He sinks his teeth into the pastry and raises his eyebrows at me. I make my way to the office and dive into the binder. It reads, "Viceroy Essential Duties and Responsibilities: Serve as the region's chief executive officer and oversees the functions of the law. Make recommendations to the general assembly and facilitate gatherings to ensure all voters can participate fully in the life of their society. Exude resilience, transparency and diplomacy to ensure the success of the new society. Deliver communications regarding the state of the world to your region. Appoint and oversee all region officers. These officers include the following:.."

Michael knocks on the side of the door and closes it behind him. I shut the binder. "So, is this a choice?"

"Everything you have done for the new world has been a choice, Leo. Have you read through the whole binder yet?"

"No. Just enough to know I will be leading an entire region of people. People who will be locked up in a bunker for months. I'm sure they will be pleasant." I spare no sarcasm.

He throws his hands up in the air. "That is true. But it's a mere four months in the grand scheme of things. I'm not here to sell you on this. It's my job to ensure you understand what is being asked of you. If you decide that you do not want to move on as Viceroy, you will still have a spot in the asylum."

My mind flashes to the flesh-eating diseases, shrieking winds and flames engulfing entire cities. "When we are able to move out of the bunker, will any of the demons still be roaming around?"

"No. They will be exiled to a lake of fire. Basically, a new hell. Regardless, you need to know that the second those bunker doors are locked shut, your 'gift' will leave you. You will step into a world without sin, but you will still have free will. Think of it as mankind's chance at a fresh slate. To live as one with Abba the way you were designed to. Initially, it will be much simpler than present day." He studies my face, awaiting my reaction.

"What do you mean, simpler?"

"Earth will be scorched, ripped and drenched in blood for months. Just keep that under consideration when you get out and take a look around. Your stretch of mountains will suffice as a good starting point. The damage will be less intense there, but you will need to work together to provide the region with sustenance. There will be a limited number of species and edible plants remaining, but luckily, you recruited one phenomenal environmental scientist." He finds himself so clever and charming. Stassi is going to have her work cut out for her.

"How far would my region extend?"

He pulls out a tablet and opens a map. "Not that it matters, since the 'United States' will no longer exist, but it will extend from Florida as far west as Louisiana, up through Missouri, east through Virginia and back down. It will be referred to as the Southeast North American Region."

He draws an outline with a red marker. In the grand scale of the entire continent, it looks minuscule. 360 people is basically a tiny town in the middle of nowhere today, but it's 360 people who will all be counting on me. Every time there is an issue, those eyes will be looking to me for answers.

I sit in contemplation until he walks me toward the living room. "Mull it over, and if you have any questions let me know. I'll need your answer by tomorrow at noon, of course. Time is of the essence!" He twirls his finger in the air and turns back to the office. "Where's my 4:30 at?" Hollis glances at me and follows Michael.

My parents vanish their way out after Michael wraps up his final role examination conference in the office. Amos, Hollis and I grab a drink and walk down to the beach. Just before touching the water line, we take a seat on the sand.

"Alright, I'll tell you mine if you tell me yours," I offer.

Hollis bites first. "I'm going to be the Solicitor General. I get to represent the Viceroy and decide which regional legal cases need to be seen by the region's Court of Justice. Basically, I get to argue with people above me to ensure everyone gets their fair shake."

I fall back on the sand in laughter. "He would want you to represent me."

"Of course, you get to continue to boss me around then! Some things never change." He falls back onto the beach beside me. Amos is still sitting up, looking out at the waves.

"Your turn, Amos. We shared, now you tell." I demand.

"I will be the Sovereign Vicar of North America."

Okay, I feel like an idiot. I have no idea what a 'Vicar' is. Please just explain. Don't make me ask.

Hollis sits up at Amos' level. "What is a Vicar?"

Perfect. *Thanks, Hollis.*

Amos takes a deep breath. "I'm going to be the spiritual leader for the country."

I sit up, too.

"So, you'll be like our pope?" Hollis asks.

"No. No one will be Catholic, or any specific religious group. Just one big spiritual country, but I guess the concept is still similar."

I turn and smile in his direction. "So a Sovereign Vicar, a Solicitor General and a Viceroy walk into a bar….."

25

JUST THE PEAKS

I scour the internet for some kind of "Leaders for Dummies" guide. Michael told me what I need to be. I should just take him at his word and leave it at that…but what fun would that be? I mean, when my parents would tell me something was important, I didn't always think they were right. Sometimes, it took a third party to teach me the same lesson. That's exactly what I'm doing right now. Looking for someone else to tell me the same thing Michael did so I can feel confident about it. As if any of these "experts" online know more than an archangel. The edges of my binder are becoming worn because I can't stop re-reading his requirements. *Be concise, get to know your people, get your hands dirty too; and when you don't have an answer immediately, listen for the Lord.* It all sounds so simple. When I decided to become a scout, I didn't have to commit to a lifelong responsibility like this. I should have asked, does this role have terms like our president? Maybe four years and then we have an election?

My mother always had the right answers to calm me down, but she wasn't just a normal, mortal mother. I fell into a mud puddle right in front of my fourth-grade crush and thought that my life was over. She played my favorite Marvel movies all day and brought me popcorn and candy. My sophomore year, Beau Green's parents found him hanging lifeless from their upstairs balcony. We were biology partners that year. He was popular, outgoing and a star athlete. I was always more concerned with embarrassing myself around him than actually getting to know him. I arrived home that day, went straight up to my room and cried into my pillow. I heard the door click open. My mother gently sat down next to me and lightly ran her fingertips up and down my back. She didn't even ask me what happened. Just waited for me to tell her. When they are losing their minds over the life-threatening challenges that arise, I'll need to be the mother. Telling people to calm down is the last thing they will want to hear, but what will they want to hear? No worries, people! This young, unexperienced woman will have the answer…said no warm-blooded American ever.

I have everyone who matters pulling for me, and yet, every story in history would not land in my favor. If I say no, then I have to take a backseat to someone else taking the lead. It's also possible that Hollis won't have the same opportunity as Solicitor General. I shouldn't assume this because he is very talented, but he might not be the best righthand man for a different leader. His instructions include an email address to send my acceptance or declination to. The thought of Michael's secretary in Heaven or some version of Heaven's embassy on Earth, sitting at a desk, responding to emails and taking calls for him brings a smile to my face. I slam the binder shut. Who am I kidding? When God sends an angel to ask you to lead, you lead. Michael knows I am going to take the role. He just needed me to know I made the decision myself. I type up the acceptance and click send.

***

I've finally found three survival schools near us that accommodate adults and don't entirely revolve around firearms. Florida residents love their right to bear arms. The interstate is littered with digital billboards advertising machine gun shooting attractions. "Come see our outdoor range or get behind the wheel of a 16-ton army tank!" Hollis is researching each of their websites to determine which one is the best fit for us. All of them provide some kind of "Weekend Warrior" course in which you learn how to build a shelter, make fire, identify edible plants, purify water and how to signal for rescue.

I point to the last lesson. "Maybe we should skip this one."

Hollis raises an eyebrow, "Ha! If we skip out early, it could attract unwanted attention. These all look the same. I say we go with this one. Their trainer's beard is the biggest. He's clearly more dedicated." He dials the number into his cell. "Should I line it up for this week?" I nod, and he sets us up for this Friday through Sunday. "Get ready to hit the bush, little lady."

Once we are registered, they send us a gear list. A lot of it overlaps with the equipment list that Michael gave us. Since we will need multiples of the items that do overlap, our local sporting goods store was about to have one very good day. I grab our list and we make our way there.

Hollis opens the door for me and suggests that we do a little scouting to determine the most deserving salesperson. We make our way up the escalator, passing stuffed grizzly bears holding canoes, and mannequins draped in fly fishing trousers. I scan the upper level for anyone in the hunter green, short-sleeve collared shirts their employees wear. They basically require them to wear camouflage because nearly everything in here is green. In the tent aisle to my left is a petite brunette girl assisting a father and son. I make eye contact with Hollis, point my fingertips to my eyes and in their direction. We move closer until we can hear the conversation.

"We really just need something for the two of us for one night max. I'm not really an outdoorsy guy," the father explains.

"But this tent has the ability to hold two more people and it's only $20 more. You really would be getting more bang for your buck, sir," she argues.

He seems unimpressed, but she continues to push. I look at Hollis and whisper, "Nope, she's trying to get him to buy something he doesn't need so she can hit some sad sales goal."

Hollis agrees, and we move on to a young gentleman helping an older man in the golf accessories section. The gloves the man is looking for are not on the shelves. It's maybe a $15 item, but the young man offers to go in back to take a look for him anyway. Ding, ding, ding! We have a winner. Once he finishes helping the man, we approach him with our list. His eyes light up in excitement. I make sure to let him know that we wanted him to help us because we noticed how he went the extra mile for the man in the golf section. He takes very little credit and humbly changes the subject to our task at hand. Once we start piling on the items, he needs to get a merchandise rack from the back to haul everything to the checkout.

The store manager approaches. "Whoa friends! Some lucky people are about to get out and rough it! Did Jackson here help you find everything you need?"

He slaps Jackson on the back, almost toppling him over. The manager is a large man with a gruff voice.

"Yes, Jackson was amazing. We really weren't sure if we would be making our purchase here, but he made all the difference. I can't thank him enough. You really should give him a promotion or raise at the very least," I respond.

It won't make his life better for long, but I'm happy to give him a good few weeks at the very least. He throws his hand up in an all-encompassing gesture, "Well, this might come as a surprise to you, but here at William's Sporting Goods, my employees work on commission. So, Jackson here just gave himself a raise!" I muster a brief, closed-mouth grin. Jackson just stares in the other direction. All of us hoping the manager will just leave. A customer approaches with a question and he finally makes his exit.

Hollis leans in. "You should get a regular bonus for listening to that guy every day." We all laugh as he starts loading everything onto the checkout counter.

The car is packed from the trunk clear up the ceiling. We're able to obtain most of the necessities on our list. I open the garage door and we each take inventory of our items. I line mine up on the shelving and start packing the astronaut food, flashlights, fire starters, pocketknife, water purification tablets and first aid kits. We both pack a separate bag with the items required for our survival weekend camp. I open one of the food packets, pour in some water, and take a bite. I force myself to keep it down. It tastes like powdery soup that has had some freezer burn. I hand the pouch to Hollis and he takes a bite.

He hands it back to me. "Let's go out for a really good dinner before survival camp. Steakhouse? Lobster mashed potatoes and shaved brussels sprouts?"

I throw the package in the trash can. "You had me at steakhouse."

Meat Cute Steakhouse happens to be just across the bridge from the beach house in a section of connected buildings. It's a staggering skyline of various textures and colors. There are numerous high-end restaurants all boasting the best in their niche. We luck out and find an off-street parking spot just in front of the horse carriage ride station. We cut through the long line of tourists waiting for their turn for a ride, and head into the restaurant. The hostess offers to take my sweater. I decline, of course. She takes us around the corner to a booth built into the wall with curtains on either side.

When she walks away, I grab the curtain. "Really Hollis? So tacky."

"Knock it all you want, but it's kind of cozy. It also happens to be your very own, secluded restaurant bunker. I thought it might be a little less chilly back here." He gestures to all the tables sitting out in the open on the main area and raises his eyebrows. He makes a good point. The light fixtures have clean modern lines, each table is dressed in a crisp, white tablecloth and the lighting is just dim enough to hide any imperfections these people on first dates may want to conceal. I pick up the specials menu. It appears to be handwritten by an employee who has taken a calligraphy course or two. It baffles me that technology has advanced this far and here we are, buying paper with age stains covered with handwritten words for patrons in an effort to appear earnest. A family seated across the restaurant roars in laughter. They are passing a picture around as they "Ooo!" and "Aww!" Then I see the blonde with the short hair place her hands on her round belly.

Hollis snaps his fingers to get my attention. "Hey! I asked, what you are going to order?"

"I don't know yet." I look back down at the menu. "Do you think there will be babies in the asylum?"

He purses his lips. "If there are, let's hope their parents are also with us."

The waitress returns and we place our orders. Hollis picks up the breadbasket and hands me a piece. He watches me spread a pad of butter across it.

"I know we would typically voice over the surrounding first date conversations, but I thought tonight we could switch it up. Let's share our peak moments of all time. Well, in this world's time."

I laugh. "Alright, I'll play. No pits?" Our family dinners always included a roundtable of our day's peaks and pits.

He sits back into the leather seat. "No. I don't think the pits matter anymore." The waitress returns with our wine. Hollis raises his glass. "Cheers, to the glorious stories of joy I've brought to your life." I roll my eyes, but I don't leave him hanging.

"The day Southeast Transcription offered me my first salary job. It was one month after we graduated. I had interviewed with four different companies, and three had already decided to go with other candidates. I had this dilapidating fear that it was my last chance for a career that would enable me to work remotely. I wasn't sleeping and barely ate. When they called, it felt like someone had wrapped a warm weighted blanket around me. I knew things were going to be okay."

Hollis nods, encouraging me to continue. "The day Michael showed up at brunch and my parents told me about my gift. Part of me wanted to stand up and gloat, 'I knew this wasn't a normal condition!' but the part of me that was in shock won over. I had second-guessed my mental health for as long as I can remember, and I don't think I could face this without that validation." I pick my glass up in salute to pass the baton his way.

He takes a drink. "I think you're forgetting the day I ate shit on my bike and joined your family for dinner. I mean, had that not happened, who knows where you would be now," he laughs. "If we're being honest, that was actually one of my peaks. My childhood would have been garbage without you and your family. Second would be the day that my parents' divorce was finalized, and he agreed to leave the house to my mother. I knew she had interest in one of my dad's business partners, and as long as he wasn't going anywhere, we wouldn't move. Any moral standards I have were learned in your family's home." I turn away to face the wait staff to distract from the tears welling up in my eyes. I don't know what's wrong with me. Get it together.

He continues. "The day you told Carl that you weren't going to move in with him after graduation. It felt like I was losing my best friend to a guy with the life mission to land a million Insta followers." I laugh, because it's true. That should be one of my peaks, too. He reaches across the table and places his hand over mine. "I don't know what the next stretch of our lives will bring, but I'm glad it's in a world with you." All the blood in my body rushes into my face. It's probably just the wine. Thankfully, our waitress arrives with the food, so we enjoy the best that fancy farm-to-table has to offer.

26

ROUGHING IT

After two hours and three cups of coffee, we turn onto the unpaved road that will lead to the Better Safe Than Sorry Survival Camp. We bounce around with every pothole the tires dive into until a roundabout appears. The vegetation is thick with tropical palms, cypress and redwood trees. A stalky man with a bushy beard comes running to greet me as I step out of the car.

"Welcome, my name is Mason. I will be your survival guru this weekend. Let me help you with that." He takes my bag and shakes Hollis's hand. "Let's hit the trail. The others are setting up."

We follow him along a narrow walking path winding through tall grass that I'm sure is teaming with snakes. The grass thins as we make our way into camp. There are two other groups setting up. To the left a middle-aged man and teenage boy. To our right, a younger guy, maybe in his early twenties. Mason leads us further along to a small clearing behind some bushes.

"This will be your home away from home. Go ahead and set up your tent. When you are done, we will all gather around the center of camp for introductions."

Hollis and I look at one another. I stop him before he runs back. "Mason, I noticed the clearing is pretty small." I point to the small burnt piece of ground by his foot. "Is this where we will be making a fire?"

"Yes, that is where the fire will go." He points over by Hollis. "And this is where you will set up your tent."

Oh, great. So, we're sharing a tent. "Ahh, okay, so just one tent. Gotcha." Of course, Hollis didn't check if we needed to register for an additional camp lot.

He nods and makes his way back to the others. Hollis throws his pack onto the ground. "Well, I hope you don't snore, because I am a light sleeper." I roll my eyes and unpack the tent pieces.

We pound the final stake into the ground, place our things inside the tent and head back to the center of camp. I'm surprised at how quickly we threw that thing up. Maybe we have knack for this survival stuff. Mason directs us to all gather in a circle and sit on the rugs he has placed on the ground.

"I could fill your weekend with a hundred quotes from those who came before us about survival, but I don't think that is what you came here for. The only thing you need to remember is that no one gets lucky without preparation. If you find yourself in a real struggle to survive, those who are prepared might get lucky. That said, I've already introduced myself to you all, but let me tell you about my background. I am a former Navy Seal and I have two decades of survival experience in a multitude of terrains. I chose to start my school in Florida because I found this terrain to be the most difficult to survive. When I am teaching others how to survive, I feel fulfilled, so thank you for being here. Now, let's go around the circle and each of you tell us your name and what terrifies you the most about surviving in nature."

The teenage boy, Kenzo, speaks up first. He and his father, Calvin, wanted to have some male bonding time away from his mother. His biggest fear was catching a flesh-eating disease. Calvin just laughs, introduces himself and announces that his biggest fear would be to die of dehydration. Not as exciting, but much more realistic.

The young man next to us waves a hand to the group, "I'm Uri. My biggest fear would be losing hope." We all nod in agreement. A little deep for survival camp, but okay. The circle makes its way to me.

"I'm Leo, I guess my biggest fear is making a mistake that could result in someone else's death." The crowd gets quiet. And I've made them all very uncomfortable. Hollis speaks up. "And I am mostly worried that she will veer us down the wrong path and I'll get torn to shreds by a panther." He throws his arms up in humor. Grateful for the comedic relief, they all laugh.

Mason starts our training with a lesson on basic shelter-building. We learn the ins and outs of setting up camp, how to find dry wood, and what plants are edible. He takes to a clearing near a small body of water. On the other side of the water, two large gators are basking in the sun along the shore.

277

Mason points in their direction. "You will never have to look far for water in Florida. However, the dangers that live there are to be taken seriously. Alligators primarily feed at dusk and in the evening. Most afternoons, you will find them sunning themselves like this. If you avoid the water, they will usually leave you alone. That doesn't mean that they can't be just as dangerous on land. It's a common misconception that gators aren't fast on land, but they are capable of short bursts of speed that can exceed 30 miles per hour."

He leads us back to camp so we can learn how to start a fire without gas or a lighter. It's a process that requires more natural materials than I had expected. He takes us through the steps from tinder, kindling and larger pieces of wood that will keep the fire going through the evening.

"Boiling water for at least one minute is the best way to kill off any pathogens that would make you very ill. And how do you do that? With fire. Aside from deterring any potential predators in the dark, this is the most important reason we must learn to make a fire with little to nothing." He grabs a flat piece of wood and carves a notch into it with his knife, placing a piece of tinder next to the notch. He then inserts a long, skinny stick into the notch and rubs it vigorously between his palms. The tip of the skinny stick starts to turn red with heat from the friction. He gently lifts the stick, places the ember near the tinder and starts blowing until it catches flame. We all watch in wonder as the miracle occurs.

I feel my stomach start to rumble. Mason looks to the sky. "We are approximately two hours from sundown, so go ahead and grab some sustenance from your camps. Then, I would like you all to do your best to start your own fires. If you struggle, I'm here to help."

Hollis and I dive into our cooler and devour the sandwiches and grapes I packed for us. It's dusk now, and I seriously question our ability to start this fire with a couple little sticks. Just as we start to take a crack at it, Uri approaches. "Let me help you guys with that." He pulls out a small knife from his belt and starts poking the tinder. Flames immediately burst from the pile.

Hollis jumps. "Whoa! How did you….?" He looks up at Uri's face. Then we know. He's not human. He places the knife back into his belt, "My name is Uriel. Some call me the Angel of Repentance and Wisdom, but Abba really created me to guard Eden. I'm here to let you know that there will be sickness and death soon. Rain for days. When the sea creatures try to grow legs, you must depart. There will be others in charge of asylum arrangements, and they will direct you to your bunker."

When the sea creatures grow legs? Does everything have to be in code? I think of the others that will be meeting us there.

"What about the others? How will they get there?" I ask.

"The others will be given the same instruction and meet you there. They will have the means to get there. Do not worry about them."

I want to ask him how they are choosing who joins us. Who are the other 352 people? Nothing adds up when I'm reading the book of Revelation. This might be my last chance. I'm just going to ask.

"I need to understand something, scripture states that only virgins will go to the new world—

Uri points at my blanket laying on the ground and stops me. "Will you throw that blanket away after this weekend?"

I'm sure there is a metaphor in this. Just get to the point. He asks again, impatiently, "Will you!?"

"Of course not," I snap.

He picks it up and hands it to me. "But it's dirty now."

"Then I'll wash it?" I counter.

"Exactly. Abba sent his son so the slates could be wiped clean. Virginity can refer to more than one's sexual experiences. That is the last I want to hear about it, understood?"

I nod in agreement.

He continues. "When the winds blow in, you must seal the doors. You will have proper ventilation and a way to produce fire. Each individual must bring the items on the supply list you were given. Other items may be wanted, but do not pack electronic items. They will be useless to you. Over much time, Lucifer and all of Hades will be cast into a lake of fire. You will all feel an instant warmth, as if a heater were turned on. Only then can you evacuate the asylum. Much of the Earth will remain uninhabitable. The mountainous area will be your home." He turns to see Mason making his way in our direction. "Complete your training and go in peace. This is the new Genesis."

Mason throws his hands around Uri's shoulder. "Look at you all, two fires already! I'm among professionals here!" Uriel leads him back into the center of camp.

Darkness is setting in quickly. I wrap my arms around my knees and watch the flames flicker. Hollis comes out of the tent holding a bag of marshmallows, a box of graham crackers, a chocolate bar and two roasting sticks. I place two marshmallows on the prongs and place them above the crackling fire. Hollis places his a few inches farther from the flame.

I smile in his direction. "Can't you let them burn just once?"

He brings them down to my level. "Just this once, I suppose. We will do this again one day."

I can't even comprehend all the things we have now that won't exist. Not until we create them again. I stare at the chipped polish on my nails. I wouldn't know the first thing about making nail polish. I only put it on because everyone wears nail polish. That's one thing I'll never have to do again, and hashtag "no makeup day" will be every day. Amen to that.

The night air is thick with the deafening sound of croaking frogs and crickets. Hollis sleeps beside me with one arm above his head and his other hand upon my thigh. I lay awake, thinking about the peace that Uriel spoke of and watching Hollis' chest rise and fall with each breath.

***

Day two and our final day of survival camp starts off with a scorching 84 degrees. It never used to be this hot in December. Thanks so much global warming. Our camp is missing one student—it appears Uriel had to cut out early. I look to the sky. "Is it really only 8 a.m.?" Hollis checks his watch. "8:15 to be exact. Let's hope ranger Mason gets a move on. I really don't want to spend our last days before…you know, traipsing through a sweaty swamp."

I scrape the last bits of scrambled eggs off my plate. "At least there was real breakfast. Who knows what we will be eating when…you know."

Mason announces our agenda for the day. "Yesterday was all about the core survival techniques. This morning, we will cover navigation and rescue." He opens a bag and pulls out a compass. "A compass is great, but today we are learning about what to do if things go wrong. Maybe you brought a compass, but maybe that compass was broken. Now what? Does anyone know?" Calvin replies. "Can't you look for the North Star?"

"Absolutely, how do you find the North Star?" Mason asks. Calvin shrugs his shoulders.

"The Big Dipper Constellation is much easier to spot. Once you find that, look to the end of the dipper's handle and you will find the North Star. Also, remember that the sun always rises in the east and sets in the west. Let's say you have figured out your directions, but you have no idea where the nearest civilization is. Stay put. You're more likely to find rescue that way. Ask yourself the following questions: Am I in an area that other people may frequent? Can this location offer water, shelter and fire? If the answer is no, then consider making the move to the nearest area that can provide these things. Follow me." He walks us out of the vegetation and into an open space. He grabs two small cosmetic mirrors out of his pocket. "Carrying two small mirrors with you is one of the best ways to catch a rescue flyer's attention." He catches the sun in one mirror then reflects it into the other to demonstrate.

"What about cell phones? I know this is for emergencies, but isn't there a chance of getting reception somewhere nearby if you have a charge?" Kenzo asks.

"My advice—if you can't get a signal within a quarter mile, don't go further if you don't need to," Mason replies. "Some seasoned survivalists will bring satellite phones or other special off-grid communication devices, but anything that allows you to communicate without a cell tower can be costly."

I turn to Hollis and whisper, "I guess that makes us seasoned survivalists."

27

WHEN LIFE GIVES YOU LEMONS

It has been one week since Uriel made his appearance. One week of days on the beach, recounting our supply stash, eating our favorite ice cream, and obsessively watching the news. Every day is precious, but the waiting is cruel. I turn on the television. *"This morning we received word that North Korean officials have alerted WHO to several severe cases of an unusual flu in the city of Pyongyang. Several of those infected frequented the Fish and Meat Shop. The virus has been deemed unknown. Health professionals are working around the clock to identify the virus. We will continue to update you on their progress. This is Sandra Clayton, Bay News Nine."* I race down the hallway and pound on the bathroom door. "Hollis! You need to come see this!"

I change channels. It's being covered on every station. He steps out of the bathroom. "It's happening? People are getting sick?"

I nod and point to the screen. We watch them recap the events of our last pandemic. Political parties start bickering about the best tactics to keep the virus out of our country. There are valid concerns, but they're mostly for political gain.

We race out to the nearest Costco and load our carts with all the essentials. Hollis grabs three packs of toilet paper.

I stop him. "Whoa there, I have a pack in my cart, too. These things last us a month."

He continues to place the third package in his cart. "I'll have you know, my mother did teach me one thing. The last pandemic that our world survived, toilet paper and face masks were the hardest thing to find. This here, pure gold. You'll thank me later."

An hour and a half later, we have everything imaginable to keep us fed, clean and entertained for weeks. It begins raining just as we pull back into the neighborhood, and a large SUV pulls into the driveway behind us. Out walks Michael and my parents. I run into the pouring rain to wrap my arms tightly around my mother. Michael side steps to Hollis and lifts him off the ground in an embrace.

He places him back down and exclaims, "Hey kids, it's about to get real!"

"Speaking of," I pop the hatch open to reveal our Costco haul, "Can't you just angel this stuff into the house so we can relax?"

Michael reaches in and grabs the largest box. "Typical privileged child, always relying on mommy and daddy's angel powers to get out of manual labor."

We spend the evening playing rummy and eating Michael's famous chili, roaring in laughter every time he loses his hand and throws a pitiful fit of defeat. I feel the time slipping away as we near midnight. Michael throws his hand to the center of the table.

"Such as my career in Rummy, all good things must come to an end. Leo, get in touch with Constance Evans to let her know that you will be picking her up when it's time to go, and let Dr. Kershaw and Lucas Robinson know that a man by the name of Naveen will be contacting them and providing them with transport to the asylum."

"Hold up, they won't all be staying in our bunker? Why not?" I ask.

"There is an algorithm used to arrange each group of the community by bunker. It's to ensure that just the right combination of skills and personalities are together. Amos will be there to guide you, and Hollis will be by your side for support. Trust your instincts and you can't fail." He places his hands around my face and kisses my forehead.

In his serious, calm manner, my father grabs my hand. "This is goodbye. You have enriched our time here and we are so very proud of you. Never forget who you are or where you come from. We may not physically be near you, but we will always be watching over you." I watch a slow tear roll down my mother's face and I break into sobs. She wraps me in her arms and rocks me side to side one last time. Hollis holds me together as we watch them pull out of the driveway.

***

On our street of beach mansions, I feel disconnected. There are little signs of life. Those leaving their home do so only briefly, hunched beneath umbrellas for a moment of fresh air. Occasionally, we see a family walking the beach, but always keeping a safe distance from others. The delivery services are backed up for weeks, and more of the employees keep getting sick. It's only a matter of time before even those with money will be forced to venture out for supplies.

We take drives into the city when we are stir-crazy. People are bustling straight from their car to the grocery store or pharmacy. Their faces are hidden behind masks. Some are lucky enough to have a medical-grade face mask. Others make theirs with whatever fabric they can cut, fold or sew into the right shape to cover their noses and mouths. One woman is in a standstill with her daughter, just waiting for the coast to clear so they can make their move into the store. Just as she finds her moment to move, two men come tumbling out of the doors with fists flying. They are grappling over a gallon of milk in the pouring rain. She pulls her daughter back and they continue the waiting game. I want to help her, bring her what she so desperately needs, but I know better. This is necessary. We make our way back to the quiet streets near the beach.

The virus is spreading rapidly through countries and their disease control systems too slow to catch up. They finally came up with a name, LAMINAED-56. When the virus is examined under a microscope they found each virion has "laminae" or "petals" surrounding it. Therefore, LAMINAED for disease, and 56 because it is 2056. There are already memes all over the internet comparing it to Lemonade. "I don't care if life gave you lemons, keep your LAMINAED to yourself." Its death rate is one of every 10 cases. They are running out of places to bury bodies. Hollis flicks on the television. The news is a repeat of seemingly abandoned cities, interviews with medical professionals, and announcements from our president.

"Those infected may not have symptoms for up to two days. That is the longest incubation period our medical professionals have witnessed. At that point, symptoms typically start with an intense headache, fever, dizziness, weakness in face, hands and legs, and dry nose and eyes. Within hours, patients display signs of stroke and pulmonary edema. Once symptoms take hold, fatality proceeds within 24 hours."

I turn it off. I can't listen to it any longer.

28

TWO DAYS LATER

As of this afternoon, the United States is on full lock down. No flights in or out of any airport. Not even state to state. Citizens are to remain at home with no access to grocery stores, pharmacies or financial institutions. The only exception is necessary utility companies to keep communication, power and water running. Weekly, the government is sending troops to each neighborhood with a food ration. It's barely enough to nourish the families patiently waiting in line at the armory truck. I join Hollis in the living room, which we have cleared to make a mini gym. He drops into a set of pushups and I join him.

"How long has it been raining?" he asks.

"Eleven days. I'm ready for the signal."

I pull myself up into a seated position. Hollis stops and faces me. "Me, too. Things are only going to get worse. I'd prefer not to witness it." I drop back into a plank, holding firmly. The days are starting to blend into each other, and I imagine what being quarantined in the asylum will be like. The 360 people will be divided into 12 bunkers, which is 30 people in each. That's enough to feel a sense of community. Sure, supplies will be limited, but isn't everyone experiencing this in a more secluded way now?

I look to Hollis. "What do you think our bunkers will be like?"

"I've been imagining a scene out of the classic movie, Lord of the Rings. That mountain can be our shire. Each bunker has its own unique, rounded door with the knob placed right in the center and surrounded with a mound of grass." He beams with excitement.

"You're a doorknob. If I have to live in a little hole in the dirt for four months with 29 other people, I may walk out into my death before seeing the new world."

He nudges my shoulder. "How do you picture it, then?"

"I'm thinking simple, but secure. Some kind of bunkbed set up to save space. Probably a couple tables. The rest of the space being used as storage for supplies. I'm sure food and water will be more important to people than cushy furniture. I just hope there is some sign of daylight. I don't want to know what happens to people locked in the dark for that long."

I look toward our windows. "Hey, it stopped raining!"

Hollis jumps up to see for himself. I open the back patio doors and step outside. Our neighbors all seem to have the same idea. They come out of their back doors throwing their arms out in celebration. Then I hear someone say, "Look! Out on the beach!"

That's when we see it.

They must go on for miles down the coast in both directions. Dolphins, jellyfish, sharks...I can't begin to count how many species. They've all hurled themselves onto the beach. *When the sea creatures grow legs.*

I look to Hollis. "I'll call Stassi. Let's go."

29

THE SHIRE

We pull up to Stassi's house and see her peering through the curtains, waiting for our arrival. As the front door opens, Hollis and I offer to take her bags. Her hand shaking, she moves a piece of hair out of her face and hands her suitcase over to Hollis. I take her hand. "We are going to be okay. Everything has been arranged for us. Now, we just take a little road trip to meet our new friends." She looks back at her home, places her other hand to her mouth and blows it a kiss. I set up our route. "Start the clock, we have 12 hours and 17 minutes until we reach our destination."

There is a scene in one of my favorite zombie movies that comes to mind as we move along the highway. It's just days after the infection had spread, and the main characters take a chance on escaping their town. Without making a sound, they move to their vehicle and make it out. Once they escape, they realize how desolate the roads are. They pass the occasional abandoned vehicle on the side of the road, and then the camera zooms out to a bird's-eye view of the forsaken world around them. That is what our world will feel like to everyone else.

To pass the time, we play round after round of trivia. Each of us takes a turn asking the questions and tallying up scores. Two hours in, and it's clear that Stassi has a superior education, Hollis knows far too much about pop culture, and I watch far too many movies. My bladder feels as if it's about to burst. "Can we pull over somewhere and find a restroom?"

"Um, nothing is open anymore. Remember, massive pandemic lockdown?" Hollis asks.

Stassi pulls out a large container of antibacterial wipes. "I could remove the wipes and place them into a ziplock bag," she suggests.

"So, you want me to pee in that container?" I respond. She shrugs, and Hollis bursts into laughter. He pulls the car over near a wooded area. We all step out and stretch our legs. Hollis wanders off to pee with ease and Stassi holds the container up in my direction. "Don't you have to go too?" I ask her.

"Yes. I should, so I don't make everyone pull over again in 20 minutes," she responds.

"You go first. I have this jacket to shield you in the case that someone actually drives by," I offer. We make our way just to the clearing before the forest and she does her business. She places the container on the ground and hands me the package of wipes in her hand. Here we are the chosen ones, peeing into a container. I set the it back down on the ground and head to the car.

"Hey, what are you doing?" Stassi asks. "You can't just leave this here. It's littering."

I tilt my head in question. "I understand that this will not be something we practice once the dust settles, but the world is about to be destroyed. I don't think that container will make any impact."

She allows it, just this once.

Every radio station is dominated by the mass beaching debate. The scientists can't come to a consensus. *"Hey listeners,* this is Roxane Rambler on the Rock 64. I have local marine biologist, Gary Suda, here with us today. Gary, what can you tell us about the beachings along our gulf coast today?"

Gary clears his throat. *"At times, whales and dolphins that hunt in pods have exhibited this behavior if their leader is sick and runs them into shore. However, that couldn't explain the other species we see here. Another instance in which this could occur would be if military sonar had been activated. However, our government has confirmed this is not the case."*

Roxane interrupts. *"Do you think it's possible for these sea creatures to become infected with LAMINAED-56?"*

He laughs at the question. "These creatures have very different respiratory systems than humans, and some of them do not have respiratory systems at all. I find it highly unlikely that this is the cause." She continues to pry for an explanation, and he continues to respond with information we already know, in a cycle of frustration.

The combination of LAMINAED-56 and the beachings today is sending everyone into a frenzy. People are leaving the protection of their homes to protest the government. They all think they are being lied to. That the government is hiding an environmental crisis in light of the pandemic. Picketing signs read, "My health and my planet are NOT classified information!" They all just want to blame someone, and there is no one there to give them an explanation.

Twelve hours and two more pee stops in—without a container—and my GPS alerts us that we are 20 miles from our final destination. We passed the last town over an hour ago. The land moves quickly now, from narrow valleys to sharp ridges. The steep slopes are thickly blanketed with oak, maple and sycamore trees. A lush layer of life for all the creatures below thrive upon. As we continue to climb higher into the forest, I feel the pressure building in my ears. Hollis hands Stassi and me each a piece of gum and places one in his mouth as well.

I gather the instructions Michael gave us and point ahead. "That's the turn that will take us to the entrance." The winding dirt road leads us closer to the mountain. Then, a sharp righthand turn around a line of trees brings us to a clearing. In the distance, I see two large openings in the base of the mountain and a huge man holding a clipboard standing between the two. His arms are as large as my legs and covered in tattoos. He holds up a hand and smiles to greet us.

"Names, please?" he asks.

"I place a hand on my chest. "Leora, and this is Hollis and Constance."

He files through the list on his clipboard, places a check next to each of our names and hands us each a small bag. In his deep, booming voice he introduces himself. "Fantastic, my name is Naveen." He turns to face me. "I, too, was a scout for our society, and it is an honor to meet you, Viceroy. My new role is Community Organizer of Mt. Asylum. I am here to ensure everyone is placed in their assigned bunkers and answer any questions before we are sealed in." He hangs his head, "You should know I was a guard at one of the institutions for many years leading up to this day."

"An institution for believers?" I ask.

"Yes. It is not a profession I'm proud of, but clearly all a part of Abba's plan." His weary eyes turn back toward the entrance.

"Inside each bag you will find a key for your bedrooms and locker, but first, please pull your vehicle inside here, into the far left spot." Hollis slowly drives the car forward into the garage. I stare up at the scaling mountain above us and recall feeling so much bigger upon the soft, flat surface in Florida. This majestic land is towering above me, a humbling force.

Hollis returns from the garage. Naveen guides us to the other entrance. "Please take a look around. I will be in shortly to give you a brief tour."

The entrance leads us into a tunnel lined with lockers on both sides. There are two large archways on either side of us at the end of the tunnel. The one on the left leads us into a greenhouse. Hollis's mouth is wide open in awe. "Welcome home to Mt. Asylum! I don't know who built this, but they get a thumbs way up from me!"

There are rows of potted plants, and above us, a huge line of triple-pane windows letting in a glorious amount of light. Across the hall and through the other archway, there is a large room filled with gym equipment. I see two benches, bars, free weights, jump ropes and two gliders. The walls are lined with mirrors. Mounted upon the wall to my right is a large, battery-operated stopwatch. Stassi is shaking her head back and forth in disbelief.

"Leo, look at this!" Hollis shouts. I follow him into the great room filled with plush furniture and two large, oak coffee tables in the center. There are numerous books placed on top of them. All the same one. Each black leather cover is engraved with gold foil "The Ahava." They feel stiff and each page crinkles as I flip through them. Clearly, hot off the press. The room is open to a dining area with two communal tables and to the crimson painted kitchen. There are rows of cabinets, and two deep sinks. Wait, there are faucets. In disbelief, I pull the faucet handle up. We all jump in excitement as water starts pouring out. I turn it off quickly, in fear that it is quite limited. Between the kitchen and dining area stands a tall stone fireplace. I peer inside the opening to find an iron grill shelf. We will be able to cook! Beyond the living room, there are doors with numbers above, like address numbers on a house. I open one to see a small room with just enough space to get in and out of the bunk beds on the other side. I knew it. There really isn't a better solution for this than bunk beds.

We continue along to see a row of doors along the back of the bunker, which lead to bathrooms. Inside each is a toilet, a drain in the floor and a shower head hanging above. A few feet in front of the row of bathrooms is a large, oval-shaped sink. The metal bowl surrounding it is as deep as a trough, and small spigots run along the inside.

Naveen enters the bunker to take us through the details. "Let's start from the entrance—the doors too, are made of concrete and fortified steel. Each of you has a locker here along the tunnel. This is to store any of your belongings that you may not use daily but would like to have when all is said and done. The greenhouse was a controversial option that we ultimately felt was necessary for the mental health of our communities. The natural light through the window into the living area and arched doorway will hopefully help any of those who may suffer from seasonal depression, and the plants will bring life to the dry goods we will be consuming. The gym is necessary for the mental and physical health of our community. Once we can return to the outside world, we will need strength and stamina to rebuild. I recommend that each bunker implement a sign-in sheet, so everyone has a chance to get exercise. Moving along to the main area, you probably noticed that there are no outlets, no refrigerator or stove. That is because electricity will not be an option." He opens a drawer in the kitchen and pulls out a bulky radio. "Here you will find a HAM radio. This will allow you to communicate with the world without cell towers or the internet. There is also an FRS radio that will connect you to the next bunker in case of emergencies. Lucky for you all, I will be in the bunker next to you. Its range will only extend to 22 miles, so do not go out of reach. Our bunkers are close in proximity, but not close enough for the FRS radio to reach one end to the other. You have the fireplace for any cooking necessary, and—," he turns on the faucet, "there is running water, but very little. Use this sparingly. Each bunker is equipped with a 5,000-gallon water tank. Once that is gone, you will have to dip into the water rations that are in storage, just behind this room." He opens the door and we see stacks of boxes. He moves on to the large, oval sink. "Here you will find a communal area for brief grooming and laundry care. The sinks are deep enough so those with small children can bathe them here. The bedrooms are all equipped with bunkbeds. Some are larger than others and have hammocks installed for families that will need additional sleeping space. Everyone must share a room due to space constraints. Your rooms correlate with the number on your key."

I hold my key up toward Stassi and see we have the same number. I see relief upon her face as she smiles in my direction. Hollis looks at his key. "Will you be in our bunker, Naveen?"

"No, unfortunately I was needed in a different bunker," he replies.

"But we could have been such good bunkmates," Hollis whines.

"I can't disagree with that, but I do need to head back out, as others will be showing up soon. Once everyone has arrived, I will be going along and sealing each bunker. No one, unless it is absolutely necessary, is to leave the bunker. When the sky turns blue again, it will be safe to come out."

One by one, the other members of our little bunker community makes their way into the tunnel and marvel at their new home. We make our introductions. Ellen Riley, a 24-year-old graphic designer, arrives with Asher Banks, a 26-year-old architect. Their scout brought them to the mountain, but today is the first day they have met one another. Asher quietly inspects the structure as Ellen clamors from one room to the next, her voice booming off the walls. She nearly runs into me. "Sorry neighbor! I'm Ellen Riley, nice to meet you!"

"Nice to meet you Ellen, I'm Leora Smith. What do you think of the place?" I ask.

Keeping her eyes glued on me, she slaps the back of her hand on Asher's chest. "Oh shit, hey, she's like our president. Sorry, I shouldn't say 'shit.' It's an honor, really. This is Asher Banks. We just met today."

I laugh. "Don't be sorry. This is your home now. I look forward to getting to know you both." They return the sentiment and go about finding their assigned rooms. A lanky young man with black hair enters with his parents. He turns his head in our direction.

"Isn't that Kenzo? From survival camp?" I ask Hollis. He takes a closer look to confirm. "It is! There's Calvin, too." He approaches them with open arms, "Bring it in guys, I see we were preparing for the same emergency." Calvin's face is flustered, and Kenzo quickly darts to the other side of the bunker without a care. He introduces us to his wife Hayden, and they get settled in. A few families later, and another familiar face arrives.

I bolt for the tunnel. "Amos!"

He drops his bag and wraps his arms around Hollis and me. Hollis grabs his bag and rummages through it. "Ha! Number seven, I call top bunk." Amos tilts his head in confusion and follows Hollis to his new bedroom. We begin his tour and make introductions to the others. A positive energy fills the space as they learn that they will be sharing a home with our new Sovereign Vicar. Upon entering the open living room, the books on the coffee tables catch his attention. He picks one up and smiles brightly.

"The Ahava. It's perfect," he says.

"I was hoping you would know what that means," I say.

"This is our new Bible. It was always meant to be stories of his love for us, and a guide to happiness and fulfillment. Michael tasked an editor with removing any misleading information so we can start fresh. The ancient Hebrew word Ahava means love. It was my favorite lesson in seminary school. The root of the word, Hava, literally means 'to offer' or 'to give.' So really, it's not an emotion, it's an action."

My jaw drops. *It really is a fresh start.*

One last family enters the tunnel and Naveen returns to take one last roll call. As the last name is confirmed, he tips his hat to us and seals the towering doors shut. The final door closes with a thundering slam. I flinch and take in a deep breath. I will never feel frozen inside again. Amos gathers everyone in the living room for a Christmas Eve service. The families with children brought a gift for each child to unwrap. They scramble to tear the sparkly wrapping paper off as quickly as possible and hold up their shiny new prizes. If Mary could give birth in a filthy manger, I can survive a few months in an upgraded bunker. Hollis and Calvin light the lanterns, and the children sing carols around the fireplace until there is more yawning than singing. We rotate through the bathroom and kitchen sink to brush our teeth, and shuffle into our designated rooms for the evening. Just as I crawl into the top bunk and shut my eyes, I hear Stassi say, "Thank you for bringing me here, Leo."

My heart fills to the brim, "I wouldn't have it any other way, Stassi."

30

TONIC IMMOBILITY

Initially, the days feel like hours. Everyone is buzzing about the bunker, organizing the space, unpacking their personal items, reading the gardening and HAM radio instructions, and getting to know one another. Hayden takes it upon herself to graph a chore chart that gives each individual, aside from three-old-Sadie, a weekly chore. They were often very minuscule, but there were only so many chores and it is important for everyone to have a purpose. Hollis and I make a sign in sheet for the gym, along with duplicates, and hang it next to that entrance. We agree to save firewood for a limited number of meals, just in case we need more as time goes on.

Ellen and Asher are the world's most unlikely pair, and yet, they spend every waking hour together. I question whether Ellen just orders Asher around or if it's a mutually beneficial relationship. She is a brazen—some might say obnoxious—artist. Her long blonde, curly hair is as wild and free as she is. She lives in a world all her own and could care less what the rest of us think. Asher is a cautious, soft spoken analyst. His build is fairly fit and lean, but not due to an aesthetic desire. Every decision he makes is calculated and clinical.

It has been over 24 hours since I last ate, and I decide to try my first MRE meal. I select the beef stew. It comes packaged in a small box. Inside I find a sealed pouch where the actual food is, and a separate thick plastic bag with instructions on it. I slip the meal packet into the other bag, add one ounce of water up to the double line mark and place the bag back in the box. Once the required time as passed, I reach to pull the pouch out of the box and find it's very hot. It's surprisingly tasty. It reminds me of a canned meal. Like eating SpaghettiOs or Dinty Moore. Ms. McCall, a 65-year-old widow, pulls a chair up next to mine and starts prepping her MRE. She is a tiny Irish woman, maybe five feet tall. Her hair is her most striking feature. The shiny silver strands are stick straight, just down to the curve of her chin. Each move she makes is deliberate and confident. She strikes me as a straight shooter.

"I just realized that I don't really know your story, Ms. McCall. What happened to your loved ones?" I ask.

"I'm afraid it's not a very heartwarming story. I had two children, Yasmin and Quin. They were 15 and 17 when the abolishment happened. My husband, Rory, and I did our best to continue teaching them our faith behind closed doors. They went to college and started their own families. We rarely saw or heard from them. Rory was diagnosed with prostate cancer and passed away in a matter of weeks. Yasmin and Quin began having me over for dinner more often…out of guilt, I suppose. I found little moments alone with my grandbabies to teach them about God. Until Delta, Quin's daughter, asked her mommy why they didn't pray together. My daughter-in-law made sure that I didn't step foot in that house again. They spread the news to Yasmin, and they eventually disowned me, too. So, here I am by myself."

I place my arm on her back. "You know, I've never had a grandma. Maybe you could fill in?" She just laughs and continues eating.

Mr. Olson announces that he is about to turn on the HAM radio. He and Mrs. Olson could pass as brother and sister. They both have the same straight, sandy blonde hair, freckled skin, and oblong-shaped faces. I've heard that the happier a couple is, the more likely they were to have an increased physical similarity. An agreement has been made that we each take a turn watching the children in the gym while the radio is on. Knowing the news will be nothing but destruction, we have agreed to only listen for one hour per day. As the children are shuffled into the gym to play duck, duck, goose, Mr. Olson tunes in. At first, we hear an emergency alert on repeat, *"Stay inside your homes. Public areas are not safe. Ration your food and water. Those exhibiting symptoms of LAMINAED-56, must self-quarantine. Any individuals arriving at hospitals or temporary care units will be turned away. This is not a test. Stay inside your homes...."*

He changes stations and we stumble upon a group conversation. *"Adam, NIRL. We are locked in our attic. This man—or thing, just broke in! We have had other looter attempts, but this was different. His shoulders looked like they had spikes growing out of them, and it's like—it's like the temperature in here dropped* to freezing the instant he broke through the glass!"

Another station announces their call sign. *"Brad, KBG. Are you sure that he didn't just have on some gothic shoulder pads? There are some real weirdos out right now."*

"Adam, N1RL. No, he wasn't even wearing a shirt, and it's December in New York... I think I hear something! Shit, I think it's back—I have to...." Just like that, he is gone. Brad, KBG, and the others wait for his response, but they are met with silence.

The days now feel like months. Mr. and Mrs. Olson filled me in on their situation this morning. Poppy, 14, is their granddaughter. The Olson's daughter, Aurora, got married at 32 and decided two years later to have a kid. Poppy arrives 10 months later, and they find that they just aren't cut out to be parents. They have too many ambitions that need their attention, and Aurora's parents would be much more suited to raise Poppy. The Olsons couldn't talk them into keeping her. In the 14 years they have had her, they have seen Aurora twice. Poppy is not aware that Mr. and Mrs. Olson are not her parents. They do look good for their age, but she must have wondered. Kenzo takes Poppy's hand and leads her into the garden. Hollis sees me watching them. "Checking out baby Adam and Eve?"

"Oh, you think so? Nah, they'll just be a fling. She will definitely move on to the only other teenaged boy in this mountain at some point. A girl has to have options," I respond.

"Is there really only one other teenaged boy in our region?" he asks.

"I don't know. There can't be that many. Based on what Michael said, every bunker was built to be balanced. We have one teenaged boy in here, and there are 12 bunkers. I guess that means Poppy has 11 other options. Good for her," I say.

Hollis' face moves from a state of amusement into a stoic stare. He shifts his gaze back to me. "Sometimes, the best option is right in front of you."

I feel my heart drop into my stomach. *Don't do this now.* Even if we could be more than friends, we are supposed to be working together. There will be so much more to do after we get out of this bat cave. I divert my attention back to the greenhouse. Kenzo sees Amos walking out of the gym, leaves Poppy in the garden and goes running after him. Amos humors him by teaching him a new handshake and makes his way to our sofa.

"How are you two holding up?" he asks.

"We are just fine. You, on the other hand, have grown quiet the little shadow with that one." I laugh, looking in Kenzo's direction.

"He's definitely a curious kid. I'm impressed with his extensive knowledge of the Ahava," Amos replies. He excuses himself to help Mara Long. I overhear her convincing Amos to lead a daily Ahava study for both the adults and the children. That would be good—we could use more structure around here. The Longs arrived with four children, and they clamor around like a freight train all day. Mara is a beautiful woman. She has been worn down by sleepless nights and countless hours of caring for all those kids. Her face, perfectly symmetrical, and her tiny nose crinkles up just the slightest when she smiles. One day, those kids will become more self-sufficient and the puffy, dark circles under her eyes will brighten again. Her husband, Wiley, didn't luck out in the genetics department the way she did. He is average height, sports a dad belly, and is starting to bald up top. Someone should tell him to just shave it off. What he lacks in beauty, he makes up for in effort. He puts the kids to bed every night and pushes Mara to go take some time for herself.

Mr. Olson makes his way toward the radio for our daily update. It's Hollis's turn to entertain the children. He summons them with a whistle and demands they all hop their way into the gym. The little ones giggle and play along in his game. Kenzo and Poppy roll their eyes and shuffle their way in. The first station we land on is just a couple neighbors gossiping about a love triangle in the area. The second appears to be a distress signal.

"Renee, A1C. Is anyone in the Nashville area? A group of men broke into our house!" She starts whimpering. *"They murdered my husband. I escaped with my daughter and we have been living out of my car. It's been days now, and we are running out of water."*

Another station responds, *"Nancy, WBC. Hey darlin', I'm not in Nashville, but I'm not too terribly far, either. Do you have enough gas to get down to Chattanooga?"*

"Renee, A1C. I'm below a quarter tank. I don't know if that will get me there. I've heard some of the terrible things happening to stranded women on the road...my daughter is only six." We are left with a long stretch of silence.

"Nancy, WBC. Renee, I want you to find something to write down my address or lock this into your memory if you have no way

to write it down. 2791 Wicker Street. I'm two blocks from the downtown pharmacy. You drive as far as that car will take you and huff your way to my house with that baby of yours. It's just me and my puppy, Brutus. We don't have much, but I can spare some water and food when you get here."

"Renee, A1C. Alright, it's four hours from sundown—I think we can make it there. If we don't, please imagine that we found a nice abandoned home to make home...don't think the worst. Thank you."

That evening, I walk circles around the plants in the garden. I tell them stories every night. Sometimes it is about the new city we will build—a city with solar streetlights, a carousel in the middle of city center and the park surrounding it. The buildings are all different shapes and lush vegetation decorates them in various hues of green. All the people leave their doors unlocked because they have nothing to fear.

Tonight, I'm telling them Renee's story. Not the way it will really play out, but the way I want to imagine it. Her car makes it just to the cusp of town, and they throw packs on their back and march their way to Nancy. The town is quiet. They take in all the beauty around them. Her daughter throws her arms out and spins in circles as she soaks up the sun. They turn the corner onto Nancy's street and see her and Brutus waiting for them in the windowsill. She welcomes them in with open arms and they comfort each other through the rest of this disaster. If I can just imagine that they didn't suffer, I can handle the inevitable ending.

I jump at his voice. "Are you in here talking to yourself?" Hollis asks.

"What is wrong with you, don't sneak up on people like that. And so what if I am?" I lie down on the floor, staring up at the night sky.

Hollis joins me on the floor. "You know you don't always have to be so strong for everyone. Amos told me about the radio update today. That's messed up. I know you want to save that mom and her little girl."

"There's nothing we can do for them. They might find refuge, or they might die trying. Either way, they're all going to die soon. I just need a good night's sleep." I pull myself up and dust off my pants. Hollis takes my hand and pulls me closer to him. "There is nothing wrong with having empathy for them. That's one of the many reasons I love you." Startled by his confession, I turn to discredit it and he is kissing me. Urgently, as to stop me from speaking and then gently. I almost fall out of consciousness. Like a tonic immobility that sharks experience when turned upside down in the water. I pull myself to the surface and push him away. "This can't happen. I'm not the last woman on Earth. There will be plenty of other options for you."

"I don't want any other options…why can't this happen? You look me in the eye and tell me that you don't want this, too." He raises his eyebrows, challenging me to respond.

"How long have you really felt this way?" I ask.

"Do you remember our freshman year of college, when we all used fake IDs to get into that dive bar on tenth street?"

"Yeah. It was called Frankie's."

"You spent most of the night talking to Yale Connor, and I spent most of the night staring at you. Just hoping you weren't going home with him."

I remember it clearly. I did go home with Yale that night. I told Hollis I was leaving on the way out. One of the many sorority girls who swooned over him was grappling for his attention. He was trying to stop me, but she pulled him back.

I look back in his direction. "I didn't know you felt this way. I've spent my life thinking that we defied all the odds as a female and male pair that wasn't about sex."

"It's more than that, Leo. Why don't you think about it. Or maybe don't. Do what's in your heart instead of your head for once." He shakes his head, walks back to his bedroom and shuts the door. The plants stare back at me, their leaves drooping down in disappointment. Don't look at me like that. They need me to be a leader, not someone's girlfriend or wife.

31

THE THIRTY FIRST

I cross another day off my calendar. It has officially been one month since the day the doors were sealed. Each day, the radio conversations become fewer and darker. Yesterday, a woman in Monroe, Louisiana, called for help in the area with no correspondence. A man in Charlotte, North Carolina, described a naked man that moved like a leopard, with unnatural white skin and black eyes. The creature was seen scaling the neighbor's house at dusk. Two other correspondents confirmed similar sightings. No one is concerned with the virus anymore, but they do stay indoors for fear of what they will find roaming outside. He laughs to himself, "And to think, I used to be such a proponent for gun control."

I change into my athletic gear, lace up my tennis shoes, and head into the gym for my scheduled workout. Hollis and I have signed up for a reoccurring time to train together daily, but here I am, alone in the gym again. I stride through five miles on the glider and clean up. Amos is setting up for Ahava study when Poppy screams, "There's a man in the windows! Come quick!"

I race in behind Amos to see a middle-aged man with long, dark hair begging for asylum. He is clearly yelling with all his might, but we can only hear a faint, muffled voice.

"Please! Help me! I won't survive out here. Something is out here. It's not natural," he pleas.

"What is your name? Are you alone?" Amos asks.

"My name is Lazarus. Yes, I'm alone! I'll do anything, please!"

Kenzo pushes his way to Amos. "He said his name is Lazarus! Just like the guy in the Ahava. Lazarus was the man that Jesus raised from the dead. Don't you see? That guy is as good as dead out there. Shouldn't we act like Christ and save him from that death?"

Stassi adds, "If we look at this logically, we have twelve bunkers full of empathetic ecclesiastical people. One of them is going to let him in."

Asher steps forward. "What if he has already asked all the other bunkers and has been turned down? We committed to keeping those doors sealed shut. Do we want to be the ones who didn't stick to the plan?"

Hayden places her hand on Asher's arm. "I understand your concern, but what if another bunker does let him in? Will you really be able to look him in the eye once we all gather together as a community? We won't be stuck in here forever. I, for one, could not live with myself."

All eyes move to me. Lazarus' intense, wide eyes are grasping for my mercy. I leave them standing there to gather paper and pens. I rip the paper into 18 pieces and place a basket in the center of the room.

I clear my throat to address the room. "I want to make one thing clear, this is a democracy, not a dictatorship. Everyone who is 18 and up, take a piece of paper and pen. If you would like to welcome Lazarus into our asylum, write 'yes,' and if not, write 'no.' Once you have finished, fold your paper up and place it in the basket. I will do a count once we have finished."

Everyone scatters in different directions. One by one, they place their votes into the basket. Within minutes, all 18 are accounted for. I assign Hollis to tally the votes as I call them. It's almost unanimous—16 votes to let him in.

I look to Lazarus and signal for him to run around to the front. "Alright, we are welcoming our 31st neighbor. Hollis, please let him in." He does as I ask. The doors open momentarily and Lazarus bursts into the tunnel gasping for air and giving many thanks. "Thank you so much, all of you. I've lost everyone to the virus and those things out there." Once he catches his breath, I sit down with him in private to walk him through our rules.

I gesture to him. "This way, we can speak in my room." He takes a seat on the other side of my bed. I smile to help calm him, "Lazarus—" He holds a hand up. "You can call me Russ. All my friends call me Russ. I don't why I gave my formal name. Maybe it just seemed more truthful." I nod. "Alright, Russ, my name is Leora, but my friends call me Leo. My title here is Viceroy. Basically, when necessary the community will look to me for answers. Did you happen to come across any other bunkers while out there?"

"No, are there more?" he asks.

"Yes, there are 12 bunkers along the base of this mountain. Every one of them is a part of our community. We were brought together to continue life on the planet once everything is wiped away."

He furrows his eyebrows in confusion. "If you would have told me that a month ago, I would have thought you had mental issues. Today, after the things I have seen, I believe."

"Good, that will make your transition here much easier. I don't know what your experience is with faith, but every person here is a believer in God. Our faith keeps us strong, and we gather in Ahava study daily. We do not have any extra rooms, but you are welcome to sleep on one of the sofas in the living room. Everyone has a weekly chore, and though it's pretty minimal, it helps gives us a sense of purpose. I will have Hayden add you to the chart. Now, follow me, I'll give you the tour."

"That sounds amazing, but what is Ahava study?"

***

It becomes clear that Lazarus belongs in our group. He gladly takes part in our activities. The children gather around him to hear stories that seem to be made up on the spot. He draws faces onto a pair of socks and sets up a puppet show for them. They snicker at his jokes and demand another show as soon as one ends. The parents can't get enough of him because of the burden it takes off them. He lost his wife and son to the LAMINAE virus, and shortly after, he was forced out of his home by a group with guns.

Finally, it is my week to tend to the plants in the greenroom. The MRE meals have sustained us, but we could use some fresh produce this week. The brightness of the room lifts my spirits, but again, I find the plants sad. Each day they appear to be worse. Today, the strawberry buds are gone, and their leaves are nearly falling off. The lettuce that was almost ready for harvest is wilted and the tomato plants have yet to produce anything. I place my fingers on the soil and find it to be moist, but not over-watered. I don't understand. I find Stassi reading on the sofa and bring her in immediately. She makes her rounds through each row feeling the soil, "They shouldn't be reacting this way. We have the perfect arrangement for these plants to thrive. Someone must have tampered with them. Do you think one of the kids got in here and poured something toxic into the pots?"

I place my head in my hands. "I don't know. That's quite an accusation. I definitely think we start by asking the parents before announcing this to the group." She nods in agreement. "You speak with the Longs and the Bryants, and I will speak with Clarks and Olsons."

Stassi and I reconnect and find that all the families claim that none of their children have touched the plants. *Great, now I get to be the bad guy.* I glance across the hall to find Hollis lying across the bench, pressing a bar with multiple plates. I watch, hoping that he will feel my gaze and look this way. He lifts the bar back into the cradle, sits up to wipe the sweat off his brow, drops the towel and looks up to see me staring at him from the greenroom. I mouth "help me" as to not alert anyone else. He tilts his head, rolls his eyes and comes to me. "What do you need?"

"Stassi and I have inspected the plants and something isn't right. They have just the right amount of sunlight and water, but everything is dying. We asked all the parents to check in with the kids and ask if they were messing around in the greenroom. All the kids said they haven't touched the plants. I figured since you are the Solicitor General you would want to address the group as a whole to determine where we went wrong?"

He pauses for a deep breath. "I'll gather everyone after dinner." I reach my hand to his arm in a gesture of thanks, but he turns and walks away. *Come on, Hollis, don't be like this.*

I take the last bite of my meal and look in Hollis' direction. He pushes his chair back from the table and clangs on his glass with a fork, "Excuse me, everyone if I could have your attention. I'm not sure how many of you are aware yet, but Stassi is actually a very talented environmental scientist. She and Leora have found that the plants in our greenroom are failing to thrive. The soil and light conditions have been favorable for every plant in every row, and we still have not yielded anything. We have already discussed the issues with all families that have children here and have determined that it was not their doing. Has anyone here witnessed anything odd or accidentally done something that could impact the plants?"

We all scan the room, looking for anyone in deep thought. Kenzo throws up his hand. "I don't mean to overstep my boundaries or anything, but weren't you in the greenroom last night, Hollis?" Hollis pulls his head back in revulsion. "Don't we all visit the greenroom daily?"

Kenzo nods. "Sure, but you were the last person I saw in there, other than Leo and Stassi, and you spend much more time there than the rest of us."

Hollis puts his hands up. "I can assure you, that I have not tampered with the plants."

I look into Hollis' eyes, searching for the truth. *I know you are furious with me but tell me you didn't have anything to do with this.* He would have motive. If that room is just a memory of me rejecting him, then why wouldn't he destroy everything in it? Russ clears his throat. "I'm not making any accusations, but I also saw Hollis in the greenroom last night."

Hollis shakes his head. "This is ridiculous." He points in my direction. "Didn't you and Stassi say that the plants have had issues thriving for some time now? Could this really happen overnight?"

"There are a lot of things happening in the world right now that don't make sense. Maybe this is one of those cases," I reply. "I trust that we will have the nutrition we need to carry us through this period. In the meantime, let's pull the greenroom from the chore chart. Only Stassi and I will be caring for the plants moving forward."

The group goes back to their previous activities, but Hollis's eyes never leave mine. I shoot him a glare and storm into my room. If he did this, I will be finding a new Solicitor General.

***

The radio conversations have become too difficult to endure, so Mr. Olson agrees to place the HAM radio in retirement. Bringing Russ into our bunker has given our group plenty detail to imagine the current state of the world. Enough to know those people were not imagining the creatures they described. The reason he ventured out into the mountains was with hopes of finding an abandoned cabin, far away from all the action. Somewhere along his journey, he started hearing things…until one day, he saw one. That was the same day he found us.

Hollis finishes wringing out his clean laundry, drapes it on the drying rack and waves for me to come his way. I should ignore him, but I need to deal with this at some point. He takes my hand. "Can we talk, in my bedroom?" I scowl. He continues, "It's just to talk about the other day. Please." I humor him and follow his lead. The children come darting in front of us in a game of tag and a couple of them come crashing down on top of one another. One by one they pull themselves up, tears streaming down their faces. The last to stand back up is little Sadie Long. Her mouth is wide in shock, a pair of garden shears imbedded in her side. Time feels to have stopped and I lunge for her. Before I can reach her, the shears fall onto the ground and a copious amount of blood spills from her wound. Her brothers race off to get their mother. She takes one look at her baby and starts shaking. "We need help. Can we still call an ambulance? Someone help!" I search for something to stop the bleeding. "Someone get me a clean cloth, a shirt, something!" Hollis throws me a t-shirt, and I fold it up and press it down onto her wound. Sadie bursts into tears. I signal to Mara. "I'm going to need you to come here and comfort her." I watch the blood flow slow, but the shirt is still rapidly filling. Hollis places his hand on my shoulder and whispers, "I know we can't get her an ambulance, but what about Isaac Kershaw? Do we know what bunker he is in?" I think back to our first day. "I don't know, but we know that Naveen is in the bunker next to us. Get the FRS radio out and ask him.

Hollis grabs the radio. "This is Hollis in bunker one, we need to speak with Naveen now. This is an emergency. Over." His deep booming voice fills the tense room. *"Hollis, I'm here. What's happened? Over."*

"We have a three-year-old girl, Sadie Long, with a serious injury. She has a deep wound on her abdomen, and we need to find our way to Dr. Isaac Kershaw. Can you reach him? Over."

"Yes, He is in bunker four. I will call over to bunker three and tell them to let bunker four know that you are on your way with the girl. Signal to them in the window and they will let you in. Be careful out there. Over."

Hollis grabs his backpack and throws a shirt, jacket, pair of pants, toothbrush and a couple pairs of underwear in. I look at Mara. "I'm going to take Sadie to a doctor. I don't know how long she will need to stay, but I will be there with her and I will be sure to update you on her progress through the FRS radio. She stares back at me, nodding. It's clear that she's in shock. Hollis overhears me. "I'm going with you, Leo. There is no way you can carry that girl all the way. I start to object. "I can do it—," "No, I will not allow you to do this alone," he interrupts. Hollis takes over applying pressure to her wound. "Now, go pack a few things for yourself and Sadie." Wiley heads to their room. "I'll bring you Sadie's things." He emerges holding a small stack of her clothes and a bright pink stuffed animal. Sadie cries out. "I can't go without my mommy!" Hollis strokes her hair with his other hand. "You're going to be just fine, Sadie girl, and your mommy will be right here waiting for you when we get back from the doctor. Is there a stuffed animal or a blanket we bring with us for you?" Mara speaks up. "She needs Mingo, her stuffed flamingo." I zip up our bag, throw it on my back and place a small, rolled up washcloth on Sadie's chest. "We have Mingo packed for you. I need you to be brave. Once we get outside, we have to be so very quiet. No matter what. If your ouchie starts to hurt, I want you to bite down on this, alright?" Wide eyed and weary, she nods in agreement. Amos walks us to the door and places his hand on Sadie. "Lord, we pray for the protection of Sadie, Leora and Hollis. Guard them in their journey and grant them discernment. Give them strength in the face of evil and lend skill to the hands of Dr. Kershaw." He lifts his hand and opens the door. "Go with God."

32

EMOTIONAL ROLLERCOASTER

The crisp air hits my face and sends a jolt of electricity through my body. Each step we take is an echo of leaves and twigs underneath our shoes. It's eerily quiet. Peaceful, even. Sadie lays her head back onto Hollis's arm and starts to fall asleep. I'm sure she is passing out from the pain her fragile little body has endured. I look to the sky to see the sun is nearing the horizon. We should have at least another 20 minutes before sundown. Look at that, I am using some of Ranger Mason's survival training after all. It hasn't been but two minutes, and I see Bunker Two in the distance. The forest is thickening, requiring Hollis to twist and turn in an effort to maneuver Sadie's body between the trees and bushes. I narrow my eyes, looking for any signs of Bunker Three. The sun has nearly set, and the light barely peeks through the vegetation. Hollis stops and points his chin up to our left. There are small wisps of smoke lifting into the sky. He turns to keep moving when we hear a shrill howl, followed by a snarl in the distance. We hold perfectly still. I can feel my heart thumping in a life-threatening beat. All I hear is the erratic pounding from my chest to my ears. Hollis signals to continue and I follow his lead. I see another smoke stream in the sky. We can't be far from Bunker Four. Making my body move nimbly through the terrain, I hear a loud snap and look down to see the broken twig beneath the ball of my foot. My teeth clench together, and a loud scratching sound reverberates off the forest. Standing still, we move our heads around in search of the culprit. The sound was scratching, like an animal climbing. I look up and out farther, and I spot it. There! Something moved at least 10 feet up into a sycamore tree in the distance. Hollis looks in my direction, and I point toward the tree. The creature is peering out around the trunk. It knows we are out here, but it doesn't know exactly where we are yet. I slowly crouch lower to get a better view through a clearing, and I see the entrance to Bunker

Four. We can't be more than 50 feet. Further into the woods I see a small rock pile next to a clearing. I reach into the front pocket of my backpack, pull out my lighter, and tap on Hollis' shoulder. He turns and I mouth, "Stay right here. When I say go, run her to the Bunker."

He frowns furiously at me. "No!"

I point at Sadie, "She needs you." Conflicted, he shakes his head, but inevitably agrees out of obligation for the little girl. I place my hand around his face. "I love you."

Then I move quickly, silently, to the rock pile. I arrange them in a circle and place a few dry branches and bark in the middle. I pull out my knife and shave pieces of kindling on top of the pile. Cupping my hand around the shavings, I flick my lighter to ignite them. The sound and smell triggers the creature to stir. Closer now, its bright, translucent skin glows amongst the dark wood. Its body is just like a human, but more limber and agile. I grab a large rock off the ground, wind my arm back to throw, and upon its release I turn to Hollis. "Go, now!" The rock lands and the creature darts to the sound's location. I make my move for the bunker, sprinting at full speed. The creature hears more movement but is distracted by the fire. Ahead, I see Hollis and Sadie running into the tunnel.

Isaac holding the door open. He sees me coming, looks in the distance behind me and his eyes widen in alarm. I can feel it catching me. I nearly topple Isaac to the ground and the door crashes shut behind us. Isaac rushes Sadie onto a makeshift hospital bed they have prepared in the dining area.

I struggle to catch my breath and crawl to standing. There is a banging on the sealed steel doors. Hollis wraps his hands around each of my arms and leans in to touch his forehead to mine. "Don't ever do that to me again." I fall into his chest and let the stress melt off me for a moment. Sadie wakes up, coughing and crying. Isaac removes her shirt and inspects the wound. A woman standing next to him hands him small sewing kit and he removes a needle and thread. He grabs a travel-size bottle of vodka off the table and pours it over the needle. Once clean, he places the thread through the eye hole and ties a knot at the end. He looks up at Sadie. "Honey, I need to give you a few pokes so you can start to feel better." In the background, *BANG! BANG! BANG!*

Isaac continues preparation to stitch Sadie's wound. "Does she have something else to hold onto? To keep her hands busy? Someone needs to make sure she doesn't grab at it once I start, and someone will need to hold her legs secure." I pull

Mingo out of my backpack, set it on her chest and place my hands on both of her arms. Hollis moves to the end of the bed and places his hands over her legs. He quickly dabs some of the vodka on the surface and she screams. I wrap her arms inside mine and hold tightly. "You're going to be just fine sweetheart. Think about all the fun things we are going to do together once you heal up. Remember, duck, duck, goose?" In between sobs she nods in acknowledgment. Isaac works quickly, pulls the last suture through and ties it off.

I scan the room to see everyone huddled around in anticipation. Sadie passes out again from the pain, and Isaac addresses the room. "The next 24 hours will be critical for her. She will need quiet and rest to heal. You did the right thing bringing her here. What on earth happened?"

"The kids were running around playing tag, and a few of them went down like dominos. Sadie was at the bottom of the pile. At some point, prior to the game, she must had found a pair of gardening shears and was running with them. When she stood up, the shears were still stuck into her abdomen, but they quickly fell to the floor," I respond. The crowd quietly gasps. Isaac looks to the sofas. "Let's get you both set up for the evening. You've endured a lot of trauma and it will do your adrenals good to get some sleep." He turns to the group. "We can get to know Leo and Hollis tomorrow, but let's all give them some space this evening." They wander off to their bedrooms and a man folds blankets into the sofa cushions and places pillows on each. He is wearing faded overalls with a cutoff t-shirt underneath and a bandana around his head. I take the FSR radio with me into the gym. "Bunker Three, this is Leora Smith. Over."

"Leora, you've got Sarah Morris here. What can I do for you? Over."

"I need you to pass this message along to Naveen in Bunker Two: We all arrived to Bunker Four safely. Dr. Kershaw has stitched Sadie back up and she is sleeping peacefully. We will update you again tomorrow. Over."

"I'm on it. Over."

The banging finally stops. I return the radio to its place and blow every lantern out except for one above Sadie. I whisper to her, "Stay strong, sweet girl."

***

I wake to the sound of fire crackling and find Isaac placing an iron pot over the flames. Hollis is still fast asleep on the other sofa. Isaac sees me stir. "I thought you could use a little coffee this morning. A special treat only for emergencies as such." He pours the water into a mug and adds a tablespoon of instant coffee. I salivate. "I knew I brought you hear for a reason." He grins. "I'm sure it had nothing to do with my surgical abilities. I will say, I am surprised to be needed so soon." The overalls man who made our beds last night steps into the room. "Look at you, up and at 'em Doc. How's baby girl doing?" And as though she heard him, Sadie turns onto her good side, rubs her eyes and asks, "Can I have some pancakes?" I rush to her. "Sadie, careful sweetie." Isaac checks her vitals and lifts her shirt to examine the sutures. She flinches as he pulls the tape attaching her gauze.

"Things are looking good, Sadie girl. About those pancakes, we are fresh out. However, we do have this." He holds up an MRE package in his right hand. "Brown sugar toaster pastry." He opens the packaging and places a small piece in her hand. She laughs and immediately hunches over in pain. Isaac scrambles to the drawers and pulls out a small bottle of children's Tylenol and a syringe. He fills it up to the top line and has her drink it all. I place another pillow at the top of her bed so she can relax while she finishes her toaster pastry. Hollis rolls off the sofa and straight to Sadie. "I had no idea you were so strong. You are one impressive little girl." She takes the last bite of pastry. "Can you read me my bug book and bring me Mingo?"

"It would be my honor, princess Sadie," he responds. He opens the cover and dives into character. Each bug getting a different pitch and tone. Lady bug's voice is high pitch and British. The Dung Beetle uses a very nasally voice since he is always crawling on poop. She is entranced, hanging onto his every word. My heart be still. Isaac walks me to the greenroom so we can speak privately about the plan.

"Wounds like this don't just heal overnight. It will be painful for a couple weeks, and sore to the touch for a month or more. If all goes well over the next day, she should be safe for transport back to her family if Hollis carries her again," he explains.

"Alright, let's see how she does. I will need to radio Bunker Three to pass that message along right away. Mara and Wiley, her mother and father, have probably been up all night long worrying."

Upon my return, Sadie has fallen asleep as Hollis reads to her. He slowly fades out of character and places the book back in my pack. I relay the update from Isaac to him and he picks up the radio to pass the message along to her family. I grab my coffee and take a look around their greenroom to find the plants not only surviving, but actually producing fruit and vegetables. The pots are filled with strawberries, lettuce, tomatoes and tiny, bright blueberries. Overalls man knocks on the side of the archway. "Hey there! I see you are admiring my handywork." He folds his fingers over, places them up to his mouth, huffs a couple puffs of hot air on them and rubs them on his chest with pride. I point to the bright red tomatoes. "You did all this?"

"Sure did, some say I got a green thumb. The name's Pete." He shakes my hand. "I was raised on a farm in the tiny town of Adams, Tennessee. Nothin' to do there but grow shit, shoot shit and shoot the shit." Hands on his stomach, he leans back into an unrestrained belly laugh.

"It really is impressive. Bunker Four is lucky to have you."

"Gosh, we all do our part 'round here. We choose one vegetable or fruit to eat every three days. Yesterday we ate some strawberries with breakfast, but I'm gonna make sure we feed you brave folks some fresh food before you head back to y'all's bunker." He winks and heads back out to the dining room for breakfast.

Hollis finds me staring up out the greenroom windows. He stands in the doorway. "The message is passed along to Sadie's family."

I take a sip of my coffee. "Their plants are looking pretty good. Are you sure you want to step foot in here?" I ask.

He marches in boldly and gets right in front of my face. "You know I didn't touch those plants. No matter how frustrating you can be, it wouldn't drive me to jeopardize the health of our bunker." He points his finger in my face. "You just wanted to tell yourself I did, so you wouldn't have to deal with your feelings for me." He pulls back upright, and I take another sip of my coffee, never breaking eye contact.

"Maybe you're right," I respond. His eyes widen in surprise. I keep a straight face and move around him, straight to the bathroom. Because I might vomit after laying that all out on the table. I sit in the stall much longer than I need to. What was I thinking? I could have at least waited until we are back in Bunker One with a private bedroom to retreat to. Now, I have go back out there and share a living room with him.

It's fine. It's just Hollis, calm down. I pull my pants back up and step back into reality.

***

Sadie pulls through her first day in Bunker Four like a champ. I can't say I'm surprised with a medical staff like this. All the women in the bunker shower her with love and attention, and she has her own private neurosurgeon to tend to her simple stab wound. I spend the afternoon getting to know everyone. Finley, a 34-year-old cognitive behavioral therapist, made the journey with her fiancé, Bosley, a 38-year-old small business owner. While most everyone else has been waiting for me to approach them, she grabs her MRE meal and pulled a chair up right next to me. We discover that we share a lot in common, and I'm reminded of the life I'll live after this. I could have friends again, and without limits. The world will be my oyster. Sure, it will be burnt to the crisp, beaten and flooded, but it will be my mess. Hollis finds me smiling to myself and pulls up a chair. "Hey, weirdo. Having conversations with yourself again?"

"Can't a girl think happy thoughts to herself?" I ask.

"I would never deprive one of such thoughts. Care to share?"

"I was just thinking about how nice it will be to go anywhere without carrying an extra jacket with me once we are out of hiding."

"I think that sounds—what's......what's happening?!" The ground beneath us is trembling. Hollis grabs my arm and pulls me under the table with him. Maybe 30 seconds pass and the earth stops shaking. I climb out and look to Isaac. "Anyone know what that was?" Heads shake across the room and people murmur until Bosley speaks up. "There are few things that can make the earth shake like that. It could have been an earthquake, or maybe a meteorite hit us." Sadie gasps. "Are we going to be okay?"

"Yes, we are going to be fine. We just have to stay calm." I smile at her, nodding to the others to play happy for her. They follow my lead and I turn back to Bosley. "What do you know about meteorites?"

"Not a lot. I mean, I kind of geek out about stuff like this, so I know a little. A good-size meteorite collision would send enough debris into the air to block the sun's rays for months, potentially. We could be looking at a drop in temperature soon. If we were in close proximity to the impact, we would see a major increase in wind gusts from the blast," he replies.

"What if it hit an ocean instead of ground?" I ask.

"I don't know if it would cause the earth to shake like that, but it would definitely cause a large-scale tsunami. We should check the HAM radio. See if anyone is chatting about it." Hollis places it on the counter and starts scanning for a conversation. We connect to a conversation in a language no one else understands. Maybe Mandarin? He dials to access the repeater and the electronic voice fills the room.

"Multiple meteorites have cut through the atmosphere and made impact today. The first meteorite touched down 20 miles north of Mexico City, zero one zero zero hours, central daylight time. The second meteorite touched down 76 miles off the coast of Brazil. Tsunamis are anticipated along the coasts of Brazil and Uruguay. Expect waves 30 to 100 feet in height. Get to high ground as far inland as possible. Evacuate as soon as possible. If you are in a boat, go out to sea…Multiple meteorites have…." He turns it off.

We look to the windows in the greenroom for any indication that this will impact us further, but it is dusk, and daylight is slipping away. If we don't bring Sadie back soon,

Mara will be heartbroken. It will only get worse out there before it will get better. With that in mind, I reach for the radio and to let the Longs know that we are all ok. The bunker is quiet. No one knows what to think or how to feel. Hollis plops down next to me. "What an emotional rollercoaster." I lean in and lay my head on his chest. "Will you be ready to make the run back tomorrow?" He gently strokes my hair the way my mother would when I was little. "If you are ready, I'm with you. You just say the word."

33

THUNDER BATTLE

There's something poking me in the face. My eyelids feel like they are weighed down with cinder blocks, but the poking won't stop. I slap my nose and giggles erupt. I lift my head and see Sadie staring back at me with a twinkle in her eye. I push myself up to see Hollis lying right behind me. Finley stomps into the kitchen, rubbing her eyes.

"That must have been some storm. Was anyone else up all night?" she asks.

"Heck yes, it was thunder booming out there for quite some time," Pete replies.

Hollis looks at me. "Did you hear anything?"

I shake my head. "I didn't even realize I fell asleep on you."

Maybe the sound is less likely to disrupt the center of the bunker where we sleep. I fold up my blanket and take a seat at the kitchen island. Pete places a plate of MRE cinnamon scones beside a beautiful pile of blueberries and hands Hollis the same. I savor every refreshing bite of the sweet berries and applaud him for his farming talents. He tips his John Deere hat and takes a bow. Our laughter is interrupted by a crashing rumble.

Finley jumps out of her chair. "See, there it is again!"

I leap out of my seat and head to the greenroom. The others follow to peer out of the window. We find a dry, faded olive-green sky. It's reminiscent of all things unpleasant; like diarrhea, mucus or the little barf face emoji. It must be far enough away that we don't have any rain yet.

Isaac inspects Sadie's wound one last time and gives us the go ahead to bring her back. He hands me some extra gauze and tape to bring back with us. I extend my hand to him. "I don't know what we would have done without you, Isaac. You saved the baby of Bunker One. Thank you so much."

"Well, I've heard there is a nurse practitioner in Bunker Five and a midwife in Bunker Six, so I'm sure she would have been fine," he laughs. Sadie runs between us and wraps her arms around his legs. He crouches down to her level. "Remember what Atticus said…," and in unison they say, "She was powerful, not because she wasn't scared, but because she went on so strongly, despite the fear." They high-five and Sadie lifts her balled up fist in an effort to flex for the crowd.

Hollis finishes packing our bags and we say our last goodbyes. My steps feel heavy through the tunnel and I hold my breath as the door opens. Let's hope they haven't started a nuclear war already. The air, thick and gritty, hits my face and Sadie wrinkles her nose in disgust. A faint melody of rumbling and howls bounce off the mountain cliffs and into our psyches. I walk in front of Hollis and scan the area for any signs of danger. Not a creature in sight. I signal for him to follow my lead. We make it all of 20 feet and stop. A loud thump followed by a familiar snarl fills the air. I turn around and find the female version of the demon we crossed on our way here. I can easily see the bald form of her head through the thinning strands of long, white hair draping past her shoulders. She sways back and forth, her head bobbling separately from her body's movement. Her eyes are black from lid to lid and spindly, dark veins grow out of the them with fervor. Her pale, white skin is exposed through a tattered red dress. Why is she wearing clothes? Then I realize, she's no different than all the other demons in human bodies I've encountered. I can feel my arms and legs start to tremble. She throws her head back and parts her lips to snicker at us. Every tooth in her foul mouth is narrow and sharp.

I place my hand over Sadie. "Look away. Put your face in Hollis' chest."

Behind the demon, the bunker door flings open. Pete steps out to expose half of his body. He draws his right arm out, points a nine-millimeter at the demon and shoots. He hits her right in the back twice. She swivels around to face him. His eyes widen. "She looks madder than a wet hen!" He pulls the trigger three more times, hitting her in the chest. She clenches her fists into balls and shrieks. He jolts back inside and seals the door shut. She turns her focus back to us and comes charging in our direction. Her arms and legs pumping and the trees blowing in the wind all fade into slow motion. Just as she is closing in on us, a warrior plummets from the sky and slams her to the ground with his sword. He yanks his sword out of her chest and wipes it clean on the gray and white feathers adorned to the wings folded across his back. He wears a chrome chest plate and thick leather boots up to his knees. Two more demons in the distance hear the clamor, and leap through the trees like feral, pale monkeys to get closer. They halt on top of the bunker, squawking to one another in their own language. One of them starts hissing in our direction. The angel slams his foot down and the earth shakes. He looks back at us and roars, "RUN! RIGHT NOW!" I move my feet in rapid succession, slicing through the thick forest in our wake. Hollis pivots and twists his body to cradle Sadie to safety. One, two…there's three! I count down the smokestacks along the way. I can see Bunker One up ahead. I dart around Hollis and take off in a dead sprint for the greenroom window. I slam my fists over and over until I see Mara's face. She drives the heavy steel doors open and we dash into the tunnel.

Mara and Wiley rush to Sadie, tears falling down their faces. Mara places both her hands around Sadie's face, looking her up and down for any sign of new injury. Wiley carefully takes her out of Hollis' arms, carries her into the bunker and lays her on a sofa.

Sadie holds his hand. "Daddy, there are scary monkey people out there, but we went on so strong….." Her eyelids fall in defeat and we step away to let her rest. I walk Mara through the treatment plan for her wound as the others swarm Hollis to hear of what we saw. He fills them in on all the gory details, and I pull Amos aside to gain some insight.

"Listen, there are…things, other than natural causes, slaughtering people out there. We saw one on the way to Bunker One and I was able to distract it long enough to get in. On our way here today, another one attacked us. One of the Bunker Four members shot it FIVE times. FIVE times, and she only shrieked at him. Then, a big, terrifying angel showed up and skewered her with his sword. If he hadn't been there, we wouldn't be alive. I'm sure of it. That said, do you have any idea what is going on?" I ask.

"Maybe," he responds. "All of that would indicate the war in Heaven is over. According to the Ahava, Lucifer was cast out of Heaven sometime after the creation of angelic beings, but before he took on a serpent's form and tempted Adam and Eve in the Garden of Eden."

"Right, when he was striving to be greater than God. He was the first to sin, and he is the reason humankind all falls to sin, but what does that have to do with what is going on now?" I ask.

"That expulsion still allowed him to manipulate freely on Earth, but there were situations when God allowed him to have temporary access to Heaven. In the book of Revelation, the prophet describes a final war in Heaven, in which Lucifer appears in the form of a dragon. He and his fallen angels are cast out of Heaven permanently. If the prophet was correct, they have unleashed hell on Earth, so to speak," he replies.

I recall the scriptures and then the angel who saved us, who must have been a part of the cleanup crew sent to throw Lucifer and the false prophet into the Lake of Fire. "All this time I thought that the war in Heaven, referenced in Revelation, was a recap of his first banishment," I admit.

"Well, there are some other things that don't line up. In Revelations, it says that Lucifer is imprisoned in an abyss for one 1,000 years before he is thrown into the Lake of Fire," Amos replies.

"What if they are just expunging Earth of the other fallen angels? Does that mean that he is just waiting in shackles for his day to come again?" I ask.

"Possibly," Amos shrugs. Kenzo takes a seat next to Amos and asks him to go over their daily Ahava study.

God wouldn't allow us to survive only to battle Satan's spawn. He knows that our frail, mortal bodies can't take multiple bullets to the chest and carry on like nothing happened. That explains why the angel saved us today. He's just out there doing his job, cleaning up the mess. Michael is probably his commander, and he wouldn't set us up for failure. If he does report to Michael, he will know that we didn't stay in our bunker. Like all things, he can find out our reasoning. I'm sure he will understand. Whether or not Lucifer will walk Earth again—well, that's just a test of our faith. Regardless, Amos and I agree to keep this information to ourselves until we are cleared from the bunker and everyone is in a better mental state. For all we know, Lucifer could be done away with by now. It does clearly state this in the Ahava, though. I don't think he would have missed removing this if it were incorrect.

Wiley and Mara radio Bunker Two to pass the message along that we have arrived safely and to send their personal thanks to Dr. Kershaw. Ms. McCall places a drawing pad on the coffee table and invites Sadie to play a game of tic-tac-toe. Memories of my childhood come rushing in like a flood. After the adoption, I struggled with feeling comfortable in my new home. I woke up in the middle of the night terrified. In the morning, my parents would find me curled up in a ball on the floor in my bedroom closet. Something about the small space comforted me. After many failed attempts to earn my acceptance, my father turned my child-sized Minnie Mouse table into our spot. He and I would play tic-tac-toe every afternoon after my nap. At first, it was frustrating. Understanding the strategy and rules wasn't the easiest for a four-year-old. He never let me win, though. One day, I drew that final X to complete three in a row. I danced in celebration and he scrambled to find a prize for me. Digging in his pockets, he pulled out a little tin case of Altoids, "curiously strong mints." I placed it in my mouth and was shocked by the intensity. He explained what the tin said. My favorite book at that time was called "The Mitten." Growing up in Florida, I had no concept of life with mittens, but it was such a common word in my little vocabulary that I always called those Altoids strong mittens. My parents would burst into laughter every time I said it. I just thought that they were so happy for me. To this day, the smell of mint makes me long to be that four-year-old girl again.

Across the room, Hollis is seated at a dining table drinking a cup of tea. He places the tea leaves into a small metal ball, clamps the compartment shut and dips it into the cup of hot water. He looks my direction and pats the seat next to him to invite me. I grab a mug and fill it with some hot water from the kettle on the counter. He raises his cup to mine and we cheers to the life we still have, despite the odds.

***

The ground continues to shake beneath us daily. Conversations on the HAM radio cease to exist, and the occasional demon wakes the group pounding on the greenroom glass in the middle of the night. It's clear they know who we are, and they know we are here. It has been one week since I have taken a full shower. I grab my things and set the timer for one minute. I'm sure I can get everything clean in 60 seconds. The sensation of the cool water invigorates me. I dry off and before wrapping the towel around my body, I glance in the mirror. I barely recognize the person staring back at me. My cheekbones are so pronounced, clavicle bones protruding, and my hair is nearly down to my tail bone. I haven't shaved my armpits or legs for a couple of weeks. I quickly look away and put my clothes back on. I can't believe Hollis, or any man for that matter, would find me appealing in this condition. I sigh, as this is probably going to be my permanent condition. How did people find ways to remove body hair back in the old days? I mean, who is going to know how to make a razor? Even if someone could, it

357

will definitely be low on the priority list. I should have gotten laser hair removal when I had the chance.

I make my way back out into the general area to find the same concerned faces. There are whispers of this phase taking longer than anticipated. We don't have enough supplies to last another month. The children still laugh and play, but the adults have sunk into despair. Amos can sense a spirit of fear among the group and calls us into the living area. Ahavas are littered throughout the room on coffee tables, opened to different pages. Throw pillows are placed in a circle on the floor for the children, and all the adults take a seat on the sofas.

Amos grabs one of the Ahavas and hands it to Kenzo. "Kenzo, please read the highlighted verse on this page." Kenzo follows his instruction. "But those who wait for the Lord shall renew their strength, they shall mount up with wings like eagles, they shall run and not be weary, they shall walk and not faint. Isaiah 40:31." He hands the Ahava back to Amos.

"Very good, Kenzo. The last few weeks have brought you," he points around to all of the adults, "to a new low. I hear speculation of broken promises and impending doom. He picks up another Ahava and hands it to Poppy. She sees the highlighted scriptures and recites them. "For I know the plans

I have for you, declares the LORD, plans to prosper you and not to harm you, plans to give you hope and a future. Jeremiah 29:11."

Amos takes the Ahava from her and slams it shut, placing it back on the coffee table. "Does anyone here know why I've chosen to have the children read the word today?" He looks around the circle to find us all dumbfounded. "Because they still have faith. They run, dance, and play around this bunker without a care while you all sulk. Our God promised us safety. He didn't promise that it wouldn't take work to rebuild, but he gave us ALL of this." He lifts his arms up and turns in a circle to marvel at the bunker around us. "God is gentle. He doesn't struggle the way we do to keep our emotions under control. This," he points out to the world, "is a result of repeatedly defying the covenant we have with him. God didn't lose his temper. If it's his will, then let that be enough. Save that empathy and compassion for one another. We are going to need it."

34

LEAN INTO THE LIGHT

The bunker was filled with buzz after Amos's Ahava study. The once sad, sluggish group had gotten its mojo back. Ellen and Asher got to work designing concepts for our first city. He sprawls out his drafts at the dining table, measuring and connecting each line with a wooden ruler. Once the structural piece is complete, Ellen takes over the creative design elements. The streets all receive tall, stylish gaslight posts and every building is preceded by flower beds or shrubs. When she reaches the point of starting to sketch actual people waving out of the windows, Asher swoops in to have her start on the next stretch of our city. Occasionally, they bicker about the placement of a structure, but they really do work well together.

Amos is hard at work creating the agenda for our next bunker meeting in the kitchen. Kenzo, never too far behind him, is leaning over his shoulder observing his every move. Amos isn't the only one with a shadow. Poppy, who has clearly become enamored with Kenzo, is just two feet away, pouring them both a glass of water. Mrs. Olson takes a seat next to me and glimpses at Poppy.

"That boy could tell her that the sun is actually the moon and she would believe him," she says.

"She's young and stuck in a bunker. He's the only kid in here her age. I'm sure she will grow out of it," I shrug.

"He's different, though. Not like other boys his age. She's never expressed interest in boys before. We have always agreed that when the time came, she would be a good judge of character, but she's just so impressionable," she explains.

"At least his interests all fall around Amos. I won't even tell you the types of boys I had interests in when I was her age. It was far too easy to deceive my parents. All it took was an extra social media account they didn't know about. Hey, she won't have any of those moving forward. Any sneaking around she does will have to be planned out in person or through passing notes," I laugh.

Hollis leans over and extends his hand to me. I accept the gesture and place my hand in his. He lifts me out of my seat and leads me to the laundry station.

"I've come to the conclusion that you are less nervous about actually having a relationship with me than you are of everyone else becoming aware of it. Therefore, I'm going to kiss you now, in front of everyone."

Before I can respond, he places his left hand on the small of my back, his right hand behind my head and presses his lips to mine. I feel all the blood in my face rush to my cheeks, and the group begins to applaud and cheer at full volume. Hollis, soaking in their encouragement, grabs my hand, pivots his body, dips me down and back up to him. His eyes, smiling with his whole face, are staring back into mine, searching for my acceptance. I want to hit him, but the fireworks surging through my veins has had a paralyzing effect on my mobility.

"It's about time!" Calvin cheers.

Hollis laughs. "Problem solved."

I raise my hands out to the crowd. "Alright, show's over. Everyone, back to work." I take hold of Hollis's arm and drag him to my room.

"I love you, Hollis. As in, I'm IN love with you. In all these years, I didn't see it, and I don't know if it really wasn't there before, or if I was just too blindsided by my messed up 'gift.' We had clear boundaries. I was the simple, sarcastic girl who would rather stay home than go to the party. You were the life of the party. Every bubbly, polished princess doted over you. Everything I've programmed myself to believe about you and I will have to change. I need to know that if things don't work out, we can go back to the way things were. Promise me."

He takes a deep breath. "First of all, nothing about you is or was simple to me or anyone else who knew you. You are just so damn intimidating that no one has had the balls to approach you. You could reject a guy with one look before he even got in front of you. Secondly, I would rather light myself on fire than go through life without you, and I know this will work. I won't promise you that things will go back to the way they were…because that will never have to happen."

I walk him to the door. "This doesn't mean we share a room now. You'll still need to impress me before I consider any kind of real commitment."

"Challenge accepted."

***

Ms. McCall places her hands on her knees to prop herself up and stretch her back. She sits back down and polishes her glasses with the small cloth she keeps in her shirt pocket. The community plans are scattered on the dining room tables in front of everyone. Amos and Hollis connect the two large tables so they can arrange them in the order that each project should be completed. There is a lively debate as to where we will decide to settle, but we all agree that it makes more sense to build just one city for the time being. If we can pool our talents and resources, we stand a better chance at survival. Poppy asks what we have all wondered: "Will we be able to see what has happened to our old homes?"

I think back to the supply list that was given to us before the journey…gas, everyone had to bring gas along. I look to Hollis. "Did you see any gas cans in the garage?"

"Just ours, but we were the first ones here." He scans the group. "Did you all bring gas, too?"

Every head nods in confirmation.

"Then there should be no reason that we can't venture out, but we need to be back by a certain day. I'm sure we will find some gas along the way there and back. Our trip was by far the furthest in this group. There may be others who came from south Florida. Regardless, one night is the most any of us are going to want to sleep in our vehicles. How does everyone feel about 48 hours?" I ask.

The group agrees in unison. Mara points to the city center again. "We really need to have some kind of community park here. The kids need a space for play that is protected, and we can gather here when the weather permits."

Amos grabs the sheet. "We will definitely put an area for play somewhere safe, but for now, it's more important to have the well in a central location. If we place the well over here," he places the plan in front of her and points to the far west side of the development, "it will be far too strenuous for anyone living on the east side of the city to get water. Eventually, we will have more sources of water, but we need to make sure everyone is taken care of until the basics are in place."

The men begin to brainstorm how to dig and hack at the ground until reaching the water table. It would be one thing if producing a well was the only project, but we may need to build houses and a church as well. Wiley's father ran a construction company, so he had some insight to the kind of equipment that would have been used to dig a well in modern times. We will all need to keep our eyes peeled for a truck mounted by a drill rig. It's clear none of us know what that looks like, so he sketches a picture for us.

Many of these decisions will be voted on once we are all together, but it's my responsibility to lay out the options. It can't just be a free-for-all. Bunker One's reaction should be a good indication of what concerns the rest of the community will have. Stassi tallies up how many individual homes will be needed for our bunker.

"Eventually, there should be eight individual homes for our bunker. Unless, of course, some of you decide to share a home with your own bedrooms or whatever." She looks to Hollis and I. "It seems to me that it would make the most sense to build the well first, then start with one home at a time. We could start with those who have small children. Until your home is built, you continue to live in your bunker. As long as we still have water, of course," Stassi suggests.

Amos places his fingers around his chin. "So, we would have to build somewhere fairly close to Mt. Asylum. That's smart, Stassi. Add that to our voting options."

I pick up my clipboard and take down the note. Conversations hum around the group. This place was our safe haven, but it was also where we experienced the most terrifying moments of our life. Can they build a new life where literal demons kept them up through the night? Hollis approaches the table and slams his mug on it a few times to get their attention.

"No one wants to stay here in this bunker any longer than we need to. This place can either be a memory of horror for you all, or it can be the place that saved you from that horror. Leo is trying to explain that we need to stick together, or no one is going to make it." He stops and looks off into space, shaking his finger at a new thought. "What if, once all the essentials are built, each of us can make and place something reminiscent of their previous community in our city? Like a memorial to your past. If it's something you wouldn't or couldn't replicate, and you see it is still there, maybe we can find a way to bring it to our community."

Sadie jumps on top of a chair. "Daddy! The doggy scraple!" He stops her from tearing her sutures out in excitement. "You mean the doggy SCULPTURE at Brookgreen Gardens. That one might be heavy, but not too big for a normal vehicle. We will try." Similar conversations crop up around the room. Stories from their past, and how they could share it with the rest of the group.

Amos takes that as his cue to move the conversation into farming plans. The assumption is that our land will be burned or flooded. No one is expecting a good first year, but we need to start somewhere. I tell them how Pete, in Bunker Four, grew up on a farm in Tennessee. He can speak from experience once we're all together, but we know that we will use the seeds we all brought with us and the potted plants we have in our bunkers. There may not be an abundance of wildlife, but nature always finds a way. If we could survive, some of them must have, too. Maybe enough to breed cattle. A chicken coup! Oh, please let there be a few chickens left. The thought of fresh eggs on a skillet makes my mouth water. I understand how those people on that reality television show Naked and Afraid ate snakes and alligators. I'm not really starving, but the MRE meals taste gelatinous and malty.

Stassi has experience calculating how much area certain species will need to get enough sustenance. She grabs a pen and talks to herself as she calculates. "If each person will need 2,700 calories per day, that's 5.5 pounds of food, then you get 490 calories per pound. Average harvest is 147 bushels per acre, so 8,250 pounds.....so it would take about one acre to feed one person for a year. I would make sure we account for growth, though."

She looks up and smiles. Every mouth is dropped open in awe of her genius. It's decided that we would need an area with at least 400 acres of land. If everyone agrees, Hollis, Pete, Amos and I will take a quick trip to scope out areas in close proximity that could work for us. It's possible that some of the towns and cities may be somewhat intact. If we find a gem like that, we can take another vote. Amos opens up the meeting for any ideas regarding future developments, and I continue to jot them down like I'm taking their order. Hollis leans over to me. "We've got our work cut out for us," he whispers.

Hours of brainstorming pass by, and eventually the thoughts became recycled versions of concepts we had already discussed. Amos closes the meeting, and everyone retreats to their bedrooms for much needed rest. I can feel them all softly breathing in a deep sleep around me, but I lay awake. The back and forth of today's debate is still playing in my mind. I look down to find Stassi sound asleep. I slowly pitter-patter my way down the bunk stairs and out of the room. The fire is still going, so I throw another log on and heat up a kettle of water for tea. The dining chairs don't appeal to my restless body, so I gather a few throw pillows from the sofa and pile them together a safe distance in front of the fire. Mrs. Olson knitted the bunker a couple of blankets, which are draped over the kitchen island chairs. I select one patterned with radiant blues and earthy beiges. They remind me of the sand at the beach meeting the ocean water. I wrap it around my shoulders and nestle into the pile of pillows with my tea. A door cracks open and Kenzo shuffles into the kitchen. I clear my throat so he isn't startled by my presence. He jumps, and squints in my direction, "Leo? What are you doing up?"

"I could ask you the same question."

He reaches into the cabinet for a glass. "I was just thirsty." He fills the glass with water, pulls a chair to the other side of the fire and takes a seat. "That was a crazy day. I'm sure you have a lot on your mind and need to decompress. If you're a little stressed out, don't worry. Your secret's safe with me."

"It was definitely eventful, but in a good way. You don't have to worry about me."

"I've overheard some people talking about what a challenge this must be for you, at your age and without any family here. I'm just saying, no one would blame you if you were struggling." He takes another drink of his water and stares into the fire.

I tilt my head, "I think we all struggle with the things inside us that make us human, Kenzo. Those things only take control if you allow them to. In fact, that's the only reason we are here, because we leaned into the light when we were shrouded by darkness." I stand up and place my mug in the sink. "I'm calling it a night. You should probably get some rest."

Kenzo nods in acknowledgment, but stays seated, his eyes on the flames.

35

ROCKY ROAD

Sadie has refused to stop telling the other children stories of the scary white face lady on our adventure back to the bunker, and they have all driven their parents insane waking up in the middle of the night with nightmares. Hollis has the bright idea to empower the little monsters. He pushes all the gym equipment up against the mirrored walls and calls them in. They all fit in the gym with just a few feet between one another. He lines them up and spaces them accordingly before explaining the rules.

"Today, you get to learn how to beat the bad guys! You are all going to stay standing in your spot, but do exactly what I do, alright?"

They cheer in agreement. Hollis pivots and throws a punch in the air and then pivots the other direction. "Punch! Kick! Get 'em!" It's kickboxing for babies. Some parents peer in and give Hollis the thumbs up. They are clearly desperate at this point. Luckily, it has been days since we have heard any pounding on the windows. I can only imagine how much worse it would make this situation. Sadie has been watching from the sidelines. She sneaks in and throws a punch at her brother's arm, prompting him to chase her out of the gym as she squeals in excitement. They go full speed ahead into the tunnel, circling around and darting into the greenroom— "AAAAHHH!" Sadie's shrill scream fills the air. No, no, no. She must have seen another demon. Mara goes racing into the room, the rest of us not far behind her. She stops abruptly. Sadie is jumping up and down, pointing overhead. "The sky is blue, the sky is blue, that means we can go play outside, right Mommy?!"

There it is, in all its cerulean wonder and not a cloud in sight. I squeeze past those behind me and out of the greenroom, so the others can see for themselves. I had always imagined everyone busting those doors open and basking in the sunlight when this day came. But here we are, in utter shock. What if it's a fluke? Mr. Olson suggests we wait until this afternoon, just to verify that the sky really is blue to signal our safety. The others talk amongst themselves and the bunker is filled with debate again. Ms. McCall pounds her fist onto the table. "Look at all of you, right back to where we were. Did you all hear Sadie? Thrilled because the blue sky is here just like we were told it would be. She's thrilled because she believes. Do none of you believe anymore?"

Silence fills the space. Shoulders crouch ever so slightly and some heads tuck into their chests. Every person in the room is doing some spiritual inventory on themselves. I take Ms. McCall's hand. "Ms. McCall makes a very good point. Let's not move backward. Let's start small and just take a few steps outside the bunker to get a look at the mountain." I unlatch the compression locks on the doors and pull the pins.

Here goes nothing.

I push the doors open wide and the light floods the tunnel. Hands go up to block the light wreaking havoc on our bat cave eyes. Goosebumps spread up and down my arms. It can't be more than 50 degrees out here.

"It's freezing out here for March in Kentucky, people. You might want to grab jackets," I suggest.

Most people go back inside and take their time getting bundled up. I remember watching documentaries about some soldiers who were captured during war and had spent years confined to small spaces. When they were rescued, some couldn't sleep in a normal bed. They would crawl into a small closet to get relief. What had once tortured them became their comfort. Let's hope a few months in this bunker doesn't do that kind of damage.

Hollis and I wait at the entrance so we can all exit together. Sadie slips her jacket on and comes darting through the tunnel, Mara not far behind. The group moves in unison into the light. I close my eyes and face the sky in all its glory. My hair is whipping across my face in the wind. Hollis wraps his arms around my waist and lifts me up, spinning in circles until I fall on top of him in a fit of laughter. I dust myself off and look back up at the mountain we have been sealed inside all this time. Where a cliff once stood about 50 feet above our garage entrance, is now a sharp, straight stump of rock. Like the cliff had been amputated. The winds, clearly stronger now, had flattened hundreds of trees. They were all knocked down in the same direction, a huge wooden set of dominos. Ugh, now I want pizza. *Note to self, get a milk cow and grow things that we can make pizza with.* I swat Hollis in the chest. "Do you remember when we went on that rafting trip in Yellowstone?"

"Uh, how could I not? We barely made it there," he laughs.

"Right, because my father forgot to set the alarm. We spent hours out there rowing away with nothing in our stomachs. I truly thought I was going to faint, but then that pizza once we got to the restaurant at the bottom."

"Best meal I've ever had. How could you do this to me?!" He throws his hands in the air. "Now all I want is pizza!"

"I'm sorry! I couldn't endure the memory alone," I laugh.

The children run in circles while their parents try to keep them in close proximity. Ms. McCall carefully bends down to sit on the ground. She closes her eyes, places her hands on her knees, and takes in a deep breath. Amos stands far left of our entrance, peering toward the other bunkers. He looks back and signals for me to come see something.

"There," he points toward Bunker Two. "They're coming out."

We watch as the group steps into the sun for the first time in months. They raise their arms in celebration and embrace one another. The group has fewer young children, but I see a handful of young adults. Amos looks at me. "Should we go introduce ourselves?"

I look back at their celebration. "Let's give them a couple minutes to soak in their freedom first." He smiles and nods in agreement. Hollis and I grab our jackets and instruct the group to follow us to Bunker Two. There isn't a clear path to follow, so we all climb over the flattened trees. To our left I see that the road leading to Bunker Two's garage is blocked by huge fallen sycamore and maple trees. Sadie hurries in front, shouting to the new group. "New people! Here we come! We are your new friends!" A large woman extends her arms in a welcoming embrace. Sadie lunges into her in a fit of giggles. The woman kneels to her level. "How does it feel to be outside for the first time in months, sweetheart?"

"Oh, I've already been outside! I had a bad ouchie and went to the doctor," Sadie nods in all seriousness.

The woman gasps. "You're the brave girl who made it to see the doctor and back to your bunker?!"

Sadie places a proud hand on her chest. "Yup, that's me."

Naveen is swinging a girl up and down in circles. He sets her back down and runs to us.

"Well done, Viceroy, well done. So, what's the plan now?" he asks.

"I think we should allow everyone the option to visit their previous homes, so long as they return within 48 hours and obtain any necessary supplies they come across along the way. Since some of the bunkers may not have an easy way out," I point to their road, "we will need some people to carpool. I'm sure your bunker, and all the rest, have come up with some ideas for our next settlement. I have put together a list of suggestions, and we can add any other reasonable ideas to that list."

"That works for me. Make sure every group takes one of the gas cans lined across the garage walls. Our bunker has made a lot of speculations, but no one has voiced any strong opinions. I think they are under the impression that the choice won't be up to them anyway. Let me get you the garage key for Bunker One."

He runs back into the bunker and returns with the key.

I place the key in my pants pocket. "I don't want them to think they don't have a say, but that's an issue for another day. For now, round up your group and explain the plan." I look up at the position of the sun. "I'd guess that it's around 8 a.m. If everyone gets packed up and leaves soon, they should be able to get to their destinations before dark. Can you send the message along to Bunkers Three, Four, Five and Six? I will send Hollis with you."

"Absolutely, let me grab their garage keys."

I fill Hollis in on our plan and he sets off with Naveen to the other bunkers. The simple padlock clicks open with the turn of the key Naveen gave me. I squat down, grab the handle at the bottom and lift with all my might. The door budges a crack. I see along the bottom there are two more handles, so I round up Amos and Wiley to help. All three of us thrust the door open to find our dusty vehicles lined up in neat rows. I gather the group just outside of our garage to determine whose vehicles are in the first row and will be leaving first. We make sure every vehicle has a full gas can loaded, and I take an inventory on how many people can fit in each vehicle and where they came from. Amos hands me a notebook and I write in big block letters the capacity number and location. He takes the paper from me and places it under that vehicle's windshield wiper.

We have one vehicle left to complete when Hollis and Naveen return. Naveen bends over to catch his breath.

"Four of the six bunkers still have passage down from the mountain, but Bunker Two and Bunker Three got hit hard. We asked that someone from each bunker stay by their radio, so you can instruct them," Hollis explains.

I nod. "Alright, thank you. Naveen, let's have everyone from Bunker Two come over here to our garage. Make sure they bring what they need for their trip but remind them to pack lightly. They will want room in the vehicle for any supplies they find along the way. I'll get on the radio to tell Bunker Three to head over to Bunker Four's garage, and I'll let Bunker Four know to expect them. Hollis, can you help everyone in our bunker get their things together and loaded?"

"I'm on it," he replies.

Each family and individual find their appropriate vehicle based on their destinations. Ms. McCall carpools with the Longs, as they already have a pretty full vehicle with their four children. Hollis, Stassi and I agree to take Marie, a forty-something widow from Tallahassee, Ellen from Orlando, and Asher, who is from Atlanta. Kenzo, of course, jumps at the chance to carpool with Amos. He and his family cram into Amos's small sedan with Russ. This leaves plenty of room in the other vehicles for the other Bunker Two passengers. I do one last radio call out to Bunker Two to confirm we are loaded and heading out. One by one, we watch them descend the mountain and into the unknown.

***

The winding gravel road down the mountain is littered with debris. Hollis swerves back and forth to avoid branches and boulders that plummeted from the cliffs above. I make conversation with Marie to pass time. She raves about what a great job Naveen did keeping their bunker in order. There were days when people didn't want to leave their rooms, and he pulled them out of their depression. Her husband passed away several years ago. He was a pilot, so he was gone for long periods of time. One day, he left for work and a semi lost control on the freeway, wiping him right off the road. He flew through the windshield and was pronounced dead on the scene. They had decided early on that they didn't want to have children if they would have to live in a world without faith. It didn't seem right to them, and they already felt wrong about hiding their beliefs. Her eyes begin to water, but she quickly wipes them dry with her fingers.

Hollis points out his window at the small town of Littcarr, which we passed on the way in. We come to a rolling stop in the town center. The houses have been burned to the ground. There may have only been a couple dozen of them. I step out of the SUV to get a closer look. There are no bodies, but the pavement is sporadically splattered with what looks like dried blood. The gas station and grocery store have fallen to the ground. Only a couple feet of brick still hold strong from the ground up. The post office's windows are smashed out, but it is the only building left standing. I open the front door to see the clerk's desk cracked right down the middle, mail sprawled across the floor and bins strewn about. Ellen and Asher search the place for any food or water and come back empty-handed.

Hollis sets a chair back up on its feet. "This would be a great church. A fixer-upper, but if it survived the apocalypse, it can survive us," he says.

"Not a bad idea," I reply. "I mean, the windows are blown out. Maybe someone can make a pretty stained glass to put in its place. Like churches used to have."

"If we can find the right materials, I know how glass is made. I would need some sand, soda ash, limestone, and some of the glass shards lying on the pavement out here," Stassi explains.

I shake my head. "What DON'T you know how to do, Stassi?"

Hollis opens the door. "We should probably hit the road if we want to make it back on time."

We drive for miles, looking and waiting to see something abnormal, but there aren't many signs of active civilization. Signs indicate we are coming up on Knoxville. In the distance, the road looks blurry, but I can't tell if it's just my vision playing tricks on me. Hollis leans forward, into the steering wheel, squinting.

"Is the road messed up ahead, or am I imaging things?" I ask.

"No, it's not normal," he replies.

As we get closer, it's clear that the road is flooded. Signs indicate that we are near Norris Lake. There is no sign of the road underneath the still water. Hollis shifts the SUV into reverse, and we head back the same direction we came from.

"I saw an exit a while back that should take us further east," he explains.

I take out our map and find our best detour route back south. Just past the Georgia border, the land west of our road looks black. I roll down my window and ask Hollis to pull over. Marie, Asher and Ellen have all fallen asleep in the back seat. Hollis and I unbuckle our seatbelts to take a closer look. Once out of the vehicle, we see a massive crevasse in splitting the earth for miles. It's unnerving. Hollis steps to the edge next to me and pulls me back. "What are you doing?! You can't just stand that close to a drop off like that!"

"Alright, calm down. I'll look from a distance," I reply.

Marie hears the commotion and wakes Asher and Ellen. Ellen steps closer in disbelief. "That explains all the ruckus."

Marie smiles. "It reminds me of the last trip I took with Paul, my husband, to the Grand Canyon."

I pick six pebbles off the ground and hand one to each of them.

"Everyone make a wish, and toss yours in," I say.

***

Asher's hometown of Atlanta looks like a landfill. Where soaring skyscrapers once stood are now massive piles of rubble. I imagine a giant toddler stomping around, trampling the buildings down and damaging everything in their wake. The damage has made the streets impossible to navigate, so we drive through the suburbs looking for any valuable stops. Asher spots a Dollar Tree store to the right and asks Hollis to pull into the parking lot. The glass door has been smashed, so we step through carefully not to cut ourselves on the shards still sticking out of the sides. The aisles have already been ransacked, but some items remain. I find a shopping basket and begin filling up the vehicle with anything we can find. Three hauls later, the back hatch is full of nearly expired Chex Mix, three beach buckets, four gallons of spring water, Fig Newtons, two cups of ramen noodles, five hula hoops, a six pack of Play-Doh, a dozen coloring books, three packs of crayons, and a package of Twizzlers.

I shut my door and whip out a box of Chicken in a Biscuit. "Looks like we have road snacks!"

Hollis smiles and slams a package on the dash. "I see your Chicken in a Biscuit and I raise you some Swedish Fish."

It's agreed that we will save everything else for the group. The flavors are intense after only consuming MRE meals for months. My body is buzzing with energy. Tallahassee turns out to be a mini version of the disaster Atlanta was. We stop at two convenience stores and one grocery store to load what we can. Asher finds a long tube that we can use to siphon gas out of another vehicle. Hollis fills the SUV with the gas that we brought with us and pulls behind a couple vehicles parked along the street. He grabs the gas can and places it on the ground next to the first car. After taking the gas cap off, Asher inserts the tube into the tank. He blows into the tube. We hear nothing, so he lowers the tube deeper into the tank and starts blowing. Bubbles! Jackpot. He sucks on the tube until the gas reaches about six inches from the end. Crimping the tube at the very end, he lowers it into the gas can and gravity goes to work.

The sun is setting and none of us feel comfortable with the idea of pulling into Tampa in the middle of the night. Marie suggests we drive to a nearby park and get some sleep so we can hit the road bright and early. Many of the park's trees are downed, but in the center, the metal playground equipment still stands.

Hollis looks in my direction. "Are you thinking what I'm thinking?"

I race him to the swings. The wind has looped them around the metal bar so many times that I can't reach them. Hollis jumps, tipping the saddle around the bar over and over until the metal chain is hanging freely. I take a seat and pump my legs until I feel the rush in my stomach on the way back and forth. Ellen and Asher race up the equipment, banging around in the dark and tearing down the slide. Stassi and Marie join us by the swings. Hollis, grasping the metal chains, leans back to look up at the sky. It seems wrong that we are still here looking up at the same starlit night sky, and everything has changed.

I hand out blankets to everyone and lay my seat back to get comfortable. Hollis grabs the tiny, battery-operated alarm clock and sets it for 5 a.m.

***

The sun rises just as we approach Tampa. The closer we get to the city, the more congested the streets become, littered with vehicles. Hollis swerves in and out until we reach the exit that could take us to the Gulf.

"I think we should just take this exit and try to work our way to Honeymoon Island," I suggest.

"Okay, but don't be surprised if we can't make it all the way there," he replies.

The roads become narrower, making it increasingly difficult for Hollis to navigate around the debris. I don't care, though. I need to see the ocean just one last time. We pass Frenchy's Rockaway Grill, and I know that we are almost there. Then I see the bridge—just another stump barely jutting out from the land. I can see the small beaches that line the bridge, where fishermen used to stand with their poles and bait all morning. The sand is a gray black, and the ocean is blood red.

"There couldn't have been that much bloodshed to make the water red, right?" Ellen asks.

"No," Stassi says. "I mean, I don't think so. There is a bloom like this that is caused by microscopic algae. It produces toxins that kill fish and make shellfish dangerous to eat."

We pull forward as far as possible and step out onto the small beach. Animal skeletons from the beaching are still scattered, no longer in a neat row along the beach. I step onto the sand and find it difficult to breathe in the thick air. It's not humidity...but a dense thickness. Stassi falls to her knees on the dark sand, tears streaming down her face. She picks up a charred seashell and starts digging. I kneel next to her and watch, until I notice the color begin to change. "The sand...it's still white underneath!" I run back to the SUV and grab the beach buckets we found at the Dollar Tree in Atlanta. Stassi takes them from me as I look for another seashell for digging.

"Does anyone want to tell me what's going on here?" Hollis asks. "You know there's not another world you can dig us to under there, right?"

"We need the sand so Stassi can make glass for our windows," I reply.

We fill the buckets to the brim and load them back up. I return to the sand one last time, take a handful and let it sift through my fingers onto the still red water below. The others follow my lead, a quiet homage to those who lost the faith, or never really had it. Hollis wraps his arm around me, and I rest my head on his shoulder. Of all the ways that God could have destroyed the world we've built, 99 percent of the destruction was done by Mother Nature. All her pent-up rage for the ways we had taken her for granted, unleashed in one fell swoop. Let's hope she got it out of her system.

36

BLUE COLLAR

We work in shifts to build our new city. Naveen and Pete have taken on the task to scour the region for gas and replenish our supply weekly, so at least four vehicles can head out to the construction site every day. For some of the tasks at hand, it was obvious to whom they would be assigned, based on their previous careers. We made a signup sheet for the other chores. Some are more appealing than others, so the tasks that we didn't have enough volunteers for were put in a weekly drawing. Those picked are assigned to do that work for the week, and then go back to their normal assignment. There are many bodies to feed and keep healthy, but also many to get work done. Even the elderly and children hold up their end. Some clean, some repair torn clothing, and some do laundry.

Every evening, we search for signs of life outside our community on the HAM radio. We haven't stumbled across any other conversations yet, but I'm hopeful. If we can connect with another group of survivors, we can learn from them—how they are finding supplies and organizing their community. I want to pass that news along to everyone, so they know we are not alone. There are other societies out there, dealing with the same struggles we are.

Lucas has upheld the law amongst the few disagreements that have arisen. Last week, he joined a crew to look for supplies and returned with a truck mounted by a drill rig. He pulls into the center of town with the horn blaring. A group had started digging a well by hand, and when they see him, they throw their shovels and cheer. They have to drill down roughly 60 feet to tap water and then insert a long, steel casing to capture the water. Lucas builds a round, brick wall surrounding the well, a wooden roof over head, and a winch to raise and lower the bucket for water retrieval.

The bunkers have served us so much more than we could have ever imagined. Three weeks after exiting them, the water supply runs out. A small group ventures out to search the mountain and finds a small stream of steady water that has saved our lives. We alternate bringing buckets full back to the bunkers twice daily. Everyone carries a pole on their back with buckets attached at either end. Days after our water discovery, a group finds blueberry bushes. We continue to gather from those, but also have brought some back to our greenrooms. Bunker One has finally found its green thumb—tomatoes, radishes and strawberries, to be specific. The MRE meals have nearly run dry. I've assigned two people to make food runs to the surrounding towns each week. They load up with the construction crew for that day, drop them off and head out to find sustenance. I thank God every day for all the doomsday preppers that were in the world. Many of their homes concealed underground shelters with stacks of shelving covered in canned goods. We can't just wait for that supply to run out, though. When Pete and Naveen are not picking up more gas, they are plowing our new fields, planting seeds for our future, and teaching the others how to handle a bow and arrow. Pete still has a decent supply of guns and ammo but wants to save them for the time when game starts to flourish again. All the farms we have passed are barren. Given the fencing has been destroyed, maybe the cattle wandered off into the wild. Some of them must have survived. Sadie has spotted a couple squirrels, and Hollis points out a hawk one day. No other signs of life have appeared.

Another group, which we call the cutters, is still working on clearing all the fallen vegetation so our roads are cleared—it also enables fires burning throughout the night. A few of them chip away at the massive trees with hand saws while the others break them down into smaller pieces with a hatchet. Once the roads are cleared, they will move on to help finish building the city. They return with blistered and callused hands. Bunker Four has grown an aloe vera plant in their green room and has been generous with their supply for our cutters.

Amos leads Ahava study in each bunker weekly, and every Sunday, he holds an all community church service outside of the bunkers. It's a bit of a squeeze, but we make do. Amos holds private counseling sessions for those who need to release any tension in a healthy way. In particular, Kenzo has a standing private session with Amos every Thursday afternoon. He volunteers to help Amos in any way he can, and he has expressed interest in becoming Sovereign Vicar himself one day. Mrs. Olson is thrilled at the idea, since he has given Poppy less attention now that his hopes and dreams revolve around becoming the spiritual leader. Poppy mopes around the mountain for a few days, and then she meets Titus from Bunker Six. Kenzo is merely a faint memory to her now. I see Mrs. Olson watching Poppy and Titus carving a heart in a tree trunk and adding their initials in the middle.

"Now that one, you should be keeping a close eye on," I point out.

"I'm not going to disagree with that. I should have taken my chances with Kenzo," she laughs.

The days are long and full of hard work, but it's honest work. Every evening, I return to the bunker exhausted. My limbs feel heavy and weak from the day's work. The second I lay my head on my pillow, it's lights out. There are no agendas or politics. It's simple. We need shelter, food and water. Everything else is just icing on the cake. In fact, if someone had many more complaints, I would wonder if they are pulling their weight around here.

Hollis has opened the bunkers and placed two of our dining chairs just outside them. He finds me tending to the plants in the greenroom.

"Join me outside?" he asks.

I follow him to the little patio he has made. We sit side by side, watching the sun slowly sink down behind the peaks and valleys. Its blinding light melts into a honey, to a gooey deep pink, and is swallowed by the dark blue night. Light spills out from the lanterns in the bunker, and shines into the forest. There is a rustling amongst our shadow painted on the leaves surrounding the bunker. Hollis looks in my direction to confirm I heard it, too. We lean forward, looking for the culprit.

"It must have been the wind, or one of the squirrels that Sadie saw the other day," Hollis says.

"Probably the squirrel...the wind didn't do that. Let's head in for the night," I suggest.

I grab my chair and— "Mhmmpf!" We both turn to see the flash of one large white tail and one smaller white tail softly galloping into the forest.

"Venison! Someone radio Pete!" Hollis hollers into the bunker.

"It was a mama and her baby! That means they are fawning," I smile.

Mr. Olson passes the message along to Bunker Two as the group romps around the bunker in celebration. If there's one fawn, there is likely more. Pete is going to have his hands full with hunter safety courses. If we limit it to one deer per bunker, the species should still be able to thrive. I've never tasted venison, but the promise of fresh meat is just what we need right now. It's not enough to just survive death. They need something to look forward to, and to work for.

***

This week, Stassi and I are a part of the construction team. I bundle up in a sweater and jacket before meeting her out front. We pack six workers in each vehicle, so 24 people total. Each house is assigned eight workers. The day begins at 7 a.m. The sun hasn't completely risen yet, but Asher fills us in on the progress we made the day prior and assigns us to our stations. Today, I'm stationed at what will be the Long's house.

They look just like log cabins when complete. We peel the bark off the logs first to avoid problems with insects. At the end of each log, we cut notches so it can hug the log beneath it. It is a challenge to build the homes without a cement mixer, but we have figured it out. We dig down a layer of the ground, lay the crushed stone and then the wood flooring. Each home has a small fireplace and a cellar built into the ground. We cut the wood flooring at just the right lengths to create a square door and attach a metal handle. A large, bottomless barrel with holes punched all around the sides is placed underneath each house for the sink drainage. The water disperses amongst the stones surrounding the barrel and out into the soil.

One person builds the compost outhouse for each house. Pete had walked us through how beneficial the compost will be for our crops, but we will need to wait a couple years for it to process. Wiley finds a few Lowe's Home Improvement Stores in the area, and every week we load the trucks with enough supplies to build the next couple houses. We knock out three houses per week and have completed six total to date. Eventually, we will need to expand our search for supplies.

Once the houses are complete, Ellen and I transport that family's furniture from their bunker to the new home. It's not much, but each home gets a set of bunk beds and any hammocks they had previously. It's up to them to build additional furniture they would like to have in their home. Upon their arrival, Ellen gives them a tour and explains how to properly use their sink and outhouse. She takes this task very seriously, like any good realtor would.

Today, I'm stationed at what will be the Long's house. Sadie asks me how it's looking at the end of every day. Her wound has healed to just a pink scar along her soft skin. She tells all the other children her tale of bravery at every chance she gets. Mara has given up trying to tame her, and she's better for it. That girl is a firecracker. The wind has finally mellowed, but the temperatures remain much colder, an effect from the meteorite strikes. Every log chopped up by the cutters is being stored for winter, as we are sure it will be frigid. The log walls have already been put in place, so today my focus will be hanging the roof. The rows of wood must overlap one another to ensure there are no leaks. I'm nailing down a wooden shingle when Stassi shouts, "LEO! Come take a look!"

I drop my hammer and race to our one brick building that still stands in city center. There she stands, waving at me through the most vibrant stained-glass window. A snowy white dove sits in the middle of bright yellow beams and geometric shapes of every vibrant color fills the background. It's a beacon of hope, shining down on us. The construction crew gathers around to appreciate the beauty. Once a shanty post office, now our sanctuary. These people, my people, carry God with them everywhere they go. In the mountains, on a bright day, and even through hell fire. Smiling, I roll my ancestors' pearl between my fingertips. This is the Church of Genesis.

KENZO

37

A SCARY NEW WORLD

Naveen asks me to gather more shards of glass so Stassi can make more windows. I pick up the pieces one by one. I'm sure she will arrange them into another hideous display upon the decrepit post office they keep calling a church. I slice my finger open and watch the blood drip onto the dirt beneath me. Any pain is better than the torment that structure inflicts. Leo notices the blood dripping from my hand and races to my aid.

"Oh no, Kenzo. Are you alright? Here, let me get you a bandage," she fusses.

Go ahead, find a first aid kit and while you're at it, fall in the well. That's actually not a bad idea. I'm sure we could make arrangements if need be. Imagine all the horror stories people would tell for years. The mighty Viceroy of the apocalypse fell into the well and her soul haunts the very water we drink to this day. It took all of my will to keep my distance from you at survival camp, but now your little gift is gone. Look at her, stopping everyone in her wake to demand they help find a bandage for poor, helpless Kenzo. Don't think you're so high and mighty. I've seen the hesitation in your eyes when they look to you for guidance. You're one of us. Our blood still runs in those veins. Your father's blood. I'll find your weakness. When I do, I will let it consume you slowly, until you wish you died with all the other sad sacks of bone and flesh. Here she comes, my hero.

"Here you go buddy. Keep an eye on it, we don't want it getting infected, alright?"

"Of course," I reply. "Thank you so much, Leo."

Off she goes, back to the construction site. I'm sure that tiny act of kindness earned her a world of praise from Abba and his haloed servants. They've coddled her and now she'll pay for it. Hollis leans in to kiss her on the cheek as she passes and then continues lifting loose bricks into a wheel barrel. He looks up to see Simone Bourland bending down to pick up a water pail. She's just the distraction he needs.

Lazarus takes my basket. "What did Leo want?"

"Just another opportunity for our little star to shine in front of her vapid flock. I have another assignment for you. You see Simone Bourland, over there fetching water?" He nods. "Hollis is actually interested in her. You should probably suggest that Simone help him with those bricks. It might be the start of a beautiful relationship."

I thought poisoning the plants with salt and vinegar would throw a wedge between them, and it did for some time. Now, the garden shears, those were for everyone. Sadie had been eying them up on that shelf for days. I just made sure she could get to them. They can tell her how brave she was, but she will live with that scar for the rest of her short, meaningless life. As for the rest of them, the terror that filled them will never be forgotten. I'm still baffled how they can ramble on and on about the Book of Revelation, blah blah blah, but not once has the Antichrist been considered as a threat. They either don't want to imagine the reality, or they've truly dropped the ball. I'll just have to remind them when the time is right.

Amos arrives to start designing the layout of the church. Will there be pews? A wooden box where everyone can spew their sin at you? I'm sure there will be a stage, so you can tower above them and shout your message of false hope. After 15 years of listening to Hayden and Calvin's pathetic, secret Bible stories, here I am again, listening to Amos's sorry attempts to justify his life. He feeds into my altar boy persona more and more each day. Once I've become his protege, my influence will reach new levels. Our little chats have begun opening his mind to question the things he thought were firm foundations of his faith. He fumbles around ways to answer my pressing questions and, in turn, questions what he really knows. It's a scary new world, Sovereign Vicar. Don't you think it's time to write the Third Testament?

Lazarus returns. "The deed is done. Let's see if she takes the bait."

Simone, her cheeks bright red, glances at Hollis as she lifts another bucket of water from the well. He notices and waves but continues working. Nice try, lover boy. She's not going to give up that easily. She places the bucket on the ground and makes her move. The offer of help is made, and he accepts.

"This is too easy," Lazarus says.

"Don't be so sure. There is still a lot of work to be done, and we only have so much time before my father returns."

* * *

ACKNOWLEDGEMENTS

First and foremost, I must thank my editor, Anna Simet. She helped me tackle my first novel and helped me grow as a writer. I couldn't be more proud of the work we've done together, and will forever be grateful.

To my husband, Kevin Saunders, without you this book would not exist. For all the nights and weekends that you took over changing diapers, making dinners, and making sure our children stay alive while I hid in my writing cave. You'll never know how much your support means to me. I love you.

To my daughters, Esme, Murphy and Ophelia—Nothing gives me greater joy than being your mother. You make me so proud. Always remember you are the heroines of your own stories.

To my parents, Roger and Terry—Thank you for always encouraging my creativity and supporting me through this journey. I'll always be grateful that you chose to be built in parents and grandparents during this time.

To my In-laws, Rick and Debbie—Thank you for creating such a thoughtful, supportive son and joining me in my love for books. Your enthusiasm means everything to me.

To my first beta reader, Jennifer Todd: I needed your meticulous eye for all those little details that can easily slip through the cracks. You are always my biggest cheerleader and you've been a part of this book since the beginning. Thank you for always being in my corner.

To my formatter, Amanda at Let's Get Booked and my cover designer, @coverbookdesigns: you have taken my precious baby, and made it look beautiful. Of all the challenges to get this story published, formatting and cover design intimidated me the most. Because of you, The Pearl in the Darkness is a book.

To the ladies of apartment 307 and everyone else that read my book or listened to me ramble on about my story—You gave me the courage to share my book with the world. Writing can be very isolating, but all of your comments and support made me feel less alone. I'm incredibly lucky to have such a talented group behind me. Thank you for encouraging my dream.

Made in the USA
Columbia, SC
13 November 2020

24477619R00245